Angel in My Heart

(Clarabelle's Story)

By

Julie Poole

Copyright

Angel in My Heart (Clarabelle's Story)
Text Copyright © 2014 Julie Poole

Angel in My Heart – First published October 2014
Angel in My Heart (Clarabelle's Story) First Published July 2015
Published by **J.P. Publishing**
Cover Design by Rebecca Poole from Dreams2Media
Formatting by Julie Poole
Editing by Elizabeth H. O'Reilly
ISBN – paperback – 978-0-9933522-3-2
ISBN – ebook - 978-0-9933522-2-5

Acknowledgements

Acknowledgements are made to the following, whose work I have mentioned in this novel:

Snow White: Walt Disney Productions (1937).

Some Day My Prince Will Come: Frank Churchill, Larry Morey, Paul J. Smith and Leigh Harline: Bourne Co. Music Publishers (1937).

Liar Lair: Universal Pictures (1997).

I have a Dream: Anderson, Benny Goran Bror / Ulvaeus, Bjoern K: Abba: 'Voulez-Vous' (1979).

It's a Wonderful Life: Frances Goodrich, Albert Hackett, and Frank Capra: Liberty Films (1946).

Special Thanks

I would like to thank the following people for their help with the development and production of this book:

Dreams2media - thank you Rebecca Poole for the fabulous book cover and your unending patience with me.

Betsy (Cuppy) - for your wonderful editing and hard work.

To my children, Tom, Chris, and Charlotte; I love you all dearly and am so grateful for you being in my heart and part of my life.

To my readers, who have asked for more - I thank you from the bottom of my heart for your support and kindness.

And finally, of course ... to the angels; I thank you.

Julie Poole

Dedication

***

I have a dream, a fantasy
To help me through reality
And my destination makes it worth the while
Pushing through the darkness still another
mile
I believe in angels
Something good in everything I see
I believe in angels
When I know the time is right for me
I'll cross the stream, I have a dream

***

(ANDERSSON, BENNY GORAN BROR /
ULVAEUS, BJOERN K.)
ABBA - "I have a Dream"

Books by Julie Poole

Angel on My Shoulder (Sarah's Story)
Book 1 in the 'Angel' series

Angel in My Heart (Clarabelle's Story)
Book 2 in the 'Angel' series

Angel in My Fingers (Frieda's Story)
Book 3 in the 'Angel' series

COMING SOON
Angel in My Paws (Fred's Story)
Book 4 in the 'Angel' series

Contents

Copyright.. 2

Acknowledgements 3

Special Thanks 4

Dedication 5

Books by Julie Poole 6

Chapter 1..1

Chapter 2 15

Chapter 3 34

Chapter 4 48

Chapter 5... 60

Chapter 6 73

Chapter 7... 86

Chapter 8 96

Chapter 9 107

Chapter 10.. 121

Chapter 11 131

Chapter 12...145

Chapter 13...161

Chapter 14...178

Chapter 15...187

Chapter 16...199

Chapter 17...214

Chapter 18... 233

Chapter 19... 249

Chapter 20 265

Epilogue.. 270

    Angel on My Shoulder 280

    Angel in My Heart....................................281

    Angel in My Fingers............................... 282

    A Note from Julie Poole......................... 283

Chapter 1

Clarabelle sat on Cloud 362 singing.
"Someday my prince will come,
"Someday we'll meet again,
"And away to his castle we'll go,
"To be happy forever I know," (Gosh she just loved Snow White! Just *loved* it!)
"Some day when spring is here," she warbled on merrily,
"We'll find our love anew,
"And the birds will singgggggggggggg,
"And wedding bells will ring,
"Some day when my dreams come true ... Oooooooo. ...!"

A huge stupid grin was plastered all over her beautiful face as she contemplated the extraordinary events of yesterday at the Award Ceremony. Had the Mighty Archangel Michael *really* stroked her feathers and been a little suggestive with her? She knew she had fainted at the pure pleasure of it, right into his arms, of course! How utterly wonderful! Clarence wasn't amused though, that was clear. Her brother had hardly said a word since the momentous event. Sulking! Typical brother, bless! He'd come round eventually, although it may take some time that was clear!

Clarence was old school Angel, First Class and didn't believe it right, or proper, that she had a crush on Archangel Michael - AA Mickey, as she liked to call him. Ideas above her station, Clarence had said, Metatron won't like it Clarence had said, it wasn't right Clarence had said, what *was* she thinking Clarence had said. Well, tough! If her Mighty AA Mickey wanted to stroke her feathers, he could and that was that! And okay, so she *might* get into trouble with Metatron, but she couldn't see how. Really, he wasn't that bad as bosses go, not really. He could be a bit stern, being in charge of all the angels *and* the Voice of God and all that, but she was just sure he'd be fine with it, just fine! And anyway, she hadn't glowed like this for eons and she had never ever seen her halo so bright, so there couldn't be anything wrong with that now could there? Okay, she admitted to herself, so it wasn't exactly normal for angels to have inter-angelcy-relations up here and okay, so yes, she'd never actually *heard* of an angelic wedding, but you never knew, there was always a first time! And besides, the Angelic Temple would make a *super* wedding venue!

Clarabelle glowed as she thought back. She had first met AA Mickey about a year ago when they had called an Inter-Angelcy-Meeting to discuss her Sarah, all very serious stuff. She had never met a proper Archangel before and had just been overawed by his beauty, majesty, power, and downright wonderfulness, not to mention that battle dress, that sword, and those *wings!* She'd been dumbstruck for days! Oh my goodness, he was just so handsome!

There had been all the normal Guardian Angels present, of course, as well as the two Archangels that they'd called in for extra help, AA's Michael and Uriel. Uriel was lovely, of course, but he was no Michael! Michael, well, he was just something else! That meeting had been the best day ever! She had been struggling so much to get Sarah on the right track that reinforcements had had to be called for, and it had worked, oh my, how it had worked! Just fifteen months ago Sarah had been a single thirty-seven-year-old 'spinster-of-the-parish'; a string of rubbish men and rubbish jobs behind her, with no clue of how to go forward, and, of course, *totally* resistant to any help from her 'Guardian Angel Clarabelle,' whose job it was to guide and assist her.

Clarabelle thought back to last year with a smile. Sarah had been such a mess, bless her. Just terrible self-esteem, zero self-worth and life was going nowhere fast for her. She had a terrible relationship with her mother, a chaotic life, and nothing of any worth to look forward to. When she had finally surrendered, that fateful day in the spring of last year, allowing Clarabelle to guide her at last, it had been the best day ever! Over the following months, they'd worked hard to sort out her worth, her esteem, her career, and finally, when she was strong enough, her mother. When all of that was done, Sarah had at last been ready for real love and in had come her soul-mate, Simon. The rest, as they say down there, is history! In the making, of course, but history nevertheless.

There was Sarah now, laying on a beach in the Maldives on her honeymoon with Simon, their hands entwined as they lay together, soaking up the sun on the paradise island. Clarabelle could feel the love and the joy radiating out from them, right up here, all the way to Cloud 362! It was so powerful, their love, it was just lovely, and she just knew that they were all going to live 'happily ever after.' Mind you, she thought, it had been hard work getting Sarah there, getting her ready, but with all the angels working together and with a bit of help from her Mickey, of course, it had all worked out in the end.

Clarabelle peeked down over the cloud towards the beach far below on planet Earth and beamed. Not their usual Cloud 322 overlooking Redfields where Sarah and Simon lived. This one, Cloud 362, was half way around the other side of the world, overlooking the paradise island where the happy couple were honeymooning. The tropical sun was shining brightly down onto the white sand while the turquoise sea lapped gently at the shore, their gentle waves soothing the happy couple as they half dozed on their sunbeds. Hands entwined, they lay together happily in their bliss. Ah, it was just lovely to watch them, bless! She was chuffed about the baby too, how exciting! They would be delighted, of course, Sarah and Simon, when they found out. Both had wanted children for ages, but without the right partner and the right life it just couldn't happen. Now, of course, it was different! All was in place and ready, and the angels could finally move things forward. Plans had been underway for the additional two souls to join them, although admittedly there had been a long delay, longer than anticipated. They'd been due several years earlier, but Sarah hadn't been ready for Simon, so practically the entire Angelic Realms had had to work together to move heaven and earth in order to stall the arrivals. Now it was finally the right time, although, with Sarah nearly thirty-nine and Simon coming forty-one, they needed to move fast.

Angelica would be the first, of course, baby number one, followed by baby number two in a year or so, a son. That had been a close call, boy or girl first! She and Clarence had argued about it for ages before deciding to toss a feather for it, he, of course, wanting a boy first (being a typical male), but she had won (smashing!), so a girl it was. Angelica was on her way, forming nicely inside Sarah at this very moment. Anyway, Clarabelle thought, it wasn't really Clarence's place to be interfering like that and she had argued with him for an age over it. After all, it was Nathaniel who was Simon's angel and it should have been down to her and Nat to sort it out, but Clarence had jumped in, insisting. To be fair, if it wasn't for Clarence, they wouldn't all be where they were now, and anyway, she'd won the feather toss; ha! Sarah herself didn't have a clue yet, of course, that she was pregnant, but she'd find out soon enough. When she did, Clarabelle would be there for her as ever with her pearls of wisdom and support, after all that was her job; she *was* Sarah's very own personal Guardian Angel.

Thinking about the baby that was due in eight and a half months, Clarabelle beamed. She was looking forward to working with Seraphina who had been allocated to be Baby Angelica's Guardian Angel. Her training and preparation was already underway and Clarabelle knew she'd be working closely with her for the rest of Sarah and Angelica's lives.

With a rustle of feathers to her left, she suddenly saw Nathaniel join her. They grinned as they watched the two lovebirds below. She and Nat had been working hard over the last year to bring the two soul-mates together and it hadn't always gone smoothly, particularly their first meeting which had been nothing short of a disaster, but then again, it rarely ever did go smoothly with humans!

The two angels sat chatting about the wedding, which had been wonderful, just wonderful! Clarabelle had loved being bridesmaid and Nat was chuffed to bits at being best man, standing next to Simon proudly. His bright orange 'Gonk' hair had even behaved and he'd been able to leave the cap that he usually wore to hide it, behind for once! Sarah had walked down the aisle of the beautiful chapel looking radiant on her brother's arm, followed by Clarabelle and Clarence, of course. Clarence was Clarabelle's brother, mentor, and saviour, bless him! Well normally, anyway, although he really was giving her *such* a hard time over this Mickey thing at the moment! It was most unlike him to be a pain, most unlike him indeed! Very out of character!

Clarabelle's thoughts were darting back and forth without rhyme or reason at the moment. Now where was she? Ah, yes, the wedding! Clarence had followed Ben down the aisle, making sure his ward didn't mess up as he gave his sister away. He was Ben's Guardian Angel so it was a nice family occasion all round; brother and sister angels looking after brother and sister humans; lovely, just lovely!

"Lovely day, lovely day!" she beamed again, "Just lovely!"

Sarah had walked down the aisle of the small chapel slowly, revelling in each step that she'd taken. The church organ had filled the room with its rich tones, its music echoing off the old stone walls and ceilings matching her footsteps to its slow beat. She'd worn a beautiful ivory, lace wedding dress with a long train, a veil over her face, and a bridal bouquet in her left hand, holding tightly onto Ben's arm with her right. It was a glorious day in the middle of June, the sun shining perfectly, as ordered from above by Clarence and Clarabelle, of course. A host of angels sat in the rafters of the church singing along with the organ, joining the happy couple on their special day.

Clarabelle beamed at the memory of Sarah walking down the aisle on Ben's arm. She was so lucky to have such a lovely relationship with her brother, wishing for a moment that her own brother was as supportive!

"Now, Clarabelle, you know I'm always there for you! How can you even *think* that?" a stern voice with a hint of hurt suddenly declared from behind her. He'd been watching her quietly for some time, but she had been so wrapped up in her dreamy state about Archangel Michael and her chattering to Nathaniel about the wedding that she hadn't noticed him at all. He smiled sadly at his little sister and shook his head. He'd been mentoring her for twenty years now, helping and supporting her to guide Sarah towards the right path and had pulled more than a string or two on her behalf. *To say, to even think that I don't support her is just sooo unfair!* "Just because I think this little crush you have on Archangel Michael is inappropriate does *not* mean that I don't support you!" he said indignantly. "Quite unfair of you, Clar, quite unfair!" and he sat down in a huff.

"Oh, stop sulking, Clarence!" she grinned. She knew he'd never understand her feelings for Mickey, himself never having put a foot wrong in all his 7000 years of angelic existence, not that she was admitting that she was doing anything wrong, mind you, *but ... okay, possibly, it wasn't quite normal for angels to have crushes on each other.* She looked at him carefully, scrutinising his 'perfection.' It was alright for Clarence, she decided, never risked his halo did Clarence, never put a foot wrong did Clarence, but that being said, she was lucky to have him and she knew it. She'd never have managed to get her Sarah sorted without him and he was a darling really, just a bit old fashioned, bless.

"Ben did a good job giving her away, didn't he?" said Clarence quietly, trying to change the subject and get them back onto neutral ground. He'd been so proud! He loved being Ben's Guardian Angel and was blessed with him being such a cooperative ward. He reflected back on his relationship with Ben over the years and knew he'd had it easy. He'd shown himself to Ben when he was just twelve years old and, bless him, he'd listened and followed Clarence's guidance ever since. Ben's life, as a result, had been easy and Clarence's job as his angel had been easy, unlike poor Clarabelle! She had taken over twenty years to get Sarah to cooperate, poor thing. "Grand job he did, aye,"

Clarence said again.

Clarabelle smiled at her brother. *Bless him, he was trying to make peace!* She thought about her comment of no support from him and knew he was right. He'd always been there for her and always would be, but she also knew she was going to have trouble with him over her and AA Mickey and she wasn't looking forward to that one, no, not at all! *Ah well,* she thought, *it'll all come good in the end I'm sure. It will all be just perfect. ... eventually!*

Suddenly, all three jumped with a start as a dark figure flew past them at speed, descending towards 'downstairs,' trailing a long cloaked shadow of blackness behind him.

"Hi, Fred!" Clarabelle shouted after the figure, waving. Fred zoomed past waving back, leaving the cloud shaking as he passed.

"Speeding again, Fred!" Nat shouted after him. "You'll get done one of these days, mate, and then you'll be stuffed!"

"Will he ever learn?!" exclaimed Clarence crossly. *They were all the same, these Grim Reapers, always speeding in their rush to get their quota filled.* "I know there's pressure down in transport to meet targets, but really, can you not at least try to keep within the speed limits!" he grumbled, smoothing his ruffled feathers down in annoyance. Seconds later, Fred zoomed past again, this time on his way 'upstairs,' creating the same shock wave as he did the first time. Cloud 362 shook violently and Clarabelle had to hang on to it so as not to fall off!

"Fred, really!" they called together. "Must you?"

"Hi, both," shouted Fred as he flew past them. "Come

on you," he shouted, looking behind him at the trailing angel. "We haven't got all day you know!" He nodded towards the retrieved soul of the recently departed that he was carrying. "Have to get this one upstairs. I've got loads more to collect today. Don't want to miss my quota!"

The trailing angel flew faster, wanting to stay with her ward that was going 'home.' She was trying her best to catch them up, *but these Grim Reapers, blimey, they just flew so blinking fast*, she thought to herself!

Then all of a sudden, Fred yanked the brakes on and whipped round, doubling back to the three angels sitting on Cloud 362. "Oh, yeah, I forgot to say, guys, I'm going off grid for a while, got a mission, dunno what!" he grinned.

"What? Where you going, Fred?" asked Clarabelle.

"Dunno, mate, just know The Boss has reassigned me, something to do with my PDP. Just wanted to say Ta-ta." He waved a dark, shadowy arm and then he was gone, trailing the black mist behind him again as he zoomed off 'upstairs' with his delivery.

"What did his PDP say then?" asked Clarabelle, wondering what could be so bad in a 'personal development plan' that an Angel of Death would be reassigned. She didn't particularly care for the Grim Reapers as a whole, bit too calculating and clinical for her liking. She knew that Fred had been in trouble for being too 'gung ho' with his collections, but she'd gotten used to him over the years, speeding and zooming in and out as he collected the departed. She knew that a few of the Guardian Angels had complained about the way he collected his wards so roughly. There had been several complaints here and there and they'd all reflected in Fred's PDP badly!

"I think it was something about the way he carts them off a bit quick. Too business-like or something," Nat said. "That's what I heard anyway. Bit too harsh is Fred, even for a Grim Reaper. I heard on the grapevine that he's got some training to do, apparently."

"Oo, that's almost a demotion isn't it?" Clarabelle asked with alarm.

"Not at all," reassured Clarence. "It's just a matter of softening him up a bit, that's all. He'll be fine. The Boss knows what he's doing don't you fret, dear."

Clarabelle, Clarence and Nat watched Fred go, all thinking the same thing - that they'd hate to be in transport like Fred, just hate it! They all loved their jobs as Guardian Angels as much as each other.

"I couldn't work in transport, Nat, be a Grim Reaper, could you?" asked Clarabelle, thinking what a chore it must be, up and down all day collecting souls that had passed on, transporting them to upstairs, unloading, then back down again for more. So boring!

"No mate, never!" replied Nat. "Couldn't do it, just couldn't!"

"I wonder what they have to do to get promoted, to get out of there and be like us?" she asked curiously.

"Not a clue, mate, not a clue." Nat shook his head. He wasn't the brightest spark in The Realms, he knew that, still had loads to learn, same as Clarabelle. He was surprised that Clarence didn't know though, Clarence usually knew everything!

The three pondered the promotions and demotions that were known to happen within the Angelic Realms for a few moments, happy in their jobs, wondering how it all worked in the other classes like the Grim Reapers, then returned their attention to the couple below.

"She's going to burn if she's not careful!" Clarabelle worried, noticing Sarah was turning rather an alarming shade of pink as she lay on the white sand, the tropical sun blazing down onto her fragile skin. "You know their skin is more susceptible to the sun when they're pregnant!"

"Clar, she's got factor 150 or something on, mate, she'll be fine!" Nat assured, "Just fine, honest, mate. Simon's plastered it on her, I made sure of that," he grinned.

"Yes, but she's pregnant now, it's different," she worried. "Won't it be just lovely when she finds out about the baby?" she declared happily, not for the first time. She turned to her brother giggling, not able to resist rubbing in the victory she had over him of the girl coming first.

"Just lovely! A girl! I won, I won!" she crooned, taking out the winning feather from her sparkly golden belt and waving it in the air in front of Clarence's nose. "A girl, a girl," she grinned. "Smashing!"

Clarence watched his sister with concern. Her light was far too bright and her halo was glowing all over the place. She was getting ideas above her station so she was! Between winning the feather toss and thinking she could possibly have a romantic venture with another angel, and an *Archangel* at that, well, it was just all getting out of hand and she was only a Second Class angel! This crush she had really had to be nipped in the bud, and quickly! And crowing about winning the feather toss, rubbing it in his face like that? Most unbecoming of a Second Class Angel! It was time she was put back in her place! "I'm off," he humphed, his mission now clear in his mind. She wasn't going to like what he was going to do next, not one little bit, but she'd asked for it. He left her to carry on watching the happy honeymooning couple far below, deciding that he had an urgent appointment that needed making, and making immediately! Clarence flew off, picking up the jet stream that Fred had left in his wake. "Time to sort this out!" he declared firmly to himself.

"Right oh then, Nat, I'm popping off," said Clarabelle, standing up from Cloud 362 stretching. "Off to see Sarah. Want to come?"

"Nah, you're all right, mate, too hot down there for me. I don't know how you stand that heat! Makes my feathers sticky, it does! I'll wait till they get back home to normal climate conditions tomorrow. Not programmed for the subtropics me, not at all. Do me a favour and keep an eye on Simon, though, would you? If he needs anything give me a shout, but I think he's fine for now. I'm off for a Harp lesson!" Nathaniel grinned and then suddenly remembered the meeting the following day. "Oh! Haven't we got a meeting with Seraphina to fill her in on the background of those two tomorrow?" he asked, nodding towards the happy couple far below. "She needs to be brought up to speed now that she's been allocated to baby Angelica, doesn't she?"

Clarabelle nodded her agreement emphatically. She was looking forward to filling Sephi in on the details and the history that was Sarah and Simon. Such a lovely story!

"Right oh then, see you tomorrow. Ta-ta for now." Nathaniel waved as he flew off upstairs leaving Clarabelle poised for take-off to 'downstairs' and their wards, though he wondered why she bothered. Sarah was so sorted now there really was little for Clarabelle to do, but he knew she'd find something. Couldn't sit still for two minutes, that one!

"Things to do, things to do!" Clarabelle trilled, and flew down to catch up with the latest news from Sarah, singing her favourite song of the moment as she zoomed down, her song from Snow White. *What was it that Mr. Disney had said, ah yes!* 'All our dreams can come true if we have the courage to pursue them!' "Yes, indeedy!" decided Clarabelle, thinking about her 'Mickey' again. "Smashing!"

She sang loudly and clearly, her song carrying across the sky as she flew, wings outstretched, grinning serenely, "Someday my prince will come. ..."

Chapter 2

Sarah was in the hotel bathroom when Clarabelle reappeared fresh from her visit to Cloud 362 and her chat with Nathaniel and Clarence. The cool marble luxury shone all around her as she cleaned her teeth in its plush sink; one of two matching ones, a 'his and hers.' The enormous bath with its gold taps and Jacuzzi jets commanded the room and stood majestically in front of the enormous windows overlooking its amazing views of the Indian Ocean. Sarah grinned, loving the opulence of the honeymoon suite.

Clarabelle dove in as always, giving Sarah a start as she got straight to the point, piping up into her nagging without even saying hello. "Have you told him yet, dear? About me, I mean? You were going to tell him right after Christmas, then Easter and then before the wedding and now here we are on your honeymoon! Two weeks you've had and you promised me that you'd tell him! So," she stared at Sarah encouragingly, "is it done?"

"Hello, Clarabelle. Long time no see. Must be at least half an hour, how did you manage that?" Sarah grinned, putting the toothbrush down and moving over to the toilet.

"Now, dear, don't change the subject; not a good sign, not a good sign. So, have you? Told him? Aye, aye?"

"Ah, well, no, not quite," admitted Sarah sheepishly to a concerned Clarabelle, sitting perched on the toilet roll holder watching Sarah as she sat on the loo in the luxury bathroom of her honeymoon suite. "I didn't want to spoil anything. It's our honeymoon!" she defended. Seeing Clarabelle's eyebrows rise at the admission she rushed in continuing her defence. "I was waiting for the right time … and … it just hasn't appeared … yet … honest!" Sarah noticed Clarabelle's sceptical face, the set determined mouth and she knew that she'd be nagged into submission sooner or later. Sure enough, the advice, lecture, interference, or whatever someone wanted to call it began in earnest.

"Fear does not become you, Sarah dear. You know that he loves you. He's going nowhere, I promise you! There is nothing to fear in telling the truth. The truth will set you free! How many times have I taught you this?" nagged Clarabelle happily. It had taken her over half of Sarah's life to get her to the point of granting Clarabelle permission to guide her and now that she had the 'said permission' she just loved these little opportunities to interfere. Relished them, in fact! She watched Sarah squirm with some concern, but not too much!

"Yes, well, Clar, it's easier said than done, admitting to your brand new husband that you have a Guardian Angel called Clarabelle, who sits on your shoulder most of the time, is about six inches tall and who you see and talk to every day. He'll have me locked up!"

"He will not have you locked up, Sarah, and you know it! He may be a little, how do you say, 'freaked out by it all,' but he will get over it and he will get used to it! Secrets and lies are not good between a couple you know; breeds doubts and before you know it those doubts have grown into more. And lies? Well, they just grow and grow and on it goes."

"Okay, okay, don't nag! And I don't lie! Well, not much and only when I have to!" She saw Clarabelle's left eyebrow rise again at precisely the moment that Simon called out through the closed door to her,

"You okay in there, babe? Sounds like you're talking to someone? Yourself again or have you got a strange man in there that I don't know about?" Simon laughed from the other side of the bathroom door.

"Singing, darling, just singing. Won't be long. Be out soon." Sarah didn't want to look at Clarabelle's face to see the triumph in her eyes at this little, nay minute, tiny weenie lie, but she couldn't avoid it as Clarabelle bent over towards her, sticking her face right under Sarah's nose as she grinned and said,

"Soooooo, you don't lie to him, aye? Of course you don't! What was that then? Aye, aye?"

"Okay, okay, you win! I've been putting it off long enough, I know. I'll tell him when we get home, I promise, but you'd better be there with some help when I do. This is going to freak him out big time!"

"But of course, child, of course I'll be there! Aren't I always?"

"Mmm, I guess so."

She watched Clarabelle's face as it changed from scepticism to disbelief and corrected her statement quickly,

"Yes, yes, you're always there. I know, sorry."

"And I will be there for you when you tell him and it will all be fine, I promise," she reassured a clearly reluctant Sarah.

"Thank you. Now could you please get off the toilet roll holder so that I can get out of here?" she laughed. "Go, shoo. See you when I get home. Go and play on a cloud or something, Clar! Enjoy your flight and with any luck, I'll enjoy mine too and there won't be too much turbulence."

"I'll make sure of it, my dear, you just leave it to me," beamed Clarabelle, popping off upstairs to order some calm weather for the next morning and the return flight of the newly wed Mr. and Mrs. S. & S. Brown. She'd do her best to make it as perfect as possible for them both, and with any luck, she may even bump into AA Mickey upstairs on her way to the weather station.

"Smashing!" she beamed. "Just smashing!"

***

Sarah pondered Clarabelle's request for the rest of the day as she lay by her husband's side soaking up the sun on the fabulous beach. She thought back over her relationship with Clarabelle through the years and pondered some more. She remembered the day, some twenty-two years before when Clarabelle had first introduced herself when Sarah was just seventeen, long before she knew or understood any of the 'weird' stuff to which she had become accustomed. Clarabelle had simply appeared one sunny morning when Sarah had been sitting at her dressing table, staring in the mirror, examining with horror the latest teenage zit on her chin, when she had looked up and saw what she thought at first was a fairy sitting on her shoulder. It was as clear as day and Sarah had frozen in shock, staring at it and thinking, *what the bloody hell is a fairy doing sitting on my shoulder?*

"A fairy!" laughed the thing in amusement and indignation. "A fairy? No, child, I am an Angel! I am your Guardian Angel! My name is Clarabelle!" She had twirled around, taking a sweeping bow and waving her arm in the air, all theatrical and everything! Initially, Sarah had decided that she'd gone mad, lost the plot and was totally bonkers, but apparently not! As the months and years had gone on, she got used to Clarabelle sitting there, interfering, as usual.

Clarabelle was about six inches tall, dressed in a long, white gown and had long, white, sweeping feathers draped all the way down to the floor. There was a light of gold all around her, apparently her halo! Her hair was golden too, curling just past her neck and onto her shoulders in soft waves, her eyes the clearest and brightest blue that the young Sarah had ever seen. She looked about thirty, Sarah reckoned, but Clarabelle had said that she was ageless and she was, of course, utterly beautiful.

"Clarabelle! What kind of name is that?" Sarah had laughed to the miniature fairy thing during the introductions. "Sounds like Clarence, that crazy angel out of that film that always makes me cry, what was it called? The one with the guy with the voice, what was his name? Ah yes, James Stewart. 'A Wonderful Life,' yes that was it. You know the one where a bell rings when an angel gets its wings?" Well apparently, (so she was informed the day of the introductions), Clarabelle was Clarence's sister! For God's sake! How you could be related to an angel in a bloody Hollywood film she hadn't quite got, even to this day, but Clarabelle had assured her that most of the ideas for the good films were put in the writers head by angels or other important bods upstairs, (that's 'Upstairs' where the angels live, so Clarabelle had said. She didn't call it heaven, Sarah recalled, she just called it, 'Upstairs'). Clarence had, so he had told his sister, inspired the writers of that particular masterpiece and had made sure his name was in there somewhere. Well, you can't have those Hollywood writers claiming all the credit for ideas given by upstairs, can you? Even angels like a bit of credit, you know. They were close, Clarence and Clarabelle, had been for eons she had said.

At that time, when she had first appeared to Sarah back then, Clarabelle hadn't long qualified up through the ranks of 'Guardian Angel-ship' and Sarah was her first ward. Clarence, her brother (the one from the film!), was her mentor apparently and according to Clarence, Sarah had been a challenging ward. Nice! Since then, of course, Clarabelle had been promoted and was now a Second Level Angel - First Class, so she said, and to be fair, she'd sorted Sarah's life out, and then some! So really, if Clarabelle said to tell Simon, then she guessed she'd better get on with it. But then again, maybe not!

***

Metatron sat at his desk in the office at the back of the

Angelic Temple and pondered. Most unusual for one of the Guardian Angels to ask for an audience with The Boss, but he'd arranged it and now there were new orders through from the 'All That Is.' He'd been slightly concerned to see Clarence's feathers so ruffled and clearly something was bothering him, but he hadn't been able to get any information out of Clarence whatsoever, so Metatron was clueless, as much as he could be, being 'The Voice of God' an' all. Usually the Guardian Angels sorted out their problems in discussion with the Archangels above them and he oversaw them, so really, this was most unusual! Angels did, of course, occasionally fall out with each other, but it never lasted long as they were incapable of holding grudges. Forgiveness and compassion were built into them at an energy level, way before an atomic level, so they always kissed and made up quickly, so to speak. He thought again about Clarence asking for this meeting. It must be something very important to have brought a Class 1 Guardian Angel up this high and wondered again what the cause of it could be. Metatron stood up, moving from behind his desk into the vastness of the enormous room. He opened his feathers wide to their full thirty feet span, tuning into the vibrations across the cosmos, feeling for anything different. His feathers ruffled gently. Yes, something had definitely changed. There was a new energy present, one that he hadn't felt before. He would need to do some investigating, find out what was occurring. He felt for it again, this strange vibration. It wasn't anything negative this energy, but it was different, something new! These were times of change across the entire Universe so this was to be expected, of course, but it was nice to be 'in the know,' especially in his position. He was, after all, the total top boss of all the angels and it wouldn't do for him to be clueless, no not at all!

"Must find out what's going on and smart quick!" he declared to himself, and flew off for a tour of the cosmos to figure it out.

**

The following morning came far too quickly for both Sarah and Simon. Their wonderful honeymoon on the amazing island paradise was over and it was time to go home and back to reality, a new reality, a wonderful reality, a reality that they were both looking forward to very much indeed; the start of their married life together. A whole new chapter for them and Sarah couldn't wait!

The long flight home was uneventful. Clarabelle had worked her magic and the plane cruised home smoothly without any lumps, bumps, or scary moments. The happy couple slept most of the journey away and awakened just before the landing announcements were made by the captain.

"Nearly back home again, Fire Girl. Happy?" asked Simon, as he brushed away a flop of stray hair tenderly from his wife's sleepy eyes. He loved her long chestnut hair. It flowed softly onto her shoulders, framing her pretty face. Sarah's turquoise eyes sparkled.

"Ecstatic, darling, just ecstatic. It's been wonderful. Thank you for the best honeymoon ever!"

"The *only* honeymoon ever, I hope!" laughed Simon

happily, kissing her nose with a grin.

The journey home from the airport seemed to take forever, but the pair eventually got home late that night and fell exhausted into their large bed, despite having slept on the plane, and for the first time in weeks, they did not make love. Both their bodies had given out and neither stirred a muscle for the next eight hours.

The early morning sun awakened them gently from their slumber, its rays filling the bedroom on the top floor of the old three-story house with its warmth as it poured in through the windows. Sarah stretched, looking at her sleeping husband in wonder, still not quite believing she was home, she was married, and this, her beautiful home was now properly *their* beautiful home. She loved this house, every inch of it and felt so blessed to now be sharing it with the man she adored. Their large ensuite bedroom occupied the entire top floor with windows on three sides; it was light, airy, and spacious. The windows were open, allowing the fresh scents of the countryside to permeate the room. The front views scanned the small town of Redfields a quarter of a mile away, the side view spanned across the valley with its trees and sloping green hillside, and the rear view reached far across open farmland.

Built some 200 years before, its old stone walls had faded gently with time. It was an impressive detached house at the end of a small lane on the fringes of the town where she had lived most of her life. Not an overly large dwelling, but the extra floor at the top of the house made all the difference. It also boasted a large garden, its boundary the tall hedge that separated it from the adjoining fields and which swept gently from the front gate, around the sides, and across the back, protecting its cottage garden, its trees, plants, herbs, and flowers within its warm embrace.

The middle floor of the house had two smaller bedrooms and a large bathroom. A beautiful wooden staircase swept down through the house and into the hallway on the ground floor with its high Victorian ceilings and stained glass front door. The sun filled the hall with different coloured lights when it shone through the glass, creating a rainbow effect on the wooden floor, its rays and warmth releasing the fragrance of wax and polish which wafted gently throughout the house. The ground floor consisted of a good sized living room with a large marble fireplace, its black wrought-iron hearth always filled with coals and logs, ready for a match to be struck and burst it into life. Large French doors opened into the garden, framed by heavy golden drapes, tied back to allow in the views from the garden. Next to the living room was a small dining room, just big enough for her table and chairs. Along the hall was the kitchen, the hub of the house, and finally a small utility room behind it. Yes, she loved this house. This home, a home that she had been sharing with Simon since Christmas when he had first moved in with her.

She felt her husband's warmth next to her stir and beamed delightedly.

"Good morning, wife," a smiling Simon said sleepily as he rubbed his eyes.

"Good morning, husband," Sarah replied, grinning back. She reached for him automatically, drawing him into her arms and rolling him on top of her in one smooth movement. It never ceased to amaze her how his 6'4" frame didn't totally pulverize and squash her small 5'4" body when he was on top of her, but it never did. They made love gently and slowly, savouring every moment of each other until their passion built, gradually reaching its climax. Afterwards, they held each other, revelling in their closeness, their love, their oneness, as they often did. Their married life had begun.

***

Clarabelle smiled sweetly at Seraphina as they sat together on their usual Cloud 322, high above Redfields, waiting for Nathaniel. She was very pretty, Clarabelle noticed. Her long auburn hair fell right down to her waist, covering half of her small dainty frame. Her halo shone brightly around her sweet face. Her eyes, the deepest blue of the ocean, sparkled with anticipation.

"Well, of course I've read their files," Seraphina confirmed, "from the Akashic Records like we're meant to, but it is so nice to be able to talk to you and Nathaniel and hear it first-hand. Helps so much, you know. Thank you for taking the time to help me."

Ah, bless her, she is so sweet! Clarabelle thought, smiling at the new angel. Seraphina had only recently qualified as a fully-fledged Guardian Angel and Baby Angelica would be her first ward.

"Whilst we wait for Nathaniel, perhaps you could fill me in on the mother, Sarah?" Seraphina asked politely.

"Of course, my dear. Where to start, where to start?

Mmm, let me think. From the beginning then, but the shortened version as you've already read the file." Clarabelle replied, grinning.

"That would be lovely, thank you." Seraphina focused, concentrating intently.

Clarabelle launched into the history that was 'her Sarah' with gusto.

"Sarah Smith, as was, now Brown. Thirty-eight years old, 5'4" tall, dress size eleven (but she thinks she's a ten, bless), turquoise eyes, chestnut hair, but you'll see all that for yourself when you meet her. Father, John, deceased, mother, Margaret, still going, brother, Ben, age thirty-three, his wife, Gina, and their son, Joe, now three years old. That's the family. Oh yes, relevant fact: Ben can also see his guardian angel, Clarence, who happens to be my brother as you know. Sarah and Ben know about each other's angels and their ability to see them and found out last summer, didn't know before, though. Keeping up?"

"Oh yes, thank you!" Seraphina smiled. "Do go on."

"I showed myself to Sarah when she was seventeen because she was having a very hard time at home and needed a lot of support, a lot of help. I thought I'd be able to give her that help a bit easier, if she could see me. Thought it would get her to trust me easier. Trouble was, see me or not, she wouldn't let me help, most frustrating, most frustrating! Made a lot of mistakes did my Sarah, went the wrong way repeatedly. Lots of boyfriends, lots of jobs, nothing stable apart from her house. Her Gran left it to her, lovely house, lovely house."

Clarabelle always repeated herself when she was getting carried away and Seraphina had already been briefed on this annoying habit. She smiled sweetly, nodding for Clarabelle to continue.

"Anyway, she finally surrendered and let me help a year ago last March. She was two years behind where she should have been, of course, stubborn, you see, very stubborn, so there was a lot of work to do to catch her up. At the time, she had just been rejected again by the latest boyfriend, Rob, and was working as a shop assistant in MacKenzie's store, you know, the one she owns now?" Clarabelle asked. Seraphina nodded. "Well, I did that! Helped her get over Rob first, of course, then we sorted her career out. She bought the shop and through that her confidence began to grow and somehow we finally managed to get her to believe in herself. She'd been bullied mercilessly by her mother for years, you know, did a lot of damage, did that! Anyway, where was I? Oh yes, well, eventually we got her to grow some grit and confront her mother, sort out the bullying, and now they have a half decent relationship. They'll never be close, but it's much, much better than it was."

"That's lovely, well done," Seraphina smiled. "You worked very hard with her, didn't you?"

"Oh my goodness me, yes! Took a *lot* of work from a *lot* of people to get her sorted, but eventually we got there. Then when she was ready, we could bring Simon in. He was due two years before, mind you, but she wasn't ready, so we had him held stuck in a dead-end relationship with a woman called Nadia. Awful woman, bless! Awful for him, I mean. Anyway, when Sarah was ready, we released the blocks and in came Simon."

"How did you get them together then?"

"Ah, my dear, it was easy. There's a flat above Sarah's

shop and we got her to rent it to him, that's how we brought them together, very clever, very clever!"

"Yes, indeed," agreed Seraphina, listening avidly. "But why did he need a flat? Didn't he have anywhere to live?"

"Oh yes, my dear, he had a lovely apartment, quite posh, lovely it was, but in the city, a long way away. We had to relocate him to bring them together. We got him a transfer you know, a new job in Redville, you know the town over there?" Clarabelle pointed towards the large town eight miles away, clearly visible from Cloud 322. "Simon works there now with Ben, Sarah's brother. They both work in the Bank as account managers. Very clever he is, our Simon, very clever!"

"Oh, I seeee!" Seraphina grinned.

At that moment Nathaniel arrived, jumping into the conversation without introductions.

"Simon's my ward, lovely chap he is too! Forty years old, 6'4" tall, looks like a Greek God, gorgeous, so I'm told, not that I notice these things, of course!"

"Hi, Nat. This is Seraphina, Angelica's angel," Clarabelle piped.

Introductions were made quickly and Nathaniel began to relay the background to Sephi.

He'd been Simon's Guardian Angel for ever, and it had been really, *really* stressy the last few years, *really stressy!* Keeping Simon stuck had been a nightmare, an absolute nightmare! He'd been ready for Sarah for years, but she, of course, wasn't ready for him! Typical woman! Nat had been forced to keep Simon stuck in dead-end relationships, long past the time he should have been happy and settled. Nat recalled the first time it had gotten really bad. He'd been sitting on the top of Simon's 42' LED smart screen television watching, with increasing alarm, the argument that had been going on in front of him between Simon and his latest lady-friend, Nadia. Oh my, that Nadia! Nat's bright orange hair had, as usual, been glowing with panic, standing up straight on top of his head, all the way up to its full six inches, making him look rather more like a 'Gonk' than an angel! Simon didn't have a clue that Nathaniel was there, of course, or that his Angel was having a seriously bad hair day! Simon was just one of the average billions of humans who couldn't see, hear, or acknowledge their Guardian Angels. That didn't mean to say they weren't there, working away in the background, just that Simon, like most people, couldn't see them.

Nathaniel picked up the story.

"Simon was going nuts stuck with Nadia. More than ready to settle down, he was, and that was never going to happen with Nadia! She wasn't the settling down kind, no, not at all! Anyway, he kept wanting to leave her, drove him nuts she did, bless, but we couldn't let him leave her, not till Sarah was ready, so we had to keep fixing things between him and Nadia so that he'd stay, well stay until Sarah was ready anyway. It was a *nightmare* I tell you Sephi, a blinking nightmare! Anyway, we held him there as long as we could and then we were finally able to let them get together, Sarah and Simon. He wanted to leave the city anyway, so we had him relocate here to Redfields. Oh, has Clar already told you that bit? Sorry. Anyway, Simon's family; mother, Linda, father, James, both live in Spain. He talks to them every week by Skype and they visit every year.

Then there's his sister, Jane, she lives in Australia so he hasn't seen her in years. So it's just him really, bless. Loads of friends, though, loads! Very popular is my Simon, very popular, lovely chap, just lovely!" Nat grinned, continuing the story of Simon. "Work - he's a financial wiz at a bank, same one as Ben, Sarah's brother, and they're mates, good mates. They're both account managers and share an office together. Now then, let me think, have I missed anything?" Nat searched his memory banks and decided that he'd covered everything that needed to be covered where Simon was concerned and declared happily to a waiting Seraphina, "Nope, that's it!"

"That's great, guys, thanks," she grinned. "The background really helps, helps a lot. Only one thing I'm a bit confused by, and that's this 'Fire Girl' thing. Why does Simon call Sarah 'Fire Girl'? There wasn't anything in the file about that!"

"Ah!" Both angels said together looking sheepish. "Well, we left that bit out of the report. The bosses don't need to know *everything!*"

"Why, did something go wrong?" she asked curiously.

"Well, only a little tiny bit." Nat looked at Clarabelle grinning, recalling Simon and Sarah's first meeting.

"Well, we had to get them together, right?" Clarabelle explained. "The problem was that whilst we got them into the same room easy enough, they weren't taking any notice of each other, none at all! So, of course, we *had* to do something! But, umm, it backfired somewhat." They were giggling.

Seraphina was now more than curious and was looking at them both expectantly for the rest of the story.

"Okay, we'll tell you, but don't you write it into any reports, okay?" they said sternly.

Sephi nodded her agreement solemnly.

Clarabelle picked up the story.

"We had them in this pub, The Crown, that's their local, well, it was Sarah's local and now it's both their locals, you know, and anyway, they weren't looking at each other, not at all! So I made an executive decision! I decided that if I showed my light, it may help her a bit. I know we're not meant to, but we were *desperate*, weren't we, Nat?"

Nat nodded solemnly. "Desperate, mate, desperate!" he agreed emphatically.

"So I sat on Sarah's head, right at the top you see, and I glowed my halo *really* bright, bright enough even for him to notice, being a human and that. Bright enough so that he'd *really* notice her and think how wonderful and special she was. It was a good plan! Well, I thought it was!" she said guiltily.

Nathaniel chipped in, "And I had to make sure he looked at her at exactly the right second as Clar lit up her halo so that he'd see the light, see Sarah, and then he'd fall right in love with her, just like they were meant to!"

"Did it work?" Seraphina asked breathlessly, excited now.

"Oh yes, it worked! Well the bit about him noticing her worked anyway, it worked a bit too well!" Nat said.

"Why, what happened?"

"Well, he saw the glow around her hair, it was bright mind you! Very bright! And then he saw the candles on the tables in the pub, and you know, being a human that doesn't get the idea of halos and stuff, he decided that her hair must be on fire!" They looked at the floor in shame, both squirming a little at what happened next.

"So what happened?" Sephi squealed, dying to know, just dying to know!

"He threw a pint of beer all over her to put her out!" they sheepishly said. "In a packed pub and in front of everyone! Soaked her, he did, totally soaked her!"

"Oh my goodness!" Seraphina giggled. "I bet she didn't like that!"

They shook their heads solemnly again.

"Hated it! Hated *him!*" Clarabelle admitted. "Anyway, that's why he calls her 'Fire Girl,' cos the first time he ever saw her, she was on fire, well, he thought she was. Took us some work to sort *that* one out I can tell you! They couldn't stand each other for a while, but we put it right. Took a while, but we put it right in the end. That was last June, then he moved into the flat in July, they didn't speak for weeks, but finally made friends in August, and then they got together properly early in September. Whirlwind it was, total whirlwind, but then, they were always meant to be together so it was bound to happen! He proposed Christmas day, so romantic, so romantic! One knee and everything! He hid the ring in a cracker, bless his cotton socks! Just lovely!"

"And it all went smoothly after they got together?" Sephi asked.

"Well, more or less," Nathaniel said, "although we nearly had a problem with Nadia, but I sorted it. Oh, that Nadia! She's a one, I tell you! She turned up at his city apartment when he went to clear it after he sold it last November. All going lovely with Sarah it was and then

Nadia the EX turns up and tries to seduce him! Stark naked, I tell you, just a long fur coat on and nothing underneath! Hell bent on getting him back, she was. I sorted it, though, don't you worry. He threw her out, right out, fur coat an' all! Sarah doesn't know, mind you, doesn't have a clue. No need for her to know, nothing happened anyway, but it was a bit of a scary moment for us, I can tell you."

"And that's the story of Sarah and Simon?" Sephi asked. "And they all lived happily ever after?"

"But, of course!" grinned Clarabelle and Nat in unison. "But, of course!"

"Right then, dear, is there anything else you need to know or have you got enough to be going on with?" Clarabelle enquired kindly to a clearly tired out Sephi.

"Oh, that's enough for now, thank you so much to both of you. I'm really looking forward to working with you," she said politely. *Enough for now?* Seraphina was exhausted! *So much to take in!* Still, she had plenty of time to assimilate all the information over the next few months, loads of time to catch up before Baby Angelica arrived: eight months, three days and twelve minutes to be precise! Perfect! Just perfect!

Chapter 3

Sarah and Simon spent the first day home from their honeymoon unpacking, sorting out the laundry, and catching up with the house and garden chores as they began their reluctant return to normality. Phone calls were made to friends and family announcing their safe return, post opened, plants watered, and photos downloaded from their digital camera onto the laptop, for a future evening of reminiscing the fabulousness of their honeymoon over a bottle of wine and a takeaway. The following morning saw their wedding presents opened, thank you notes written, and by the end of the second day, it was almost as if they had been home for two weeks rather than two days as it had gone so fast!

Sarah was in her own little bubble and enjoying every moment of it until Clarabelle showed up the following afternoon as she wandered happily around the large supermarket doing her weekly food shopping. Appearing without warning, as per usual on her left shoulder, the angel announced brightly, "So, what did he say? Take it all right did he? When you told him?"

"Ah, well, no, not quite. Haven't quite got round to it yet, Clar, sorry. But you knew that anyway didn't you?"

"Yes, dear, of course, I know that. If you had have told him I'd have been there wouldn't I, but as you *clearly* had no intention of telling him these last few days I thought I'd leave you to it."

"Really? Wow, that's not like you at all! What's going on? What are you up to, Clarabelle? You've been acting weird for days!" she hissed as quietly and discreetly as she could to a mysteriously acting and definitely weird Clarabelle. She wasn't normally weird, well, not weird apart from being an angel, of course!

Sarah hated these interactions in public places, being very aware that she looked totally potty talking to her bloody shoulder. It was a wonder that she hadn't been locked up years ago! People in the supermarket were looking at her, noticing her whispering to herself around the fruit and vegetable aisle, so she tried to be a bit more discreet in her questioning and interrogation of Clarabelle. Something was definitely going on, but what? She turned to the glowing Clarabelle and demanded, "Spill! Spit it out, tell me all, now! What are you hiding, you little minx?"

"Well, dear, you may want to... Ah, umm, no. Never mind. Must go, things to do, things to do," and she was gone!

"Bloody hell!" said Sarah to herself in frustration. "I hate it when she does that! Repeats herself and then goes all mysterious and you just know that she knows something and she won't tell you, and she's the one lecturing me on secrets, bloody hypocrite!" She smiled at the irony of it, at the same time seeing a way out of having to tell Simon about her angel. *If Clarabelle had a secret or two, which she clearly did, then I can use that as a reason to get her to back off until I'm ready to tell Simon, as opposed to being nagged to within an inch of my life to do it before I'm ready. Secrets went both ways! You tell me yours and I'll tell you mine kind of thing. Ideal!*

Sarah felt the pressure lift and continued her shopping in a far more relaxed state than when she'd come into the store. "Yes," she decided, "I'll tell him in my own good time, preferably when there's something else going on to distract him so that he won't freak out too much. Yep, good plan, good plan." She hesitated for a moment and burst out laughing in the beans aisle at the realisation of her last statement. "Ye Gods, I sound like bloody Clarabelle again! I'm repeating myself just like she does. Ah well, hay ho!" she giggled, and continued her shopping.

Sarah's thoughts drifted to the following day. It would be their first day back at work and life was well and truly getting back to normal. She'd be in her store before eight o'clock in the morning to check the books and to make sure Tim had followed all of the instructions that she'd left. Hopefully her beloved store was still standing, but she knew it would be. Tim had been with her since the beginning when she'd first bought MacKenzie's store and he had been a rock, bless him. Yes, she was looking forward to going back to work very much.

***

Metatron had followed the new orders that had come through a few days earlier and ensured that all was in place, as instructed. He agreed with the new plan and wondered why they hadn't thought of it in the first place, especially as the time scale was so short. Still, it was sorted now and all was ready. He knew he would have to speak to Second Class Angel Clarabelle about the orders that had come through following Clarence's visit to The Boss. That could wait, though. Far more pressing was this new vibration that he was still feeling. He'd flown right across the entire cosmos over the last few days and he was now definitely aware of the energy, but not what it was. It felt alien, like it didn't belong, and he was determined to get to the bottom of it. His next plan was to visit every planet in the multiverses to see if he could identify this new energy that seemed to be present in the Angelic Realms. Once he could put his finger on it, he could sort it, but the multiverses were a big place and it would take some time, not that time was an issue for Angelic Beings, being ageless, of course! He'd just have to fit it in amongst his other tasks. He certainly couldn't delegate it, not without admitting that there was something he didn't know! He'd lose kudos, respect, awe, and all manner of things right down through the ranks. No, this was something he and he alone would have to sort out and he wouldn't rest until the problem was solved and he was returned to his normal state of being, 'The All Knowing, All Seeing, Mighty Metatron.'

***

Sarah walked into the semi-darkness of her store early

the following morning with a grin. She loved this old place with its low ceilings, adorned with many rows of electric strip lights, each overseeing one of the small, narrow aisles. She noticed, as she usually did, the shadows bouncing off the mirrors and glassware by the door as they vied for position with the early morning sun peeking through the small windows. Musty with the smell of time, old wood, and love, the shop stood, as it always had, oozing character from every crevice, its shelves piled high with every conceivable item that the local townsfolk might need. Sarah looked around her with a satisfied smile then headed to the back office.

She soon got to work checking the books, the banking, the orders, and the sales and then set about reorganising a few things in the storeroom. Tim wasn't the tidiest soul bless him and Sarah, being a typical Virgo, just couldn't stand a mess. She was humping stock boxes around quite happily when Clarabelle showed up.

"Nooooooo!" she screeched loudly, making Sarah jump right out of her skin, dropping - with a huge smash - the large box that she'd been carrying.

"What the hell, Clarabelle! What did you do that for? You scared me half to death, you dozy fairy!"

Clarabelle glared at Sarah. "Fairy? Fairy! Sarah, did you just call me a fairy?" she scolded. She was most unamused. Sarah glared, furious about the lost stock not to mention the fact that Clarabelle had made her jump out of bloody skin! Clarabelle glared back. Calling her a fairy was one of the worst insults possible, but Sarah was cross! God knows how much stock was now broken because of bloody Clarabelle screeching at her!

"Okay, I'm sorry. You're not a dozy fairy!" she conceded reluctantly. Clarabelle, at times, was not to be messed with and by the look on her face, one of those times might be now.

"Thank you! Not that there's anything wrong with fairies, of course. They have their place, lovely creatures, lovely creatures, but angelic they are NOT! Fairy indeed! Humph!"

"Yes, okay, I said I'm sorry. Now why did you scare the life out of me like that?" Sarah demanded. "What is wrong with you?"

"Ah, well now, umm, I ..." Clarabelle mumbled. "I can't remember. Sorry. Never mind."

"What?" demanded Sarah, her hands on hips, she was a force to be reckoned with as she stubbornly refused to let the subject drop. "What's 'nooooooo'? A screamed nooooooo at that! You never scream, so what's going on, Clarabelle? Spill right now or we are going to fall out big time!"

"Oh dear, oh my, really, Sarah dear, it's nothing. Umm, let me see, yes, I .... I just think it's a good idea for you *not* to be carrying heavy boxes! Not good for your back, not good at all. You'll slip a disc, my dear!"

"Hmmm. Why don't I believe you? Maybe because your halos gone dim! It always dims when you're lying."

"Lying? Me? Don't be ridiculous, child! I don't lie, angels *can't* lie!"

"Why's your halo dim then? Aye, aye, answer me that?"

"It's just that umm, oh, dear. My, my, what shall I do?" she panicked.

"Just tell the truth, Clarabelle," Sarah laughed and

added with relish, "THE TRUTH WILL SET YOU FREE! Ha-ha! Gotchya!"

"Umm, yes, quite, child! I can see where you are on this, but this is neither the time nor the place. However I will make a bargain with you, a deal if you would. I shall tell you what I know when you tell Simon about me, how's that? Shall we say tomorrow after work? Or even tonight? Yes, tonight!"

"No, no, no, that's not fair! That was gonna be my line, my deal!"

"Sorry, child, I got there first. So do we have a deal? You tell Simon about me and I shall tell you what I know," she beamed.

"So you do have a secret! I knew it!"

Clarabelle smiled serenely, staring at Sarah intently as she waited for a response. Sarah hesitated, although she didn't know why really. She had the curiosity levels of a million cats put together and now that Clarabelle had admitted there was something that she wasn't telling her, Sarah would just have to find out. It would kill her if she didn't! "Okay, deal. You win," she agreed reluctantly. "I'll tell him tonight after work. Just make sure he doesn't fetch the men in white coats or anything, okay?" she groaned. "I mean it, Clar, if this goes wrong and everything falls apart because of me telling him about you I will never, ever forgive you!" she declared dramatically.

"Of course, my dear, of course. Nothing *will* fall apart and I shall be there, of course, I shall be there! And all will be well, very, very well!" Clarabelle grinned and then quickly disappeared again.

She'd been disappearing a lot lately, Sarah noticed. "I

wonder if the disappearing is anything to do with the secret that she's holding? God, the suspense is killing me!" Sarah shook her head and went back to work. Her first task was to clear up the mess in the box that was upside down on the floor where she'd dropped it. "Sods bloody law that is, just like toast - it has to land on its arse-end to make the worst damage possible!"

The day passed quickly as Sarah caught up with everything at the store. Tim had done a sterling job of holding the fort as temporary manager, along with Mary and Sam, the assistants. It had ticked along like clockwork, just like she'd known in her heart that it would. For a start, she'd had Clarabelle check up on them every day and report back to her at the beach - there were definitely some perks of having an angel even if she was really annoying sometimes, bless her!

As five o'clock loomed Sarah started to get nervous. How the hell was she going to broach it? What on earth should she say? What in heaven should she say was more like it! *Ben!* In an 'Ah-ha' moment, Sarah reached for her mobile, texting Ben in a panic, **'ring me wen u finsh wk. urgent, ta. X'**

Two minutes later he rang, darling Ben! *Thank God for little brothers!* Admittedly she hadn't always thought that way, but since he'd grown up, he'd been fantastic and she loved him dearly. The fact that Ben had his own angel, Clarence, really helped things on the 'understanding-and-having-a-clue' level and Ben would be sure to know what to do. "Oh, thanks, Ben, thanks for ringing. Can you talk?" she asked as she picked up the mobile, knowing full well that he must have snuck out of work to call her.

"Yes, go ahead. What's the problem, Sis?"

"Is Simon within hearing distance?" she whispered. Ben and Simon shared an office and it would be a bloody disaster if he overheard this conversation!

"No, I'm outside. What's wrong, mate?"

"Bloody Clarabelle is what's wrong! She's insisting I tell Simon about her and I'm scared to death! Have you told Gina about Clarence? Does your wife know about your angel and that you can see him and talk to him?" she asked, near hysteria.

"God no! Are you mad? Gina would have a fit!" her brother laughed. "She'd have me committed! Why on earth does Clarabelle want you to tell Simon? Clarence has never pushed me to tell Gina. If he did, I probably would mind you, cos he's always right, always knows best. It's odd this. Let me think for a minute." Ben paused and collected his thoughts. He knew the angels never forced you to do anything you didn't want to do, but when they were insistent it was always because it was important for some reason. "Sis, I reckon if your Clarabelle thinks that it's right for you to tell Simon then that's what you have got to do, hun, bite the bullet and go for it. If he's in work tomorrow asking me to have you locked up I'll do my best to calm it down. Try not to bring me into this though, aye, not unless you have to?"

"Okay, Ben, thanks anyway." Sarah's face fell.

Ben could hear the disappointment and panic in his sister's voice, but this was one that she was just going to have to handle on her own. *Tough for her though*, he thought. He knew he would be worried if he had to tell Gina about Clarence! *She must be petrified!* "I know it's not the answer you want to hear, Sarah, but it's the only answer I can come up with at the moment, hun. If Clarabelle thinks it'll be okay then I'm sure it will be. She's never let you down yet now, has she?"

Sarah hesitated. "No, she hasn't. Okay, I'll do it. Nut house, here I come! Laters and thanks, Ben." She ended the call and sat with a bump on the nearby stool. *God help me now!* she thought to herself with trepidation. "Let's just hope Clarabelle's right and Simon is going to be okay with this."

***

Sarah walked slowly home in the summer sunshine, praying all the way to herself. "Please, God, don't let him leave me. Please, God, don't let him hate me. Please, God, don't let him lock me up for being crazy." On and on the prayers went as she walked along the pavement, into her lane, and right up to her front door. On and on they went right through the hallway and into the kitchen. Simon, thankfully, was nowhere to be seen; neither was Clarabelle, and with the thought that maybe she was going to be spared this ordeal, Sarah was just beginning to relax when Simon walked in at exactly the same moment as Clarabelle appeared - perched on top of the kettle.

"Honey, I'm home!" called Simon in a loud fake American accent as he approached the kitchen and an increasingly nervous Sarah. He pulled her into his arms and gave her a huge kiss along with a massive bear hug, nearly crushing her ribs in the process. "God, I missed you!" he declared emphatically. "Two weeks together day and night and it was really hard not being with you today, babe, first day back and that."

"I know, hun, me too," replied Sarah as she clung to him. Seconds passed and then minutes and Sarah had still not let go of her vice-like grip of her husband, fearing that hug may be for the last one forever.

"Don't be silly now, child," piped up Clarabelle. "I've told you that it will be fine. Trust me now!"

She popped onto her usual perch on Sarah's left shoulder and began to pour love, healing, and light into her. It descended through Sarah like an injection of Radox, bringing an instant calm to every part of her previously tense body. She relaxed and released her grip from a bemused Simon and gazed up at him. *God, he is beautiful*, she thought for the millionth time! His deep blue eyes shone intensely, his blond hair flopped over his tanned and handsome face as he looked down at her with both concern and with love.

"What's wrong, Fire Girl?" he asked gently. "Has something gone wrong at work?"

"No, work is fine, darling, marvellous, in fact. Tim's done a wonderful job holding the fort at the shop while I've been gone. Takings are good, the banking is all in order, and the stock is fine. Well, nearly fine. I dropped a box at work and lost a fair bit from breakage, but everything else is fine."

"What is it then, sweetheart? Something's bothering you; that much is clear. Want to tell me about it?" He kissed her nose and smiled at her reassuringly.

"Well, yes, I do, but after tea. Let's eat first, aye? It's been a long day, babe. We'll have a chat after, okay?"

"Of course, it's okay, honey. You tell me whatever it is whenever you're ready. Now, what do you want to do about food? Eat in or out, takeaway or cook, pub or something else?"

"Oh, cook. I'll do it. You go and get showered," she replied quickly. Cooking a meal would give her time to think and work through what to say and how to broach it. She set about with the wok and began to prepare a stir-fry. By the time Simon came back from the shower it would be ready and then after dinner they would talk. He kissed the top of her head, ruffled her hair, and went upstairs, taking the stairs two at a time with his long legs. Sarah sighed. "I hope you know what you're doing, Clarabelle?" she said nervously.

"It will all become clear, dear, just trust me." She grinned at Sarah, smiling serenely, and took up her perch on the top of the kettle again. She loved to watch Sarah cook - she was so creative!

Sarah contemplated as she threw ingredients into the pan. Simon would be the first person she had ever told about Clarabelle, apart from Ben, of course. She'd confessed all to him one drunken night last summer after she'd confronted her mother and Ben had come over later to support her. It had just spilled out, and when it did, she had been amazed to discover that Ben had an angel too - Clarence - and he admitted that he could see Clarence and talk to him just like she could see Clarabelle and talk to her! That had been so funny, that they'd both been keeping their own secret from each other, the same secret, and for over twenty years! She'd never told anyone else. Her friends Frieda and Angie, friends for more than thirty years now, didn't have a clue, no boyfriend had ever known either, and certainly not her mother! This would be a first, to tell her husband, and she really didn't know what to say or how he'd take it, but if Clarabelle said it had to be done, then it had to be done! Since she'd started listening to her fifteen months ago, her entire life had turned around and she'd never been happier, so if Clarabelle said spill, then spill it was! "Ho hum, wish me luck," she said to Clarabelle as she dished up. "Nothing's ever going to be the same again!"

**

Sarah was so busy eating her food and trying to figure out how to tell Simon that she hadn't noticed Clarabelle popping off. If she had, she'd have panicked, but Clarabelle was on a mission and had snuck away quietly. She knew that Simon would need evidence, proof of some kind, in order to accept his wife's 'gift,' so she had disappeared off upstairs to see Nathaniel. Under the Angelic Privacy Code she was unable to divulge any information that wasn't directly related to Sarah, unless, of course, she had direct permission from the recipient, and it was all so terribly complicated! Universal Laws of Free Will and Integrity had to be obeyed at all times and to achieve this she would need Nathaniel present and co-operating.

"So, Nat, I'm going to need you, if you have a mo, a tick, a spare few minutes, okey dokey?" she smiled.

"Sure thing, Clar. What time and where?"

"Right now, Sarah's sofa, and we need to go! They're just finishing loading the dishwasher so we need to beam down now. We haven't time to fly, no time, no time!"

Beaming into the living room just as Simon and Sarah walked in, the angels took their posts. A curious Simon and a nervous Sarah settled together on the big, comfy, suede sofa in front of the fireplace. Clarabelle and Nathaniel sat on the top of it grinning expectantly at Sarah, waiting for her to start. Nat was nervous, Clarabelle noticed. His orange hair was doing its 'thing,' spiked up to its full six inches in a perfect Gonk impression. He squealed in horror as he saw his hair in Sarah's mirror over the mantelpiece and pulled his cap urgently out of a pocket in his robes. He quickly pulled it down over the offending hair with a shriek. "Stress!" he yelled, "You know what it does to my hair, Clar!"

Clarabelle patted his hand reassuringly, but she was grinning as she looked at the state of him, his hair still spiked up high with the cap balanced precariously on top of it at a funny angle. She pulled it down firmly, poking an orange spiked strand under the side of the cap. "There, it looks fine, Nat, stop stressing," she scolded. "Look, they're ready, pay attention now, we're on!" she urged.

Chapter 4

The logs crackled in the hearth, despite it being early July, Sarah having lit it earlier while their dinner was cooking. Looking into its flames and feeling its warmth across the room had always helped her think, helped her to focus. Soft music played, creating a soothing atmosphere. Sarah just hoped and prayed it would help soothe her troubled nerves!

"Well the thing is, Si, I need to tell you something about me, something that you don't know. I should have told you before I know, I just didn't know how to," Sarah said hesitantly. She watched Simon's face for reactions, but it gave nothing away, so she continued, "I don't know how you're going to take it and I'm a bit nervous of telling you. I've never told anyone before, only Ben, so this is a bit scary for me."

"Okay, babe, you're making me nervous now, but whatever it is, I'm sure we can sort it together," Simon replied. He wondered what this secret was that his wife was keeping from him, but he smiled reassuringly at her and nodded his encouragement for her to go on.

"The thing is, babe, umm ... the thing is that I'm a bit psychic. I see things, well, one thing actually, but it's changed my life and it works and it's a good thing and I know it's a bit freaky, but, really, it isn't scary, it's safe and it's good," she blurted and rambled on without pausing for breath.

Simon's eyebrows rose sceptically as he looked at Sarah. "O k a y," he said slowly, "Psychic? Right ... umm ... things ...? What kind of things?"

"Well, it's only one thing really, only she's not a thing, she's an angel and her name's Clarabelle. She's my Guardian Angel and I've been seeing her and talking to her since I was seventeen."

"Angel? Mmm, right, angel ... okay. ..." Simon looked more than sceptical now, he looked downright disbelieving and more than a little concerned.

"And I know it sounds mad and I don't want you to think I've lost the plot and I'm sorry I didn't tell you before, but it's not the sort of thing you broadcast easily, but Clarabelle made me, well, told me I needed to, and Clarabelle's never wrong, so I had to, you see?"

"Clarabelle's never wrong. Right." Simon was speaking very slowly, just as an adult would talk to a child when explaining something really, *really* grown up! "And this angel, this 'Clarabelle,' she's here now? Right now?"

"Yep!"

"Right..." Simon stared at his wife. His mind was struggling to compute what she was saying. He tried to process, tried to understand, tried to believe, but his rational educated mind just refused to accept her words, and yet he knew she didn't lie. She clearly believed this herself, which was even more worrying! Simon scratched his head. She was normally so rational, a down-to-earth and head-screwed-on kind of person, but here she was spouting about angels and seeing them and talking to them. She'd clearly lost the plot! *Oh shit, what was he meant to say?* He didn't have a clue! She was looking at him expectantly, waiting for support, understanding, acceptance, but he couldn't give it. He just couldn't! Simon felt totally helpless and scared to death!

"Clarabelle, help me!" Sarah said out loud as she looked convincingly at the top of the sofa.

Simon's jaw dropped. He stared at her in disbelief. "You're talking to the sofa?"

"No, darling, I'm talking to Clarabelle, my angel."

"So this angel, this Clarabelle, you're talking to her now?" he questioned in amazement.

"Yes, darling. She's sitting on the top of the sofa in between us."

Jesus Christ, this was worse than I thought! She really is nuts! "Umm, yes, dear," he said, "of course she is. And what, umm, does this Clarabelle look like exactly?"

"Well, she's about six inches tall, that's most of the time, but now and again I do see her in her full size, which is about six feet tall; but right now she's about six inches tall."

"Mmm, right, six inches tall. Like a fairy? A goblin? An elf? How about a space man? Does she have a space ship too? Silver one, maybe?" He couldn't hide the sarcasm now. He was doing his best to play along with this ridiculous farce, but really, this was getting a bit much! *Maybe she's picked something up abroad on their honeymoon, got some mad cow disease or something that was making her talk so crazy? I really must get her to the doctors tomorrow and have her checked out!*

Sarah smiled at him. She'd expected this and more, much more, so she wasn't at all surprised. She didn't rise to any of his scepticism or his sarcasm, she just went along with it and with the most patient voice she could muster she answered, "No space ship, no. She has wings and she flies, dear, she doesn't need a space ship."

"Bloody hell, you really are serious, aren't you? You really believe this stuff? Jesus, hun!"

"I know it sounds mad and far-fetched and all that, but it really is true. I can prove it! Honest I can! Ask anything, anything you like and you'll see!"

"Right. So this ... this 'Clarabelle,' she knows everything then, does she?"

"No, darling. She doesn't know everything, but she can *access* everything. Like there's a great big bank of knowledge, all knowledge, of all time, and she can access it. Ask something and I'll show you."

"Sarah," Simon said in a firm voice, "I don't like this game and I don't want to play!"

"Clarabelle, tell me something that only Simon would know," Sarah implored.

"Yes, dear. Nathaniel, spill please," Clarabelle ordered, smiling at Nathaniel and waiting expectantly for some little gem.

"Who's Nathaniel?" Sarah asked

"Oh, that's Simon's angel, dear. He's here with me."

"Simon, your angel is called Nathaniel and he's here too," Sarah explained to a now totally freaked out Simon, passing on information as she got it.

"Sarah!" Simon's tone was warning now.

"And he says to tell you ..."

"What are you going to tell him?" she whispered to Clarabelle.

"Tell him that he should forgive himself for the little reaction he had when Nadia came round to his flat that day he went to clear it."

Sarah looked at Simon with shock.

"What?" he questioned.

"And when *precisely* were you going to tell me that Nadia came to your flat the day you went to clear it?" a furious Sarah accused her husband.

"How the f...?"

"Exactly! I couldn't have known that! Cos *you* never told me!" Sarah glared at Simon. Simon was dumbstruck! He stared at the top of the sofa in a combination of fury, disbelief and quite a bit of fear.

"And she was wearing a fur coat, a long one," Clarabelle informed the fuming Sarah.

"Fur coat? Long one?" Sarah enquired with raised eyebrows at a guilty looking Simon.

"Nothing happened, babe! I swear to God, nothing happened! She tried it on, I threw her out! I promise you!"

"Clarabelle, is that true?" Sarah asked the top of the sofa.

"Yes, dear, true," came the reply.

"Okay, you are forgiven. Forgiven for not telling me, I mean. I know nothing happened cos Clarabelle confirms it and she never lies!"

"Bloody hell, Sarah! This is mad!" said a shocked

Simon, "Totally bonkers!"

"I know, but it's also true!"

"Tell me something else?" Simon asked, curious now that his mind was beginning to accept the strangeness of events unfolding before him. He pinched himself hard, just to make sure that he was actually awake and not dreaming.

Clarabelle was beaming from halo to feet with the biggest grin ever.

"Ready? I'll tell you the secret I've been keeping now. Hold hands, please!"

Sarah grabbed Simon's hand and waited. God she loved secrets!!! Well, finding out what the secret was!

"Ready? You're ... drum roll, please ... pregnant!" Clarabelle yelled, jumping up in glee and throwing her arms in the air for extra effect and dramatisation.

"Pregnant!" a shocked Sarah exclaimed loudly!

"Pregnant?" Simon questioned with shock.

"Pregnant!" Clarabelle and Nathaniel confirmed in unison (although Sarah couldn't see or hear Nathaniel).

"Wow!" all four of them said together.

"How long?" Sarah and Simon asked at the same time.

"Seventeen days, eighteen hours and thirty-five seconds! Your wedding night to be precise!" replied Clarabelle. Gosh she was showing off now!

Sarah relayed the details to a stunned and happy Simon before they threw their arms around each other, both bursting with delight.

"Do you want to know if *she's* a boy or a girl?" asked Clarabelle, adding a happy 'Oops!' and then laughed.

"Clarabelle wants to know if we want to know the sex, only she's already let it slip so I already know!" Sarah grinned.

"No, don't tell me. You might be the font of all knowledge, wife of mine, but I prefer the normal cause of things and knowing what I know, when I'm meant to know it, thank you very much!"

"I understand, darling. Isn't it wonderful news! A baby! Oh my God! We're going to be parents!" Sarah was suddenly incredibly excited. She'd managed to suppress maternal instincts for years, but now with this news those instincts were surfacing and surfacing fast! She was suddenly overwhelmed with emotions bubbling up inside her and she began to cry. Simon held her gently in his arms as she sobbed, listening to her short statements between her gulps and between her pulling back to blow her nose periodically. "I thought I'd never be a mum," she gulped. "I thought it was too late. I thought it would never happen," hiccup, blow, snot, gulp. "And now it is, finally, at last, wonderfully, happening," gulp, snot, hiccup. After a final blow of her nose, Sarah suddenly declared, "shop, now, test! I want to have it all confirmed properly, scientifically, come *on!*" And she jumped up and raced out to the hall for her coat and bag, running back into the living room to grab Simon's hand and drag him with her to the nearest large supermarket that would still be open at eight o'clock in the evening.

"But if this Clarabelle of yours is never wrong, why do we need a pregnancy test?" asked a confused Simon, still trying to get his head around everything that had happened in the last hour.

"We just do, come *on!*" Sarah implored, impatient to see the evidence of the little blue line on the stick thing that

she'd seen advertised on the telly over the years. B[e]
which, her GP would want proper evidence. There was n
way she was going to tell her doctor that she knew she was
pregnant because her angel had told her so! "I want one of
those ones that don't just tell you that your pregnant, I want
one of those stick things that tell you how far you're
pregnant!" she exclaimed.

"Yes, dear, fine, dear, whatever you say, dear, let's go!"
a happy Simon acquiesced.

An hour later, an ecstatic Sarah and an equally
delighted Simon sat staring in wonder at the little blue line
on the pregnancy test, squealing in delight at the 2-3 week
indicator that was displayed, proudly confirming it all.
They had huge grins on their happy faces.

"Clarabelle, I love you!" Sarah screamed.

"Tell her I love her too!" smiled Simon, suddenly more
than happy to allow his wife, his pregnant wife at that, to
have as many six inch fairy folk or angel folk or any other
folk as she liked! "And I love you, you wonderful, clever
girl!" He grinned, hugging her as gently as he could, scared
of breaking something, anything, in her body that was now
housing his son or daughter. Sarah suddenly had a thought
and turning to Clarabelle she squealed, "That was why you
had a screaming fit in the store room this morning, isn't it,
because I was carrying a heavy box? You're not meant to
carry heavy things when you're pregnant, are you?"

"No, dear, not good for either you or the baby, and yes,
it is why I shouted. I didn't mean to, it just slipped out when
I saw you lugging that weight. I am sorry, dear, really I am.
I will sort the broken stock for you, don't you worry my,

st leave it to me. It's an age since I did a little age!" They smiled at each other as a bemused ...ked on. *My wife is having a one-way* ...on *with the top of the sofa, but really, it doesn't seem to matter anymore, not at all!*

"Can we tell people?" he asked. "Is it safe? Or do we need to wait till after the scan thing?"

"Clar, what do you think?" Sarah asked the smiling Clarabelle.

"Oh, child, you can tell who you like. The baby is safe, safe as houses. Just stay away from heavy lifting and all will be well; we'll take care of that. She's been waiting a long time to come in and nothing's going to go wrong, I promise you. You have my word."

"Thank you, Clarabelle." Sarah turned to Simon and confirmed smiling.

"Yes, Si, we can tell. You call your parents and I'll call my mother and Ben, or shall we do them all together?"

"Together!" Said Simon, Clarabelle, and Nathaniel in unison.

The next hour was spent on the phone to a delighted family, as news spread. Angie and Frieda were the last, but certainly not least, until the happy and still slightly wondrous couple fell into bed and each other's arms.

***

It was more than a week later when Sarah realised that she hadn't yet got to the bottom of why Clarabelle had insisted that she tell Simon when Ben had got away with keeping his wife Gina in the dark. She was sitting by the till in her store, questioning the unfairness of it to herself when Clarabelle appeared.

"Quite simple, dear, Ben isn't pregnant!" Clarabelle answered, even though Sarah hadn't said a word. *God, it was so unnerving when she read her mind!*

"Well, I know Ben isn't pregnant, silly! That'd be a miracle and a half now, wouldn't it?" she laughed. "What's me being pregnant got to do with it, though?"

"Simple, my dear. You are already quite psychic. The gift you have to see me comes from your soul energy being in line, attuned, harmonised, and things like that, but now with not just one but two souls in your body at the same time, well, my dear, your psychic abilities will be stronger, much stronger! You will have double the energy, so to speak, you see? And it's only going to get stronger, so he had to know, do you see?"

"Mmm, I think so."

"And there is also the fact that Angelica will be psychic too, of course, just like you and Ben, so poor Simon really does need to get used to it all well before she learns to talk. You know that you can't shut children up! Telling a two-year-old to keep her angel a secret from her father just won't work at all, no, not at all, my dear!"

"Who's Angelica?" A confused Sarah asked, trying to take in this rather startling news.

"Why, your baby girl, of course!"

"Her name is Angelica? The name is decided already? And she's going to be able to see her angel too?"

"Yes, dear. Names and the dates of birth, right down to the time of birth are already decided. All part of the energy they bring in with them, planned you see, planned. All to do with astrology and numerology, but don't you worry about that." Sarah nodded, although she was totally lost now! Clarabelle continued on with her explanation as Sarah tried to take it all in.

"You see, although Ben has the gift too, it was his wife who housed the new soul as he came in, your nephew Joe; and Gina is not psychic and neither is Joe. That is why Clarence never needed Ben to tell Gina about him, it had no bearing, no relevance, but it does in your case. Do you see now, child?"

"Umm, I think so." Sarah was confused, startled and overawed, all at the same time.

"And Sarah, you need to be aware that you will begin to see and know more and more over the next eight months, my dear, as the new soul gets stronger. You will need to be prepared and really it isn't something you should be keeping from your husband. He will get his, how do you say it? Ah yes, I know, he will get his 'head around things,' eventually, I promise. Although I do take exception to being called a fairy, a goblin, or a space man! Silver ship indeed! Nothing wrong with my wings, nothing at all, perfectly fine!" she declared firmly, flapping them theatrically.

"Mmm, so my baby is going to be called Angelica? Do I get a say in this? What about free will and choice and all that?" Sarah felt slightly annoyed, railroaded by this decision being taken out of her hands in this way.

"Oh, my dear, you would have chosen that name yourself anyway. We lot upstairs would have put the name in your head and you would have thought that you'd chosen it yourself, but really, it was already planned long ago. Trust me on this. I simply gave you the name because I can, alright?"

"Yes, alright." Sarah was smiling. It was a lovely name for her little girl, beautiful in fact. "Angelica!" Angel...ica, very apt really considering! And it did make sense now why she'd had to tell Simon and Ben hadn't had to tell Gina. Clarabelle was always right and she didn't know now why she'd got so upset about it all. It made perfect sense!

"Right oh, dear, if all is square and happy I shall pop off. I have a date, I mean a *meeting* that I need to attend. Ta-ta for now!" and she was gone. *Date? She has a date? Wow!* Sarah thought with wonder. She didn't know angels dated but then she still had so much to learn about upstairs.

Had she known that angels did not indeed, 'date,' she may have been rather concerned for what Clarabelle was getting herself into!

Chapter 5

Clarabelle was sitting waiting on Cloud 903, the furthest cloud out from the Angelic Realms, waiting for her 'AA Mickey.' She had polished her halo, preened her feathers and smoothed down her robes in an effort to look her absolute best. Her golden hair flowed in waves on her shoulders, her blue eyes twinkled with anticipation and for some reason her breathing was inexorably tight! She wondered why he had chosen this particular cloud as it had taken an absolute age to get here! *It couldn't be so that no one would know, as that would imply they were doing something wrong! No, no, not at all, it was simply a matter of privacy!* She was so excited at seeing him again that she thought she'd pass out with pure delight! "No, no! No passing out!" she said to herself. "We've had quite enough of that!" Clarabelle suddenly felt the cloud she was sitting on begin to move across the sky at a rate of knots! "Oh my!" she squealed.

Archangel Michael popped his head up from the edge of the cloud and smiled at her "Good morning, my dear," he grinned. "You're looking fabulously beautiful today, if I may say? Fancy a little ride? I thought we'd pop over to the Garden of Peace for a stroll together by the lake. Would you like that?"

"Oh my goodness! Oh yes, oh my!" Clarabelle beamed adoringly. His handsome head disappeared just as suddenly as it had appeared as he popped back under the cloud, carrying it and Clarabelle to their destination. She felt somewhat like a princess on it, being quite literally 'carried away' by her beloved Mickey! "Oh my, oh my!" she breathed (as much as she could 'breathe,' being an angel without any actual lungs, and being as her chest was strangely very, very tight)!

She peered over the edge of the cloud and watched him as he flew them across the sky. His thick dark hair fell in curls around his handsome face and over onto his large muscled shoulders. His massive wings were outstretched to their full twenty feet span, rustling in the wind as they flew. His battle dress of the warrior shone in the sunlight where it had clearly been polished. *For me?* she wondered in awe. She fell back onto the cloud in wonder. "Oh my, indeed!" she beamed. "How very exciting!"

Sometime later, Cloud 903 floated happily down and hovered gently over the Garden of Peace, the only cloud in the clear blue sky that adorned this special place.

Michael popped his head over the edge of the cloud once again and grinned at her. "Ready, my dear?" he smiled, as he floated up from underneath the cloud, hovering in front of her with his hand held out towards her.

"Oh yes, ready indeed!" she replied blushing. She put her hand in his and felt his fingers wrap around her own.

As they did, she felt a heat rise up in her, from where she couldn't comprehend, but she seriously thought that she was going to spontaneously combust it was so intense! With immense effort she managed to calm herself down and stepped off the cloud towards him. They floated down together into the centre of the garden holding hands and came to rest on the grass beside a beautiful white fountain. Clarabelle gasped. She'd been here before, of course, it really was an incredibly wonderful and special place and today it seemed even *more* special than usual!

Michael led her up to the white marble fountain. It had three tiers and the water sparkled and twinkled in the sunlight as it cascaded down the tiers and into the large pool below it. Around the bottom tier were a row of golden goblets. Michael picked one up, placed it into the water, and filled it, handing it to her. Each goblet had a word engraved on it and on this one was the word 'JOY.'

"Oh my! I don't think I need any more joy," she exclaimed. "I couldn't be any more joyous, truly I couldn't! 'Calm' might be a good one though, perhaps I could have a drink from the cup of Peace or Tranquillity? It may stop me feeling so, umm, let me see, what is the word I'm looking for?"

"Excited?" he smiled. "Happy?"

"Umm, no, well, yes, but no." She truly was not making any sense at all and was getting increasingly flustered as she tried to identify what it was that she was feeling. "Flustered, yes, flustered, that's the one I do believe!" she declared triumphantly.

"And why is that, my dear?" he enquired, stepping up

close to her and pressing his feathers against hers teasingly.

"Oh my, oh my! Really, Mickey, do give me a chance to catch my breath!"

He smiled and as he did, the entire garden lit up as if someone had just turned up the sun. Michael's energy, normally incredibly powerful anyway, seemed to have increased in both voltage and size and the entire garden was now glowing like a beacon. Clarabelle wasn't doing too badly on the energy-level-glow score either! Her own light emanated around her, radiating a reddish tint, most unusual for her. It was normally a golden glow like most of the angels.

"You're looking incredibly beautiful today, Clarabelle, my dear," he said, "Did I say that already? Well, then I shall say it again my dear! Just beautiful! Shall we go?" he motioned.

Clarabelle didn't know if her legs would actually carry her, but she nodded her assent anyway. They walked, they talked, they smiled, they grinned, and they giggled as their time together passed. They swam in the lake, dried off in the sun, walked some more, giggled some more. Clarabelle truly felt that she'd never been so happy in all of her three thousand years of existence! When it was time for them to go she turned to him smiling, "Same time tomorrow, Mickey?"

"But of course, my dear. Shall I pick you up again or meet you here?"

"Oh, pick me up! That cloud ride was just divine!"

"Collection it is then, my dear."

As they returned to Cloud 903 he suddenly swept her up into his arms, winding his feathers around hers.

Holding her against his chest, he held her and as he did, their hearts touched each other's in a unity, bringing them together as their energies merged and collided. A connection and a oneness engulfed them both, a oneness that would last for all eternity.

***

At that exact moment, in his office at the rear of the Angelic Temple, Metatron suddenly jumped up as the entire heavens shook. "What in heavens was that?" he exclaimed in alarm, feeling the wave of strange energy sweep across the cosmos like a tornado. The door burst open as dozens of panicking angels poured in, all talking at once, and all looking to Metatron for answers of the cause of this blast of energy that had just shaken The Realms. "Calm down, calm down!" he commanded, waving his hand across the room in an effort to soothe the turbulent energies and angels alike. "All is well, all is safe. Leave it to me, go back to work."

They filed out dutifully, all wondering what had just happened, but if The Mighty Metatron, the 'All Seeing, All Knowing' Mighty Metatron said it was safe and well, then it was safe and well. He'd sort it!

Metatron looked at the closed door and sat down in alarm. For the first time in his eons of existence he didn't have a clue! 'All Seeing, All Knowing'? Not quite! Not yet, but he would get to the bottom of it and he would find out who or what had shaken the normally peaceful Realms, and shaken them with such fervour, and when he did, he'd have their feathers for a pillow; he'd have every last one!

Sarah clutched Simon's hand as they waited in the corridor of the local hospital. "If I don't get in soon I am seriously going to pee myself!" she stated for the hundredth time, and that was in the last ten minutes alone. "How can they expect you to sit with a full bladder for this long? It's ridiculous!" she exclaimed crossly. "Drink a pint of water an hour before your appointment they say, then they leave you there for another two hours after your appointment time! Do they do it on purpose, just to watch you suffer?" she complained.

"No, dear, I'm sure they don't. I'm sure they're just busy. It'll be our turn soon, hun, just hang on in there. Try to think of something else," he suggested patiently. Seeing her squirming around on the hard waiting room seat in her flimsy gown with her legs crossed, he did feel sorry for his wife. Her face was pinched with the concentration of trying to control her increasingly swollen bladder. "Can your Clarabelle help at all? Make it go away?" he suggested hopefully.

"Bloody good idea! Well done that man! Clarabelle, I need you!" she said out loud, the desperation evident in her tone. Several faces looked at her from the other expectant mums-to-be, also trying desperately to hang on for their turn before they wet themselves in public. They assumed Clarabelle was her mum or a friend that she was calling for, but no woman was with her, just the lovely looking man holding her hand and patting it reassuringly every now and again.

"You only have to ask, child, and it is done!" Clarabelle

beamed, doing her best to help the uncomfortable Sarah. She turned down the volume level on the bladder trigger in Sarah's brain as they all waited together. Nathaniel sat patiently as ever atop Simon's head as he watched and waited the comings and goings of the department. He'd never been in a hospital before and was quite amused by it all.

All of a sudden the door near them opened and a voice called out, "Sarah Brown, please?"

"Oh, thank God!" a hugely relieved Sarah whispered, getting up as slowly as possible so as not to shake or disturb her bursting bladder and empty its contents all over the corridor floor.

Lying on the hard bed Sarah looked up at Simon in anticipation and then with shock. She was staring at the top of his head as if he was having the worst hair day ever!

"Something wrong with my hair?" he asked, watching her face as her mouth hung wide open in surprise. She closed it and got a grip quickly.

"Umm, no dear, tell you later," she replied, still staring at his head. Sarah couldn't take her eyes away. She was agog, staring at the male six inch tall angel in amazement, who was evidently quite comfy on top of Simon's head. He had bright orange hair which was almost as long as he was tall that was sticking straight up like a Gonk, with a strange cap perched on top of his rather strange hairdo! He appeared to be about thirty years old, same as Clarabelle, and was preening his feathers absently as he watched the proceedings. "Nathaniel, I presume?" she asked silently in her head to the chap on her husband's head. Nathaniel grinned and smiled at Sarah. "You can see me?"

She nodded and slowly smiled back.

"Am I having a bad hair day again?" he asked. Looking at her shocked expression he assumed that he was and pulled his cap down a bit harder over his puffed up hair. "Well, I mean, it's a stressful time, isn't it!" he chirped. "My hair always does this, sticks up when I get stressed, but don't worry about it. I am actually an angel not a Gonk, but I'm sure you know that. You do, I hope?" he added expectantly. Sarah just nodded, still taking it in. At the same time she noticed a larger, older angel out of the corner of her eye hovering in the doorway discretely. He was rather rotund with greying hair. His eyes smiled at her and she felt very safe although she didn't have a clue who he was. He put his fingers to his lips, motioning silently a 'shh.' She smiled, nodding at him, and looked back at Nathaniel and 'the hair'!

"Well, this is all happening rather quicker than I expected!" announced Clarabelle in surprise. "Your abilities are turning up more than a notch if you can see Nat. Lovely hair, hasn't he? Just lovely! So orange and shiny!"

Clearly Clarabelle hadn't noticed the older angel at the door and it was also clear that he didn't want her to. Sarah kept his secret, although she didn't know why, it just felt right to.

"Focus now, Sarah, you are about to see your daughter. Pay attention!" Clarabelle ordered. Sarah obeyed immediately, focusing her attention on the woman in the white coat brandishing a steel wand thingy, which was attached to a monitor by her side. She watched initially with awe as the nurse poured thick jelly over the end of the steel thingy and then the awe slowly turned to horror as she watched the evil masochist proceed to press said instrument down firmly, right on top of her extremely swollen and overly full bladder.

"I'm going to pee myself!" she screeched in alarm.

"No you won't, dear, just breathe. Good girl."

The nurse, or whoever this evil person purported to be, smiled sweetly at her encouragingly! *Why is it*, Sarah wondered, *that all hospital staff have the ability to regress me back to when I was six years old and I find myself mutely obeying without question or argument? Maybe it was the white uniform?*

"Ah, there we are!" the masochist said. "Lovely! Do you see?"

Sarah looked at the screen obediently. Nope! Didn't see a thing! What was she meant to be looking at? That blob or that blip? That shadow or that one? How these people could see she didn't know, but she clearly didn't have the x-ray eyes that they did! Had they been Clark Kent in a previous life perhaps? Where was the kryptonite when you needed it?

The evil masochist continued to press the steel thingy down on her bladder even harder, scraping it across her lower stomach whilst managing to still retain a sweet and innocent look on her pretty face. "There!" she exclaimed, "Do you see now?"

Sarah peered again at the screen obediently. God knows what this woman was capable of if she dared to disobey! Blimey, yes, she could see something now. She couldn't make out what it was, not quite, but there was definitely something there.

"Ah!" smiled the evil one, waving the steel thingy about in an even bigger frenzy, "We have two! We have twins!"

"Twins?" both Sarah and Simon yelled.

"Twins?" both Clarabelle and Nathaniel yelled.

"Twins!" all four of them yelled.

"No one told me it was twins!" said Clarabelle in a quiet, hurt voice.

"Nor me!" said Nathaniel in a disappointed, annoyed voice.

"Nor me!" said Sarah in a scared, trembling voice.

"Nor me, what?" said Simon, in a frustrated being-kept-in-the-dark voice, not being privy to the conversation that was going on other than hearing Sarah's side.

"Nor me knew that it was twins, darling! Clarabelle and Nat didn't know either!" she said startled. This wasn't meant to be twins surely?

"I thought they knew everything?" Simon asked, confused but delighted at this turn of events.

"Normally yes!" said a confused Clarabelle, "but someone has clearly arranged this behind my back, without informing either me or Nathaniel. Totally *not* acceptable! I should have known, should have prepared you! Both of you! How very, very unacceptable! Not okay, not okay!" she trilled, near hysterics.

All four of them stopped their complaining for a moment to listen to the evil masochist as she interrupted their wailing, saying now, "It looks as if it's not full twins; its fraternal or superfetation twins."

"Aye?" all four exclaimed.

"Super what?"

"Frat what?"

"Fraternal superfetation! It's when a second foetus begins to develop after there is already one developing," she explained, but Sarah looked confused. They all did! The nurse continued her explanation in a slower, 'you-are-very-stupid' voice. "They have not come from the same egg and the same sperm. Sometimes it happens like this." She looked at Sarah expectantly, wanting to see her nod her head in confirmation of total understanding. Sarah stared mutely back at her. "Hmm, let me see, how to explain? The mother releases eggs at different times and they are then fertilised by different sperm at different times. In your case, I would say about two weeks apart judging from the difference in sizes of the foetuses. One is approximately twelve weeks, the other around ten weeks according to the measurements, although we will know more at your next scan. It's not uncommon, around seventy-five percent of all twins are fraternal or superfetation. There is nothing to worry about, Sarah. It does mean that they won't be identical though, as they will share only half of the genes, which is normal for any siblings anyway. Identical twins have all the same genes. These two of yours could be the same sex or different sexes, again we will know more at the next scan. Your due date will also be brought forward; twins rarely go full term to forty weeks, usually two or three weeks before, so that will be around the second week in March, all right?"

"Wow!" all four exclaimed.

"Can I have a pee now, please?" Sarah begged, running for the door as soon as she saw a nod from the 'evil one,' leaving the others to make their way out of the scan room in their own time.

Clarence watched the chaos from the hospital doorway with a grin on his face. Make him wait two years for boy? I don't think so! He'd never lost a feather toss in three hundred years and he wasn't going to lose one now! David may be two weeks behind Angelica, but he'd make sure he came out first. Last in - first out! Clarabelle would go nuts mind you. She wouldn't like it that he'd gone behind her back to The Boss to ask for the second soul to come in now, alongside the first, but not only did that plan mean he didn't have to lose the feather toss, it would be better for Sarah anyway. After all, she was thirty-nine now, quite old for a first time mum! Yes, definitely best to get it over in one, bring the two souls in at the same time and then it was over and done with! Two souls had been booked for Sarah and Simon many years ago and he didn't see why they couldn't come together, especially with the delays they'd already had.

He saw Clarabelle look in his direction and quickly hid behind the door. He'd deal with her later! He was still annoyed with her for her ridiculous crush on Archangel Michael, although to be fair, his 'twins' stunt was making up for it. He'd definitely got his own back there judging by the look on her face. He laughed. His sister and AA Michael? As *if* for goodness sake! Angels don't romance, and even if they did, which they don't, the Mighty Archangel Michael would never look twice at a Class 2, Level 1 Angel like Clarabelle! Romancing and all that passion, not to mention lust and flirtation, well, they were all human traits, not angelic traits anyway! Totally insane!

Whatever was she thinking? She'd see the light sooner or later and hopefully sooner, before Metatron got a whiff of it. There'd be hell up if he found out! Literally!

Chapter 6

Sarah relayed the startling news to a shocked Margaret Smith as she sat in her mother's kitchen drinking tea and munching on her eighth biscuit. The late September sun shone in through the kitchen window filling the room with warmth. "So twins, Mum, twins! How am I going to manage? I don't know what I'm doing with one baby let alone two! Will I be all right? Will it be okay? I've started the folic acid and stopped drinking alcohol, of course. I'm trying to be careful, but will it be okay?"

"Yes, dear, it will be fine, I am sure." Margaret nodded, being surprisingly supportive for her. She was trying so hard these days, trying to build the bridges that had been missing for a lifetime between mother and daughter and she wasn't doing a bad job!

"Gran or Granny?" Sarah asked, "Or Nan or Nanny? Or Grandma?" she suggested.

"Well, Joe calls me 'Nan,' Sarah, so I think we should stick to Nan. Besides which, your twins could not possibly call me Granny. I am not an apple, Sarah, and I refuse, simply refuse to be referred to as Granny Smith!"

Sarah giggled. "Yes, Mum, Nan it is."

"You will need equipment, Sarah, lots of it. Two cots, two car seats, and two high chairs, not to mention two changing mats and all those nappies! Such a lot to think about!" Margaret worried. She was incapable of not worrying so Sarah just smiled and let her. That part of Margaret would never change, although a lot of other bits had over the last nine months since she'd come round. She'd been trying hard to mend fences with her estranged daughter. She'd softened, been kinder, more tolerant, and more accepting than ever before, ever since Sarah had finally confronted her last summer. Somehow, it had shocked her out of her bullying abusive behaviour towards her only daughter and with Ben's support, Margaret had begun to accept that Sarah was not the useless daughter, person, or human-being that she had always thought that she was. In Margaret's' mind now, Sarah was actually, surprisingly, quite acceptable! She was also looking forward to having more grandchildren. Sarah had done well there; twins would be nice - busy but nice! "I shall help you, of course, Sarah. I shall be available for babysitting and advice when you need it. Are you going to breastfeed or bottle feed? It will be difficult I imagine, to breast-feed twins, but perhaps the midwives can advise you on that?"

Sarah thought about this practicality with a start. How on earth would she feed two babies at once? How did other people manage? Blimey, there was going to be a lot to find out! Still, she had plenty of time and she had Clarabelle, as well as Frieda and Angie; they both had kids and they'd tell her everything she needed to know. She must talk to Clarabelle, find out about the other baby too. She'd been surprised that Clarabelle hadn't known about this. Clarabelle always knew everything! *I wonder what's changed,* she thought. *I wonder what's going on! Ah well, I'm sure she'll get to the bottom of it.*

***

Clarabelle was indeed, 'getting to the bottom of it' as she sat outside Metatron's office waiting for an audience with the boss of all angels. The huge doors swung open and his voice boomed out, "Come in, Class 2 Angel Clarabelle."

She walked in with shaky legs, nervous as ever of the Mighty Metatron.

"Ah, Clarabelle," he said as she entered the vast room, "This is Class 2 Angel Elijah. He will be working with you and Seraphina and has been allocated to be David Brown's guardian angel. I am sorry for any confusion, but plans were changed at the last minute by the 'All That Is,' so all of this was put in place rather quickly. We didn't have time to brief you and for that, I'm sorry."

He smiled at her, noticing something different about her, something amiss, but he couldn't put a finger, or a feather, on what it was. Brushing it aside, he continued, "David is developing nicely alongside Angelica and all is being prepared for their arrival into the earthly world next March. Both, of course, will be Piscean, strongly psychic like their mother and both have been briefed on a soul level, although, of course, they will have no recollection of this once they arrive. Do you have any questions?"

Clarabelle shifted from foot to foot. She didn't dare to question either Metatron or the 'All That Is,' but she just couldn't get over how this had happened without her knowledge! "Would it be possible to ask, do you think," she hesitated, "umm ... the thing is ... I just wondered what had prompted the plans to be changed?" She stood nervously, not sure if she was over-stepping the mark to question him in this way.

"I believe it has something to do with Clarence's visit some time ago. Other than that, I can tell you no more," he said.

Clarabelle was gobsmacked! *Clarence had been up here? To the boss? Clarence had had an audience with the 'All That Is'? No way!*

"Now if there is nothing else, I have things to do. If you'll excuse me." Metatron looked down at his files and refocused his attention on the map of the universes. How many planets were left to visit? He'd covered more than half of them and still hadn't come across that strange energy that was still rumbling in The Realms every now and then. He was getting impatient to know what it was and he planned to visit more planets that day in his search for clues. He looked up, surprised to see the two angels still standing there. "You may go," he glared at them, dismissing them with a wave of his hand.

Both Clarabelle and Elijah hurried out of the room, aware that they had overstayed their welcome and rushed away. As soon as she was clear of the Angelic Temple and on her own Clarabelle screamed out across The Realms in the loudest voice that she could muster, "Clarence ... you are *sooo* dead! When I find you I'm gonna de-feather you! You, you *traitor!*"

She flew off quickly to Cloud 903 hoping to catch Mickey and tell him this disastrous news. She'd known that Clarence had been really cheesed off with her about losing the feather toss and on top of that, she knew that he was very cross with her about her and Mickey. Goodness knows how much trouble he may have caused! The only one who could change souls once they had been ordered was God himself! Clarence must have asked God to change the baby to twins and whilst he was there it was very possible that he'd also dobbed them in about Mickey's and her clandestine meetings! They'd better be prepared and quick!

***

The late summer sunshine poured into Sarah's kitchen as she made a pot of coffee for Frieda and Angie. They were having a girlie afternoon, catching up and chilling out together. Simon was out playing the last cricket match of the season with the local club and wasn't expected back till God knows when. There'd be celebrations and jubilations afterwards, win or lose, and it would be a late one, probably involving copious amounts of beer! Angie's husband was part of the team too, so they were both cricket widows and loved every minute of it! Not only did it mean their men were happy, it also meant the girls had peace and quiet every other Saturday! Frieda was the only one of them single, currently between husbands and fiancé's and she'd had three - of both! There wasn't even a whiff of a boyfriend on the scene at the moment, which was most unusual for her!

"Glorious day! I love it when we get an Indian summer,"

Frieda smiled, piling several large spoons of sugar into her coffee and munching on her third cake.

How did she stay so stick thin? Sarah wondered. By rights she should be at least nineteen stone, but no matter how much Frieda ate, she remained her usual ten stone and size twelve. Being 5'8" this wasn't at all big on her and she looked amazing for nearly forty! Sarah envied her the ability to burn off the calories, knowing that she herself only had to look at a cake and an extra ten pounds would mysteriously appear on her hips the next day. Being pregnant now though, wow, it was different! She was going to get huge anyway, especially with twins, so this was an absolutely fan-dabby-dozy opportunity to stuff whatever she wanted, whenever she wanted! There really was a God!

"How's the preggers coming, hun? Any sickness or anything yet?" Frieda asked between mouthfuls of cake. Sarah shook her head triumphantly.

"Nope, not a jot. Bloody marvellous! I feel full of beans, just great really. It's a doddle this! Dunno what you lot were all moaning about when you were carrying yours!" She grinned at them both, aware that this statement was akin to a red rag to a bull. Both Frieda and Angie had suffered horrendously throughout all of their pregnancies, five between them - two for Angie and three for Frieda, one from each marriage bless! There had been sickness, bloated this and that, swollen this and that, and that was before you took into account the horror stories of the births themselves - hours and hours of agonising labour! Holding up her hand before her friends had time to retaliate to her inflammatory remarks she jumped in quickly, "I'm joking, I'm joking, peace, peace!" She waved her hands dramatically and giggled. "I know its early days for me at just fifteen weeks and I guess I'll get my time sooner or later and when I do, I'll probably have double the crap cos it's twins."

"Mmm, we'll see. Be very careful there, Miss Perfectly Healthy, Miss Unsickly, Miss Boundless Energy! If you know what's good for you, I'd quit while you're behind before I batter you!" Frieda threatened, but she was smiling.

"I dunno, she may get away with it and have a fabulously easy pregnancy, you never know?" a helpful Angie suggested.

Clarabelle nodded her agreement to this statement. "No doubt about it, I'll make sure of it!" she chipped in.

Sarah smiled and tried to ignore the interruption from the fourth guest, uninvited at that, but never mind, she was one of the gang really, well kind of!

"This pregnancy is going to go swimmingly if I have anything to do with it and as I do, then it is a given!" She beamed at Sarah from her perch on the handle of the kettle. Clarabelle loved these girly chats too, but being one-sided from their point of view, they didn't generally go too well for her. Never mind, at least she was here being part of it all, smashing!

"Really? That's great!" Sarah declared, hugely relieved by this statement from Clarabelle.

"Really? What's great?" the girls enquired, looking confused.

Sarah tried quickly to cover her tracks and think back to the last bit of actually spoken conversation that they could all hear, trying to make the interruption seamless. Ah yes, Angie's remark! "Angie saying I may have an easy pregnancy, of course!" Phew, that was a close one! One of these days they were going to figure out something was up with Sarah, but for now, she'd got away with it, again!

"Why don't you just tell them?" Clarabelle enquired politely. "It would be sooo much easier for everyone if you did! Think about all those secrets and lies that would be out in the open. You know, Sarah, the truth. …"

"Will set you free! Yes, I know, ta very much!" She finished the sentence for her. God she was annoying sometimes!

"If it was good enough for Jim Carey!" Clarabelle piped up.

"Aye?" Sarah said, looking bemused at her angel.

"Liar, liar, silly! Remember?" Before Sarah had a chance to reply that yes, she remembered the film, she was interrupted.

"Aye?" both girls said in unison.

Shit! Had she said that out loud instead of in her head? Most of her conversations with Clarabelle when she was in company were silent, kind of telepathically, but now and again they slipped out of her mouth instead of her mind and it looked, from the raised eyebrows on both of her friends' faces, that she'd done that now.

"See!" triumphed Clarabelle. "You'll have to lie again now, but there is no need, truly there isn't! Just tell them the truth; they'll think it's hormonal or something. They'll be fine with it anyway and you'll be able to help them … lots and lots!"

This was new! How very interesting! To be able to help her friends, the people she loved dearly. But how? What did she mean, help them? Her, help them? "I'll think about it," she stated. This time the thought was clearly in her head and not coming out of her gob! "But not now! We'll talk later, shush!" she ordered.

Clarabelle 'shushed' and decided to pop off upstairs and leave the girls to it. It was high time she tracked Clarence down. He couldn't avoid her forever!

Mickey had told her not to panic, to just ask Clarence if he had dobbed them in. Angels can't lie, so the sooner they found the elusive Clarence and found out the extent of the damage the better! If he hadn't told on them then it was high time that they made up. This rift between them really couldn't go on for much longer! They hadn't spoken since just after the award ceremony - not properly - and that was June, months ago! Angels didn't normally hold grudges and it felt wrong, very wrong indeed, not to be meeting happily with her brother and chatting nicely as they always had. She missed him! Yes, definitely time to make up, but only if he hadn't told on them. And if he had? Well, then … then what? She really didn't know what she would do if he had told or what trouble she would be in!

"Things to do, things to do!" she shrilled nervously and popped off to try and sort it all out.

***

Sarah had a lovely time with her friends for the rest of the day. They, of course, both moved from coffee to wine as the afternoon drew into the evening, whilst she herself moved onto an unexciting orange juice. Humph! Still, it had to be done. How many weeks left before she could have her usual Pinot Grigio wine again? At least twenty-three and then there would be the breastfeeding time to add to that, assuming that alcohol went into milk, and she thought that it probably did. If she didn't want to see either of her newborn twins tipsy then it would mean no wine for an age! *There really was no choice about it, so best get used to it*, she thought to herself. That was, of course, if she could work out how to breastfeed two babies at a time! She turned to ask Clarabelle about it and noticed that she had disappeared, again! She was doing that a lot lately, disappearing, and it was most annoying! Really, she must find out what was going on there! Something was definitely amiss with Clarabelle!

***

Simon sat in the bar with Tom enjoying his fourth pint. It had been a great day. They'd lost, of course, always did, crap team really, but it had been fun! Most of the players in the team were there to enjoy the cricket, have fun, and have a few beers afterwards. This was after all, a village cricket team in a sleepy town, hardly 'The World Series'! There were a few, of course, that were there to win, win, win, and win at any cost! Simon smiled as he thought of the disappointment on some of their faces. Gutted they were! He'd had his years of being competitive; the years of drive and of winning when nothing else mattered except the victory, but he'd changed his priorities since leaving the city and these days it seemed more important somehow to just enjoy the game and have some fun. He clearly wasn't the only one who thought that way - judging by the results!

Just then Liam, a young competitive, 'win, win, win' type of chap, sauntered up to them waving his pint of lager at them disparagingly, commenting sarcastically, "Of course, if anyone bothered putting some spirit into it we might *actually* win a game!"

Simon just smiled, nodded and returned to the conversation with Tom, leaving Liam to go and moan to someone else. *Maybe he'd be better off in the football team?* he wondered. *Far more testosterone there! Much more suitable for the likes of Liam!* Cricket was a gentle game and Simon refused to get het up about the result. They'd had fun, the sun had shone, and it had been a good day so why spoil it by getting pissed off about the result?

He turned his attention back to Tom and the conversation he wanted to have about pregnancy. Tom and Angie had been married forever and had two boys, so as far as the inexperienced Simon was concerned, Tom was the font of all knowledge on the subject.

"Well, mate, me and Angie got married when we were twenty-four. Chris came a year later and then Martin two years after that. I tell you, Si, she was a bloody nightmare on both of them! Hormones raging like a mad cow! Don't expect any sex, any peace, or any love for the next three years at least and then you'll be fine!"

Simon looked totally horrified!

"And grow a very thick skin! Everything will be your fault, from her boobs being sore, to her feet aching, to her back aching, to the price of milk, and anything else that's wrong in the world. She'll moan about being fat - for God's sake never agree - fatal! She'll moan that she's ugly - again, never, ever agree, no matter how crap she looks, always tell her she's beautiful to you! Learn to lie and learn to lie fast!"

Simon laughed. "It can't be that bad, surely?" He saw the sceptical look on Tom's face. "Really?" he asked, seriously concerned now.

Tom nodded solemnly. Simon took a very large gulp of his pint as his mind began to comprehend what he had in store for the coming months and then he took another!

"Oh, mate, you have no idea! That bad and more! Imagine the worst PMT she's ever had - times it by a thousand and you'll begin to get the idea. Just prepare yourself for the worst and then you'll get through it, somehow!"

"Moody? All the time?" a pale Simon asked.

"Up and down, but mostly down."

"And no sex?"

"Ah well, now, that's a hard one to call. That's up and down too. One minute she can't get enough of it, like a rampant animal on heat - the next she can't stand you touching her at all." Simon paled even more.

Tom patted Simon on the back in a comradery way that only men with pregnant wives know. "And when she gets too much and you want to kill her, just smile sweetly, tell her you need to walk the dog and get the hell out of there."

"But we haven't got a dog!" Simon exclaimed.

"Well, get one! You'll need it, trust me! Best excuse to suddenly get out, get away when she turns from your adorable loving wife into the evil wife from hell. It won't last long mind. Up and down like bloody yoyos, they are. Hormones! One minute she'll love you and the next minute she'll hate you. The dog's the answer, mate, definitely! Either that or a shed! Always need an escape route, trust me!"

Simon pondered the advice. *Yes, dog! I've always fancied a dog and it would be nice for the kids to have a plaything. Yes, definitely a dog.* He'd sort it soon.

"And if you can, start doing some work-outs on your hands. If you haven't got time to go to the gym use a tin of beans. Do squeezy exercises to build up the muscles in your hand."

"Aye?" Simon was blank on that one!

"For when she goes into labour! Doh! She'll squeeze your hand so tight she'll break every bone in it if you haven't prepared. I'm telling you, mate, they turn into bloody tigers when they're giving birth! Dunno where the strength comes from, but don't mess with them, bloody lethal!"

Simon was a member of the gym and worked out quite frequently, although he rarely used any of the muscle building equipment. He was more about running and keeping fit than trying to turn himself in Arnie. Mind you, Tom had a point. Maybe he should start working on his hand muscles. He could quite see his Sarah turning Tigress! Yes, definitely a dog, but no matter how grim Tom made it out to be, he was still looking forward to it and if Sarah did turn into the Mad-Wife-From-Hell every now and then, it didn't matter - he loved her to bits and he'd cope. A dog was a good idea, though, and maybe he'd invest in a shed too!

Chapter 7

Metatron had checked half the cosmos and still hadn't found this strange energy that was rocking The Realms. Angels were beginning to talk and it was really most annoying! He'd had to cut his visit short today just as he had been about to enter the Milky Way and check out the planets around that particular sun, and all because of yet another shake up in The Realms, he had been called back and his tour was interrupted. Still, they were getting nervous and he needed to go back and reassure everyone that all was well. He would continue his investigations tomorrow!

***

Clarabelle and Archangel Michael were sitting by the side of the lake cuddled up together happily in the Garden of Peace when they heard the call for angels of all levels to attend a special hearing in the Angelic Temple right now!

Metatron himself had called the emergency meeting and it wouldn't do to miss it, no not at all. The pair reluctantly got up and flew back, splitting up half way there so that no one would know that they'd been off together, again!

Clarabelle entered via the south gate and saw Clarence standing in the pew with Nathaniel and some of the others. *Ah ha!* she thought with glee. *At last, my elusive brother, he can't avoid me now!* She slipped into the pew behind him quietly, but just as she was about to confront him, Metatron walked in and took his stance on the stage. Waving his arms, he quieted the waiting crowd and began to speak. *Oh, bother!* Clarabelle thought. *No time now, what a shame!*

"Angels, Archangels, and Trainee Angels I bid you welcome," he boomed. The room fell silent as everyone waited with bated breath for him to address them. "We are gathered here today for me to inform you that we have a rumbling, a change, a new energy, a disruptive energy at that, within the Angelic Realms."

The sounds of whispering angels could be heard across the temple. Someone brave shouted out, "Are we in trouble? Is it dangerous; should we worry?"

Before Metatron could reply another shouted, "No, really, disruptive?"

"Wonder what it is?"

"Is it dangerous? How dangerous?"

"Is it the Demon Angels come back again from the other side?"

Questions were being shouted out from all across the huge hall now and from every direction. Metatron lifted his arms once again and the room quieted. "I," he boomed, "The Mighty Metatron - The All Seeing, All Knowing Metatron, *will* find this energy and *will* banish it for all time! Of that you may be assured. There is no danger, no risk, it will be dealt with and it *will* be banished, for eternity!" A huge cheer raised the roof as all of the angels yelled and clapped in rapture. "Angels of Light, do not despair, do not worry. I, Mighty Metatron will conquer this disruptive energy and peace *will* be restored to our Realms!" The roof nearly took off with the cheering this time!

Clarabelle herself cheered wildly along with the rest, but she noticed that Mickey, standing with the other Archangels on the east side of the hall was clapping rather quietly and looking rather nervous! She couldn't understand why. She'd have a word later if she got the chance, but right now, Metatron was finishing his speech and then was dismissing all the angels. She turned her attention to Clarence before he had time to escape, grabbing his wing as he went to file out with the others. "I need to speak to you," she hissed. "Now!"

Clarence nodded and turned to her he beckoned, "Follow me, Clar. I agree. We need to talk, oh yes, indeed, we need to talk!"

She followed him out of the hall and down the corridor. Looking around him discretely, checking for any signs of anyone around and seeing the corridor clear, he pushed her into a side room, closing the door quickly. Before she'd had time to open her mouth he jumped straight in. With an urgency to his voice that she'd never heard before he hissed at her between gritted teeth, "Have you *any* idea how much trouble you're in?" he panicked. "Do you know what's going to happen to you if he catches you? If he finds out it's you? You'll be demoted, de-feathered, and probably kicked out of the Angelic Realms altogether!"

Clarabelle looked at him in horror. "What are you talking about, Clarence? What in heaven do you mean? I've done nothing wrong, nothing wrong at all?"

"Nothing wrong?" he practically spat! "Nothing wrong? You do realise it's *you* that he's looking for? *Your* energy? You and Archangel Michael?"

Clarabelle looked shocked and began to tremble.

"You! Yes, you! Both of you! The energy that's been rocking The Realms is *lust!* Lust and passion! From you and your blinking Mickey!"

Clarabelle sank to the floor and burst into tears. "It's not lust, Clarence, nor passion! It's romance! Romance and love!"

"That energy, Clarabelle," he hissed insistently, "is flirtation! Flirtation, lust, and passion! It's an *earthly* energy and an energy that does not sit well in the Angelic Realms! It does not belong here! It is why it has been shaking up here, ever since you and Michael started your torrid affair!"

"It is *not* a torrid affair!" she cried. "We are in love! We are angels! We are meant to love!" she implored.

"Not *that* kind of love you're not!" he cried, although he was beginning to thaw a little on seeing her tears. He'd never seen her cry before, bless. In fact, he'd never seen *any* angel cry! Angels didn't cry, ever! That was a human trait, another one! Oh dear, this was worse than he thought! He calmed down, sitting himself heavily on the floor besides her he took her hand gently. "It's not your fault, my dear. Not his either, really. Both of you have spent so much time on the earth, too much time clearly, that you have been contaminated by some of their rather less appealing emotions."

"I don't understand!" she sniffed.

"My dear, most of us work with our wards quite easily. We are in and out, up and down between here and there. We don't spend that much time down there, not in one go and not all the time. But you, you see, had such a hard job getting Sarah to work with you, you spent more time there than is normal, much more! I believe that you began to pick up the human energy that emanates from many down there, the energy of flirtation, and you can clearly see where that's led!" he triumphed.

"But what about Michael, my Mickey?" she questioned, still teary eyed.

"Oh, well, that one is simple. Archangel Michael is *the* most well-known, *the* most popular, and *the* most used of all the Archangels by the humans. They are always calling on him from far and wide, right across the globe! He spends more time down there than up here! He is the Angel of Courage, of Protection, of Confidence, The Warrior, and The Fighter. He is the one they call on when they are scared, lost, and nervous, and as most humans are most of those things most of the time, Michael is a busy boy! Do you see?" he asked, more kindly now. Clarabelle nodded. "All of those are the things that humans lack in bucketfuls, so they're always calling on him for something or another. It's not at all surprising that he's picked this up, almost human he is, almost human!" Clarence declared.

Clarabelle understood. She looked back over the last twenty years or so and counted the hours that she'd spent 'downstairs' with Sarah trying to sort her out. It was so many compared with Clarence and the others! He'd had an easy ride with Ben who had cooperated magnificently right from the very beginning, unlike her Sarah! If Clarence advised Ben on something, Ben got on with it without question, leaving Clarence free to return home to The Realms. Her Sarah on the other hand, well! She had stubbornly, pigheadedly, independently refused to accept any help, any advice, any *anything* at all for years! Clarabelle had practically lived in the human world, so yes, she could see what Clarence meant. But to give up her Mickey? Oh my! No, no way! They'd just have to work around it! If it *was* their energy that was rocking the Angelic Realms by being together, then they would just have to do their courting elsewhere, and where better than from where it was coming - planet Earth! Yes, they'd meet there instead of in The Angelic Garden, then Metatron wouldn't find out and all would be well. Smashing!

Clarabelle smiled at Clarence. He was only looking out for her, she knew that, but this was none of his business and it was best that she kept him in the dark. "Alright, Clarence, dear. You have my word. I will no longer see Mickey in The Realms. I will no longer meet him in The Garden, alright?" She smiled at him reassuringly. The relief on his face was evident!

"Thank goodness for that! I'm so glad you're seeing sense, my dear. Such a risk, such a risk, for you both! The red tint to your energy practically gives it away too, so obvious, and it's around you both! You know what that is, don't you? It's passion! The red tint of passion! Up here! Not okay, not okay! Your energy is meant to be the golden light of unconditional love, not the red glow of passion! Contaminated, contaminated! You need to get in the healing temple and get it washed off, right now, before someone else notices and get your Mickey to do the same before you get caught!"

"Yes, dear," she acquiesced, having no intention whatsoever of getting anything washed away! *Blimey, was that a lie I just did? Gosh, yes! I really am getting more human by the second! I've just lied to my brother without even hesitating! Oh dear!* Oh dear, indeed!

***

It was the end of October. The late summer sun had faded into the autumn golden glow. The leaves had turned in Sarah and Simon's garden to the most beautiful golden colour, creating a landscape of light that radiated all around their home. Sarah was almost half way through her pregnancy and Simon finally understood what Tom had been on about! Hormones! He stared at the advert for the golden retriever puppies in disbelief. How much? Dear God alive! He was buying a bloody dog not a house! Still, if that was what they cost then that was what they cost! He dialled the number and made the appointment to view the puppies at lunchtime. An appointment to view? A dog? Really? It was just like buying a house and nearly as expensive!

A few hours later Simon was holding the puppy as it

licked his nose happily. It wasn't so much a case of him choosing it as rather he being chosen by it! The thing had bounded across the kitchen floor of the breeders house and lunged itself into his lap as soon as he had crouched down, nearly knocking him off his feet. God it was sweet though! Jesus, was that him saying 'sweet'? Well, he had to admit it was very cute indeed! Its floppy ears and chubby body was covered in golden puppy fur and it was the softest, loveliest thing he had ever seen! Simon was smitten!

Nathaniel was delighted. He had picked out the best pup as soon as he had seen the litter. He'd had a little angelic word in his floppy ear (animals were so easy to work with, bless them!), and the little thing had bounded over to Simon immediately. After payment was made, the paperwork was completed, to Simon's amazement - never having bought a pedigree dog before. He didn't know that it came with a birth certificate - First of September it said, an insurance certificate, and all manner of other 'ificates,' then arrangements were made to collect said pup at five thirty pm. Simon left to return to work at the bank with the biggest smile on his face ever. Nat grinned as he watched Simon. Gosh, if this was what a pup did to him, imagine how he's going to feel when it's his own children! Better help him with the rest though, bless him, he doesn't have a clue what he's going to need, or what he's letting himself in for! Nat whispered the word 'equipment' into Simon's ear, followed by 'dog food' and it had the desired result.

Simon left work a little earlier than usual and stopped off at the pet store before collecting the pup. He walked around the huge store completely overwhelmed and not a little terrified by what he saw. Dog's beds of many sizes and shapes, toys of more types than he could ever imagine and when he came to the food aisle, he was gobsmacked to see thousands of bags, tins, and boxes of so many varieties, it beggared belief! He knew when he was beaten and without hesitation, marched over to the customer services counter for reinforcements. Half an hour later Simon surveyed the back seat of the car stuffed full of 'equipment.' The boot was also full to bursting! The young girl had been amazingly knowledgeable and helped him choose the right size and type of bed, not soft and cuddly as he would have bought. God no! She said he'd chew that to pieces within a month! She'd recommended a hard plastic bed and a mat to go in it. Then there was the clock - a clock for God's sake! She said the ticking would help him settle, something to do with mistaking it for the mother's heart beat or something mad. Many chewy toys were also collected, as well as flea stuff, worm stuff, leads and collars, and bowls and bags. Simon just couldn't believe how much was involved with this dog business! It cost almost as much as the dog by the time he'd gotten to the till and he needed a trolley to get it all to the car! On his way around the store though, he had come across a particular toy that he liked. It was called Fred for some reason, although quite why the manufacturers had decided to give a toy a man's name, he didn't get, but he picked it up immediately, liking it immensely. Yes, Fred, great name for a dog!

Nat was delighted! Simon was getting good at this, picking up what Nathaniel was trying to do, very good really for a 'closed human' who couldn't hear his angel. He had a word with the pup earlier about his name and the little bundle of fur had decided that he'd like to be called Fred. As Simon had walked around the store with Nat whispering Fred, Fred, Fred, over and over into his ear, Simon had suddenly noticed a toy with the same name and bought it, so Fred it was!

Sarah was making tea in the kitchen noticing how big her bump was getting and thinking how much her back was aching when Simon came home from work. He was late and he hadn't even rung! She felt quite cross about it which was unusual for her. Simon saw the scowl on his wife's face and thought to himself, hormones! Here we go, we're just in time with Fred! "Ta Dah!" he announced brightly as he walked into the kitchen holding a struggling Fred out to a shocked Sarah. "This is Fred. Say hello, Fred!" he said to the pup, holding the puppies paw out and waving it at Sarah in greeting.

"Oh my God! He's gorgeous!" she squealed, grabbing the puppy out of Simon's arms. "Hello, Fred!" she beamed at the bundle. Fred licked her nose and then promptly pee'd himself all down her dress and her bump in both his panic and excitement! "Oh, Si, he's just beautiful!" she said, not even noticing the wet patch down her tummy, and then she burst into tears.

"Yes, definitely time for a dog," Simon thought to himself. "Maybe a shed too!"

Chapter 8

The next few weeks passed by so quickly that Sarah really didn't know where the time had gone. Fred had settled in well, only going through three beds so far, bless him!

"She said they were unchewable!" Simon had wailed more than once, but Sarah had just smiled and sent him out to buy another.

"Better his bed than our house, darling!" was all she had said as she packed him off to the pet store yet again. Fred's training was coming on nicely with the help of Nathaniel and Clarabelle, who were both working hard on getting Fred to cooperate. He was fully house trained now so no more puddles and slide shows of Simon skidding down the hallway, which had happened more than once over the last six weeks! He'd had all his injections and had started going for walks, getting used to the lead, the outside world, and the local duck pond, which he had managed to jump into more than once, despite the lead and Simon doing his best to keep him out of there!

Sarah had taken to going into work late, having long

lunches and coming home early so that Fred wasn't by himself too much. When she couldn't, Margaret had stepped in to dog sit and had surprisingly become quite attached to the bundle of chaotic fun that was Fred. Despite this flexibility and help, Sarah knew that things needed to change. It wasn't just that Fred needed her home more, it was her body! Her back ached so much these days with the weight of two babies getting bigger inside her and as for her ankles, well, they'd just completely disappeared they'd swollen up so much! Her feet now seemed to grow right out of her legs and looked awful! Simon said she looked beautiful, of course, but he would! The only saving grace of all these bodily changes was her boobs. They were just magnificent! Sarah had never had boobs, not really, not without the help of the essential accessory number one, the wonderful 'push-em-up-pull-em-in' heavily padded gel bra! But now, oh wow, she had boobs to die for! She even had a cleavage, a real one!

All that aside, she was getting very tired, very moody, and very achy, and she knew it was time to let go of her beloved store a little bit. Clarabelle had suggested this for weeks, of course, but she'd resisted, thinking that she could manage, but Clarabelle had been right, again! It was time to let go. She'd call a meeting with Tim soon and begin the hand-over. It was definitely time to begin the preparations for being a mum and the changing priorities that came with it. Sarah smiled. She was ready!

***

Clarabelle sat under Sarah's tree with Mickey chatting

to her beloved. Holding his hand, she gazed adoringly up at him with love and admiration. Fred lay on her lap snuggled up against them quite happily as he listened to them chatting about work. He loved it, just loved it when Aunty Clarabelle was her full size and he could snuggle up with her! When she was outside with Fred, she did the full six-foot version of herself instead of the six-inch thing that she did with his mum! He felt very honoured indeed! Uncle Mickey was telling her all about his latest mission and she was listening with rapture. He had just come back from India apparently, he'd said, another disaster, bless. So busy! He told Aunty C that he'd done what he could, of course, helping the people to release their fear from the recent typhoon that they'd just had and then he'd moved on to the next job, a flood in Pakistan. Aunty Clarabelle was much more relaxed, Fred noticed, since things upstairs had calmed down. They'd moved their courting from the Angelic Realms down to the earth plain she'd said, and it was all just fine and dandy!

Fred loved them both and didn't see what the problem was with these two being together! It was all right for his mum and dad, Sarah and Simon, to kiss and cuddle, so why wasn't it okay for his Aunty Clarabelle and Uncle Mickey? He didn't get it at all, but then again, he was only a dog! Fred shook his head in disgust. Apparently Aunty C said that she hadn't heard a whiff of any rumbles in The Realms for ages. *That's good then,* thought Fred, although he had no idea what rumbles were, but they clearly weren't good!

Clarabelle ruffled Fred's head as he gazed at her adoringly. She'd never been happier and he could see that! She was glowing like a lighthouse, shining her light across all the winter flowers and helping them to grow beautifully! It was a shame about her having to lie to her brother Clarence, of course, he knew she definitely didn't like that bit, but needs must! Fred agreed with them completely. They had his unending loyalty and love, but that was what he was here for. It was a dog's duty to be loyal whatever the cost! He looked up into the tree and spotted Clarence again, damn him, spying on them as always. Fred woofed loudly at the spy in an effort to shoo him away, making both Clarabelle and Mickey jump. It didn't work on the spy though, not at all. It may only be a small woof; he was after all, only four months old (nearly), and hadn't developed his full bark yet, but he was practicing as much as he could and he was doing his best!

"Shh, Fred," Clarabelle said to him as he continued to bark, "Shush! It's alright, dear, calm down."

"It's not alright, it's not" Fred barked. "He's here again, Aunty Clarabelle, he's here, up in the tree!"

Clarabelle patted the dog's head absently as she continued to listen to Mickey telling her about the flood. Fred gave up and just glared up into the tree at the intruder.

Clarence sat in the tree above the two angels and the glaring dog watching them in horror. He'd just known it! He'd hoped it would blow over by now but by the look of it, they had become even closer! What in heavens was he going to do? He loved her to bits, but this really was not okay! Mind you, they did look happy and surprisingly, nay *unbelievably*, Archangel Michael seemed to be as smitten with his little sister as she was with him! This was a turn up, huge actually, momentous! This needed some thinking about. What on earth was he to do? What in heavens, he meant! Clarence wracked his brain, his knowledge banks and his internal library for an answer. Daniel! Yes, Daniel. He was the Angel in charge of Marriage, Romance, and Earthly Love. He'd know what to do! Clarence popped off upstairs to have a word with Daniel before either of the lovebirds saw him. There was always an answer and maybe, just maybe, Daniel may have it! This romance just had to stop, just had to!

***

Christmas was coming fast and Sarah decided that this would be the right time to leave full-time work and hand over the reins to Tim. She'd still be around, of course, she couldn't imagine herself twiddling her thumbs, but the bulk of the day-to-day running of the store would be down to Tim. She talked it over with Simon and he was more than happy for her to do whatever she felt best. It was, after all, her store and he knew how much she loved it. Fred barked his agreement to her spending more time at home. He'd gone into the store with her more than once, but he didn't like it there. He wasn't allowed to play or anything! Expecting him to sit still nicely for hours at a time? For goodness sake, how silly! He was a puppy and they were designed to play! Sarah had given up on that notion after the third time he'd wrecked her storeroom in his attempts to find something to play with, so the idea of her being home more was more than appealing to Fred, smashing in fact! (He'd picked that up from Aunty Clarabelle, 'smashing'! Great word, just great!). "Smashing, smashing,

smashing!" he barked, although he knew that they couldn't understand the doggie language. *So limited, these people!* He himself could understand three languages. There was doggie, of course, the second was Angelic, and third was Human. *He was a bloody genius,* even if he did say so himself! He could only actually *speak* one language, mind you, and that was doggie. Sometimes they understood him, but most of the time they didn't. He'd be shouting something like 'ball' and they'd say, "what is it, Fred? You hungry, Fred? Food, Fred?"

"No, stupid!" he'd bark in reply, "I want my bloody ball!" But they never got it, *dumb humans!*

Fred loved living with his mum and dad. They were really happy, seemed to love each other to bits, which was nice. Made for a nice atmosphere, happy home, and all that. Smashing! And he got lots of walks, which was great! Dad seemed to love his walks bless him and Fred came along with him just to keep him company, although he could do without the rainy ones himself! Dad seemed to need them though, so Fred came along to keep him happy. Things were changing at home too, he'd noticed. Mum was getting fat for a start. She didn't seem to care though, stuffing cream cakes and crisps like they were going out of fashion! And what were those fetishes about pickled onions about? Really! Someone should tell her she definitely had weird taste buds! He'd tried one once but he'd spat it out in disgust. How could she eat that muck? Yuk! And the gas they gave her! He'd seen her tummy jump more than once after she'd eaten those stinky gas bombs. Jumped like mad it did, but she didn't seem to care, just patted her tummy and spoke to it like it was a real person or something! He didn't understand her at all, but he liked her lots.

She and Aunty Clarabelle had lots of chats and were great friends, so she must be nice even if she was a bit fat and stank of onions most of the time! And moody? Wow! Dad had changed her nickname from Fire Girl (what was that about?) to Yoyo! Fred had complained himself to Dad about the moods with a few woofs here and there, but he had just patted his head and reassured him absently, saying things like, "She can't help it, Fred, it's the hormones. Give her a bit of space, Fred, she'll be alright," and other stuff like that, and then Dad would go to his new shed (that had appeared last week after yet another jar of pickled onions!), or he'd take Fred for another walk. They had a lot of walks! Fred didn't know what hormones were, but he didn't like them, no not one bit!

Christmas was coming (whatever that was), and so was Granny Smith and Joe. He liked Joe - Joe was great fun! He was kind of a miniature version of Uncle Ben, though much more fun, as three-and-a-half-year-olds are, apparently! He did notice that Mum's mum, Margaret, didn't like being called Granny Smith for some reason, though. She said she wanted to be called Nan, but Fred liked calling her Granny Smith cos it seemed to wind her up and it was funny! Joe's mum and dad, Gina and Ben, would be there too for this Christmas thing, which would mean that 'The *Spy*' would be there! He wasn't sure about him at all, the spy that is, but wherever Uncle Ben was, the spy was there too and as Ben seemed to like him, Fred put up with him for his sake. If he didn't, he got locked out and he didn't like being locked out at all, no not one bit! It was imperative that he be where the action was! He was the bloody guard dog after all, wasn't he! How was he meant to protect them and keep them safe if he was bloody locked out? Quite mad! *Anyway, enough gossiping for now,* he told the tree with much seriousness, *there's play to be getting on with. Now, where did I put that bone?*

***

Sarah and Tim sat together in the back office of the general store that was MacKenzie's, drinking tea. She'd asked him to stay on after work to have a word about the future. It was the day before Christmas Eve and they were both exhausted. The new range of gifts that she'd brought in last month had sold out and takings had never been higher.

"So the thing is this, Tim. As you can see from the size of me," she patted her huge belly, "I need to start thinking about the future."

The lanky lad smiled at her nodding, wondering who the new manager would be that she would bring in when she went off on maternity leave, and whether he'd have to alter his rather unusual hairstyle. It was mainly bright pink at the moment, with green and blue streaks, although the colours did get changed on a fairly frequent basis, and stood up from his head at least three inches on a good day, gel permitting, of course.

"You've done a fantastic job since I took you on, nearly two years now, wow it's gone quick! And this last six months in particular Tim, covering me for the wedding and everything, I know I can trust you." She smiled at the young lad encouragingly. "You're still young, only twenty-six, but I think you're ready. So I'd like you to take over properly as Manager at MacKenzie's."

Tim looked gobsmacked and then delighted as Sarah continued, "I have a new contract here for you. You'll see I've put your salary up a little and I thought maybe you might like to move into the flat upstairs with Tracey. It will, of course, be rent free and come as part of the package as Manager for you."

"Wow! Blimey, yes, thank you, that's fantastic!" Tim beamed. He'd been working in shops since he left school and he had hoped that one day he would work his way up to Manager, but he never thought it would be this soon. And the flat, wow! He and Tracey, his girlfriend of two years, were living at his mum's in her spare room as they couldn't afford their own place, even though they'd both been saving hard for ages. This was a dream come true!

"Happy Christmas, Tim." Sarah smiled, delighted at his reaction. She could see his happiness and it all felt right and as it should be. Clarabelle's idea, of course; as all the good ones were.

The flat had been empty since Simon had moved in with her last Christmas and it would be good to have it occupied once more. They hadn't wanted to re-let it to anyone else until they'd sorted the access issue out, which had taken months to arrange, never mind saving up to pay for it all! The stairs had previously come down into the shop making it a high security risk for Sarah to rent it out, as whoever had it would have full access to the shop and its stock, and so would their visitors. They had jointly decided that it was better to leave the flat empty until the work was done. She had saved up and just a month ago the new staircase had been completed, with new external access to it from the back of the building. She had considered re-letting it then, but Clarabelle had suggested giving it to Tim as part of his new package. She knew that she couldn't afford to give him a proper manager's salary, what with the huge loan for the shop she had to pay for too, so this was a good compromise, a lower salary but with free accommodation.

When she had first bought the shop she had taken out a big loan, secured against her beloved house, and whilst the store had supported the repayments reasonably comfortably, with her going off now on maternity leave, plus increasing Tim's salary, and needing a new member of staff, things would be much tighter. That being said, Clarabelle had told her not to worry and all would be well, so she had trusted and put it all in place. Tim was happy, she was happy, and she would be able to start letting go now and focusing on her and the twins for the next few years, knowing that her store was in safe hands. "I will still be around, of course, Tim, but you will have full control, full say. After Christmas I intend only to be involved in the buying side of things for new stock lines and with the marketing and promotion sides, but I will discuss everything with you. The rest will be up to you. You'll need another assistant and I will help you with it, but the decision of who to take on will be yours."

Sarah handed Tim a set of keys for the flat, telling him that he could move in whenever he liked and then sent him home to tell his family the good news. "Bless him, that's made his Christmas!" she smiled at Clarabelle. "Good idea, hun, thanks."

"No need for thanks, best idea, best idea!" the angel shrilled happily. "Come on now, Sarah, time to get you home too. Your ankles have disappeared again, look! Far too much time on your feet you spend, far too much time! Still that will all change now that you've handed over to Tim, smashing!"

"Smashing indeed," a tired Sarah agreed and packed up to go home to her husband and mad dog. "Smashing." But as she looked around she noticed that she was talking to herself. Clarabelle it seemed had disappeared yet again!

Chapter 9

Sarah arrived home from her chat with Tim smiling. As she strolled into the kitchen, she was startled to see Clarabelle outside in the garden with Fred. She'd been looking out through the window absently, her mind on Tim and the store whilst putting the kettle on, when she'd looked up and nearly dropped it in surprise. It wasn't that she was surprised to see them together, she knew they were great friends. No, what surprised her was that Clarabelle was not only her full majestic size of over six feet tall, which was more than rare, unheard of actually, but on top of that there was also another angel with her, a very huge and powerful angel at that, and he was holding Clarabelle's hand! *Oh my good God!* Sarah thought with astonishment as she looked at the pair! *She's got a boyfriend! Mind you,* she grinned as she looked at him, he was bloody gorgeous! *No wonder she's been glowing lately! And talking about glowing, it's the middle of the winter. The garden should be pitch black at this time of night but it was fully lit, better than a football pitch!* The light was coming off the two angels like stadium floodlights. *Bloody Nora, someone might notice!* she worried. Thank God Simon wasn't due back till later. He was playing squash after work tonight with Ben. *Just as well,* she thought with alarm. *If he'd seen this he'd have had a coronary!* She opened the back door and called out into the fully lit garden, "Clarabelle, hun, a word if I may?"

Clarabelle came running in, transforming herself to her normal miniature size on the way and reappeared perched on top of the kettle. Always her favourite perch as she liked to use the steam from the kettle as it boiled to clean her feathers and give herself a steam bath. "Yes, dear?" she smilingly said, preening away absently, "Good day?"

"Umm, yes, fine, thanks," Sarah replied, really not knowing what to say about this turn of events. "Umm, do you think, hun, that you and your boyfriend could turn the lights down a bit? I reckon every house in the street can see my garden lit up like it was the middle of the day rather than 6pm on a winter's night!"

"Oh, dear, oh me, oh my! I do apologise, yes, dear, sorry, dear, right away, Sarah!" Clarabelle turned totally beetroot with embarrassment and then she was gone!

It was over an hour later before she reappeared on her usual perch of Sarah's left shoulder apologising for any inconvenience caused.

"Never mind that, what I want to know is, who's the chap? Bloody yummy if I may say so, Clar! And how come you were full size and how come the garden was so lit up? What's that about?"

Fred barked the answers trying to be helpful, but as

usual, Sarah told him to shush before he'd even had time to finish. *Just sooo stupid, these humans! Really she should learn to speak Dog if she's going to have one!* Fred thought in disgust. Aunty Clarabelle didn't seem to mind her being stupid though. "Patience of a saint that one," he muttered to himself, going back to his bone and leaving them to it.

"Ah, Mickey! Isn't he just divine? So macho! So totally amazing!" She gushed.

"Mickey?" Sarah laughed. "So who's this Mickey then, Clar?"

"Archangel Michael, *the* Archangel Michael, the *mighty* Archangel Michael, no less!" Clarabelle boasted.

"Wow, an Archangel! Isn't Michael the chap who battles demons?" Sarah asked in surprise. "The one with the sword?"

"The very same!" Clarabelle triumphed, "And we're in love! Isn't it wonderful?"

"Wow! I didn't know you lot dated? Do you ... You know ... do the whole thing? Have sex and everything? I bet he's amazing, isn't he?" She asked excitedly, wanting all the girlie gossip and intimate details.

"*Sarah!* No we most certainly do *not!*" Clarabelle screeched. "As if! The very idea!"

"But why not? It's a wonderful part of being in love, the sex!"

"Well, aside from the fact that we can't, we don't need to!" Clarabelle replied, turning red again.

"What do you mean you can't?" Sarah asked in horror.

"We're not made that way, dear. We don't have any 'bits'!"

"Aye? No bits?" *Bits; what did she mean bits?* Sarah

wondered. *Unless she meant sexual organs! Oh God, that's what she means isn't it?* She looked at Clarabelle in surprise and whispered, "What, none?"

Clarabelle shook her head solemnly. "All angels are androgynous, Sarah, that means we are neither male nor female," she explained.

Sarah looked stunned, sad and horrified all at the same time. "But you're a girl angel and he's clearly a boy angel! I don't get it!" Sarah was very confused.

Fred shook his head in the corner listening to the conversation and waited patiently for Aunty Clarabelle to explain to his lovely but clearly very stupid mum what she meant. Sure as bones is bones, Aunty Clarabelle was continuing on with her teaching to her eager but very dense pupil.

"We have a male or female *energy,* of course, but not a male or female form. We don't need it, you see, Sarah. We connect with each other on a soul level, an energy level instead. We do not need to connect physically as you do because we are already joined and we are joined all of the time."

"She ain't getting it, Clar," barked Fred, "you'll need to spell it out, love."

"Yes, thank you, Frederick, I can quite manage without your two-pennies worth!" an indignant Clarabelle replied.

"Yeah, yeah, don't get your feathers in a twist, babe!" Fred barked. "I was only trying to help!" He shook his head disparagingly and skulked off, flopping into his bed in disgust.

Clarabelle spent the next hour explaining to Sarah how

the universe works in terms of energy and connections until her ward had gleaned some understanding, finally managing to comprehend real love that didn't involve the act of copulation to prove it. "So you see, Sarah, as we are pure energy just simply by opening our energy to another fully, do we connect with that other and are then joined. Do you see, dear?"

"I think so," Sarah hesitated. "So are you like, married to him now, cos you've 'connected'?"

"Oh, wouldn't that be wonderful, just wonderful! To be able to declare your love in front of all of your friends and loved ones as you do down here. But sadly not. It is not permitted. In fact, dating at all is not permitted and neither is romantic love. This is why we meet here, in secret."

"*What?* That can't be right? Oh shit, mate, that's awful! Why not? Why is it not permitted?" Sarah was outraged!

"I think it's because angels are beings of love, unconditional love for all. I'm not really sure. It's just never been. Clarence says it's a human energy that I've picked up from being around you too much and things like that. He says I've been contaminated and have to go and get cleansed, so I, I ..." she trailed off and hung her head in shame.

"What, hun?" Sarah asked gently, wanting to comfort her friend, desperately wanting to help in some way.

"I *lied* to him!" Clarabelle whispered, and then burst into tears.

God this was bad! Sarah knew how Clarabelle felt about lies and if she'd refused to do this cleanse thing, and was lying about it, then she must love this Michael chap very much. If anyone asked her to give up Si, she couldn't do it and she didn't bloody well see why Clarabelle had to either! *It was a disgrace!*

"Right, well, I'm not having it!" Sarah announced through gritted teeth. "It's not bloody right! You leave it with me, my friend. I'm going to sort this out for you and that's a promise!"

Sarah had no idea whatsoever how she could 'sort this out,' but she would do anything for Clarabelle and she'd find a solution if it killed her. "No romance in the Angelic Realms? Never heard anything so ridiculous in all my life!" she declared, and patted Clarabelle's wings gently in an effort to comfort her. "You just leave it with me, darling!"

Clarabelle nodded, drying her tears with her feathers and pulled herself together. "You wanted to know about my size and light too, dear?" she sniffed.

"Oh, darling, never mind that now, you can tell me another time. Let's just get you cheered up and happy. Why don't you invite your Mickey for tea? Oh, you don't eat do you! What about a chat? A walk?"

Fred seriously could not believe his ears from his bed in the hall. *Tea, chat, walk? An Archangel, for tea? Yeah, right! She really is even more stupid than I thought! But, God love her, she couldn't help it!* Deciding magnanimously to forgive her clear limitations and total thickness, he lolloped out of his bed and over to Sarah, putting his paw on her knee he looked up at her with sympathy and devotion, and woofed in the slowest, clearest bark that he could, "You are incredibly stupid, mother, dear, but I love you!"

"What Fred? You want your tea?" she said.

"Argh!" he replied. "There's just no getting through to

some people!"

***

Sarah relayed the events of the evening to a shocked Simon as they lay in bed together later. "And not only are they not allowed to get married, they're not even allowed to be in love? How bad is that? Especially when this is meant to be heaven we're talking about! What kind of heaven's that? Bloody disgrace!"

"Yes, dear," a tired Simon agreed, almost dropping off before sleepily adding, "It's a bloody disgrace, dear," and began snoring softly.

Sarah couldn't sleep at all for ages. She lay in bed tossing and turning as she mulled the problem over and over in her head. *Why didn't Clarabelle argue against this stupid rule? Why didn't she and her Mickey just tell them? Probably to do with being an angel, all love and light and 'niceness,'* she decided. By three o'clock in the morning Sarah concluded that she didn't know nearly enough about 'upstairs' to be able to help her friend so there was only one thing for it. She would just have to learn! If these angels couldn't argue, well then she could, on their behalf. If it was one thing that humans were good at it was arguing, and if she knew enough about their silly rules, she may be able to put some kind of defence together for Clarabelle and get this stupid 'no romance' rule overturned. "Yes," she murmured sleepily, just before she got yet another kick in the ribs from an annoyed Angelica who was trying desperately to sleep, "I shall learn everything I need to know about 'upstairs' and get this stupid bloody rule overturned! As soon as" (yawn) "Christmas" (another yawn, kick, yawn,) "is out of the way." And then Sarah fell into a deep sleep, dreaming of being a high-flying lawyer taking on huge corporations in the courtrooms and winning a huge victory for her client, Clarabelle!

***

The following morning, Sarah woke late. She had intended to go into the store at nine o'clock but it was now ten-thirty and she was knackered! It was Christmas Eve and there was loads to do before the family arrived tomorrow. Their first Christmas as a married couple! Fantastic! She rang Tim sleepily from the phone beside the bed. "Sorry, Tim, I overslept. I'll be in as soon as, okay, mate?" she mumbled drowsily in her half-awake state.

"No worries, it's all under control here. Take the day off! I'm the boss now and I order it!" he laughed.

Bless him, she thought. *He's getting into the swing of it already, even though officially he doesn't take over till after Christmas.* "Thanks, Tim, but I'll be in a bit later. See you soon." She hung up the phone, climbed out of bed, and stepped wearily into the shower, hoping it would bring her round from her lack of sleep. *Was it really three o'clock before I'd dropped off? No wonder I'm knackered!* Still, she'd found some sort of resolution; fight for Clarabelle, learn what she needed to, and sort it out for her. Her angel had done so much for her, so there was no way she wasn't going to try to repay the favour and do what she could to help Clarabelle in return.

Simon had left for work ages ago. He finished early today with the bank closing for a half day. Mr. Godwin, the Bank's Manager, had insisted, so the bank would close today at two o'clock. Maybe she would take Tim's advice? Not the whole day, but finish early like Simon, why not? "Yes," she grinned to herself as the warm water washed over her, waking her up, "I'll just go in for an hour or two, give them their Christmas bonuses and come home. Good plan."

"Smashing!" agreed Clarabelle from her perch on top of the toilet roll holder, "Do you good to slow down, my girl. And you've still got some wrapping to do, don't forget?"

"Oh, God, yes!" she exclaimed. "I'd forgotten about that. Ta, hun."

The day passed quickly, what was left of it! Sarah handed the staff their Christmas bonuses, told them to close early at four o'clock and then she herself went home to finish packing and wrapping. She'd bought Simon some lovely things and couldn't wait for him to open them tomorrow. Everyone was coming to her again, same as last Christmas, but they'd all promised to help and not let her do it all. She was more than six months pregnant now and everyone was rallying round. Her mum was doing the vegetables and bringing them with her, Gina was doing the Christmas pudding, and Simon was sorting the wine and drinks, so all Sarah had to do was the turkey itself. She couldn't wait! She loved Christmas, always had and always would, turning into a six-year-old each year, jumping up excitedly at stupid o'clock Christmas morning shouting, "It's Christmas!" She was no different this year.

Fred couldn't believe his eyes or his ears when he saw Mum and Dad running excitedly down the stairs the following morning! He just couldn't believe it! *Was this a dream? It wasn't even light yet, for Dog's Sake!* They never ever got up before six-thirty and the clock said five o'clock! Five? No way! They were sitting on the sofa now by the twinkly funny tree thing, shoving packets and parcels at each other and hugging and kissing and all sorts! He was just about to go back to bed in his disgust at being woken up so ridiculously early when they called him over. Apparently he was to be part of this madness! Mind you, it was fun, opening the parcels they had for him with his teeth and finding a host of new balls and bones and toys. *Hmm,* he thought, *perhaps this Christmas lark is all right after all?* He even got doggie chocs! *Oh, yes indeedy, these were to die for! No wonder these girlies raved about chocolate so much! Totally yummy!*

After the madness was over, Fred was just about to relax, thinking that the house had returned to some sort of normality. He had watched Dad put the kettle on for a pot of coffee, though how they could drink that muck he didn't know! He'd tried it once, bitter horrid stuff! Dad had even remembered to let him out for a wee God bless him, and then the next thing he knew, Dad was handing Mum a small parcel thing saying it was her main present. She'd opened it excitedly and it was an envelope. Boring or what? An envelope, a *brown* one at that! Not even a pretty sparkly one! You'd have thought Dad would have come up with something more exciting than that for a main present! The next thing Fred knew was that Mum was crying her eyes out as she read this letter and was cuddling Dad like he was the best thing since chocolate! (Yes, Fred had decided that the best thing in the entire world was chocolate! Even better than bones and that was going some!)

Fred tried to read it to find out what all the tears were about, but he couldn't figure out the squiggly letter things. "I guess I'm just going to have to wait for her to read it out loud, or for Aunty Clarabelle to fill me in when she arrives. So annoying! But wait, it's okay, Mum is reading it out loud now! Smashing!"

Dear Mrs Brown, *(she read)*
Account Number 986045624 *(boring!)*
I am pleased to inform you that the deeds to your property, Rose Cottage, have been released following the full settlement of your secured loan, number 278476/jp9 on 24th December. *(What's deeds? What's a loan?)*
The deeds are currently in safe keeping at the branch. However these can be released to either yourself or a solicitor at your behest. Perhaps you could inform me following the Christmas Break where you wish the deeds to be kept.
With kind regards
Mr. J Godwin
Branch Manager

"But how? When? Oh, my God!" she was screaming, the reality of this enormous gift hitting her. "Simon, oh, babe, thank you! I can't believe you've done this!"

"Darling, the money was just sitting there. Better to pay off the loan on the shop and make sure the house is safe, especially with the twins coming."

"But it was your money, your investment, your savings, from the sale of your city apartment! I thought you were going to buy a property with it to rent out?"

"I did, kind of. I made sure that we are secure, darling, and that's the priority. Anyway, what's mine is yours and all that, wife of mine!" he said grinning.

Sarah felt like a ton weight had been lifted from her shoulders. She'd been scared to death to use all of her savings as well as putting her beloved home on the line as security to buy the shop, but it had paid off and she had no regrets for doing it. To know now though that her house was secure, *their* house was secure? Wow, that was just amazing! *God, he must trust me to do this! It would have been almost everything he had, to have paid it all off!* Sarah thought about it and made an instant decision. It was time to share Rose Cottage with him properly. She needed to put as much trust in him as he had in her. "Well, then I shall change the deeds of the house to joint names, darling, that's only right and proper too!" she declared. "What's mine is yours too, you know, it goes both ways!"

Simon shook his head. "You don't need to do that, sweetheart. I wanted to do this for you, for us. You don't need to do anything."

"I know I don't have to. I want to, end of!" And she threw her arms around him and cried some more.

Really, humans are sooo strange, Fred decided! How an envelope could have this effect on her, he really didn't know, but they seemed to be happy tears so everything was fine. "Is it time for my walk now?" he barked, fetching his lead from the kitchen door where it hung up and dropping it on the floor in front of them.

"Yes, Fred, we'll go for a walk. We'll all go," they said, and once the turkey was in the oven they were off for a little gentle walk around the park, his absolute favourite!

"Maybe the ducks will be there, woohooooo!" Fred barked and ran around chasing his tail at the exciting thought of the ducks, "Death to all ducks!" he barked repeatedly as he jumped up and down. "One day I may even catch one!" he thought with delight!

When they got back (no ducks, poo!), Aunty Clarabelle was there and Uncle Mickey and they'd brought Uncle Nat too, and before long Ben, Gina and Joe turned up, with 'The Spy' (that Clarence chap). There were two new angel ones too, two new friends to make. Clarabelle introduced Fred to a pretty girl angel called Seraphina and another chap angel called Elijah. They had something to do with Mum's diet problem they said, or something like that. Fred hadn't quite got that bit, but it was definitely something to do with her fat tummy, which would be going soon, they said. Just as well, she was bloody huge!

Anyway, then Granny Smith arrived, along with the sprouts and other smelly stuff, though why she bothered, Fred really didn't know! Disgusting things! Even worse than pickled onions and that was saying something! Just as Fred was about to moan about the stinky sprouts, it happened! All the lovely angels went! How bizarre! Right in the middle of Christmas dinner, saying they had to go to some bloke's birthday bash. They were expected, they said and no matter how much he barked his disapproval, they insisted. Who was this Jesus bloke anyway? And why did he have to have his bloody birthday bash on Christmas

Day? *Most inconvenient if you ask me!* thought Fred in disgust, but they just smiled and left.

Chapter 10

It was early January and Clarence was waiting for Daniel on Cloud 607. Things had quieted down after Christmas and it was time he found some help for Clarabelle before Metatron found out what was going on. He'd heard rumours that Metatron was still trawling the universe for clues and it really was so risky! Sooner or later, he'd find out, that was certain. Trouble was, the wait and the chat turned out to be a waste of time! Daniel said he couldn't do anything, not a thing! He was the Angel of Romance and Marriage, but for humans only, he had said. "Why?" he had asked. Clarence just mumbled something about wanting to know more about Daniel's brief and then made an excuse to leave before Daniel got suspicious. Really, he was so worried about Clarabelle! He just didn't know what to do for the best to protect her, no idea at all. It was a terrible worry indeed!

***

Sarah wasn't worried at all. She was determined to find a solution for Clarabelle and her mission was coming along nicely. She'd learned about the hierarchy of the angels over the last few weeks and had now moved onto understanding the universal laws. Clarabelle had described the Angelic Realms as being a little like an army, only they were an army of light-workers. There was Metatron at the top, the boss of the angels. Under him were the seven Archangels - Michael, Gabriel, Uriel, Raphael, Chamuel, Zadkiel, and Jophiel. They all had responsibility for a task. Michael was protection, Gabriel was communication, Raphael was physical healing, and Uriel was emotional healing. She couldn't remember what the others were, but it would all come in time. Under them were a whole host of angels for all sorts of things and then under them were the Guardian Angels. She knew what they were for! They were like the foot soldiers, so Sarah understood now why Clarabelle couldn't argue about silly rules.

She'd insisted that she be brought up to speed about how it all worked up there, as she was trying to get a law changed, but Clarabelle had suggested that she read some books on the universal laws and other stuff. Sarah had studied diligently and she'd learned a lot, but nowhere, not anywhere in all the books that she'd read so far did it say anything about angels not being allowed to get married!

Sarah was enjoying her learning and wondered why she hadn't done it sooner, considering that she'd been chatting to Clarabelle for over twenty years! Really, she should know all this by now, but she'd never been interested before. It had all freaked her out a bit in the past and she'd pushed away any suggestions by Clarabelle about learning about how the universe worked, until now that is. Now it was different! She was on a mission to change the law so that Clarabelle didn't have to keep lying to her brother and so that she could be with her Mickey properly.

She'd learned about the Angelic Temple, The Realms, and The Levels. Apparently there were many levels, many realms, and many dimensions. There was just so much to learn! Earth was on the third dimension apparently and spirit people were on the fourth, which was like dead people and ghosts, sort of thing, before they came back again for their next life. She'd been surprised to find out that reincarnation did indeed exist and was part of the programme, whatever that was! Then above them were Guides and Masters and then above them Ascended Masters. Then there were The Ancient Ones and The Elders and not only that, but there were STAR PEOPLE! Good God alive, aliens! Clarabelle had just laughed at her reaction saying, "Did you truly believe that you were the only beings living across the multiverses? That planet Earth is the only planet capable of sustaining life?" She'd found it highly amusing that Sarah was having such a hard job accepting it all. Above all The Realms and all the levels and in charge of absolutely everything, was the 'All That Is,' 'The Creator,' aka 'God.'

Today, Sarah was on universes, trying to get her head around the fact that there were many of them! Clarabelle called them the 'multiverses.' She said that there were lots of planets in each of the different universes and that some of the planets were higher and more developed than Earth and some were lower. The people on them we could refer to as our 'space brothers and sisters,' she had said. Blimey! And then there were the actual 'star people.' Apparently there really were space ships travelling through the multiverses and the people who lived on them were real life 'star people'! Wow! Apparently, these were beings of very high knowledge that came close to the Earth's atmosphere in their space ships so that they could transmit their knowledge down to certain people here, kind of teaching from afar. That bit blew Sarah away! "So what's it called, this transmission thingy that they do?" she had asked in wonder.

"Channelling, dear. It's called Channelling. People, earth people, humans, I mean, those who are highly intuitive with loving, open hearts and minds, and who have developed their meditation abilities to a highly advanced state can receive these teachings from the star beings by 'tuning in' to their vibration. They absorb and process the learning and then they pass the learning on to others. These are the spiritual teachers of the earth if you like. Do you understand?"

"I think so," Sarah had gulped. "It's all so, umm, weird though isn't it?"

"To you, at the moment, yes, my dear. Your mind is trying to comprehend things beyond your current understanding, but if you will just open your heart, you will find that these new understandings 'feel' right and will allow you to absorb them and accept them. Alright?" She had smiled kindly, patiently, at the confused Sarah. Clarabelle knew that Sarah was struggling, but she also knew that she would get there. Sarah was destined to be one of Earth's healers and intuitives and she herself would be channelling sooner than she realised. This was just the beginning!

"And then there's time travel too?" Sarah asked. "We can go back and look at past life stuff?"

"Yes, dear, and future life stuff too, in time."

"Wowey!" she had gasped. "I wouldn't mind having a look at that!"

Clarabelle had just laughed saying, "One thing at a time, Sarah, one thing at a time."

And so the teaching had gone on, and on, and on! Just as well, because Metatron was getting closer, and closer, and closer!

***

It was the end of February and Sarah had come home from her latest baby check-up to find Fred humping his bed, again! When he wasn't doing that he was licking his balls and not his toy ones either! "Fred, you are truly disgusting!" she had admonished.

"Me, disgusting?" he had replied in surprise. "You want to take a look in the mirror, lady! Have you seen the size of your stomach lately? You want to get off those cakes!" he'd argued, going back to humping his favourite cuddly rabbit toy again, ignoring her disapproval.

"Simon," Sarah had yelled, "we need to talk!"

The next thing Fred knew was that they were whispering in the kitchen behind his back something about him being a teenager now, followed by that bad word 'hormones'! *This could mean another shed or even another dog,* he thought with alarm! Now Dad was defending him (good old Dad), saying something like he couldn't help it, but yes, he would ring the vet and get him in for the op.

"What op?" he had barked, "What bloody op?" But no one had answered him, both of them looking guiltily away. For some strange reason, for the rest of the day, neither of them could look him in the eye. "What are you up to?" he woofed, determined to find out. "What the bloody hell is going on?" he'd barked repeatedly for the rest of the evening, but they just 'shushed' him and clearly had no intention on filling him in whatsoever. Most unfair!

The next morning Dad had taken him for his walk and was saying things like, "Now, buddy, it won't hurt. You won't feel a thing and I'll be there when it's over. It's for the best, promise. It's time; you're six months old now, that's like a teenager in our years, so it's got to be done. You understand don't you, buddy?"

"No, I bloody don't! What op? What's an op?" he'd barked, but despite that, he'd been shoved into the car and taken downtown to the vets where Dad had left him. *Left me, mind you! I ask you, is there no loyalty in this world? Just dumped, and dumped in a bloody cage of all places, with some mad woman in a white uniform who'd decided to starve me. God, life was shit!* The next thing he'd known was that someone was sticking a needle in his paw (another one - he remembered them doing that ages before, when he was a puppy, only it had been in his neck then!), and then he was waking up feeling sick. Something was very sore, but he couldn't figure out what it was, so he fell asleep again, dreaming happily about chasing ducks across the pond, and this time he'd manage to catch one! Just when he was about to rip its head off, the mad woman in the white coat was waking him and telling him that Daddy was here.

"Where the bloody hell have you been!" he'd barked at Simon as he walked towards him down the long corridor, but he was so relieved to see him he couldn't stay cross. He'd gone to run over to him, but for some reason his legs didn't work quite properly, so he had staggered instead. *And what the bloody hell is this between my legs? Some white bandage thing! And even worse, what's this thing on my head?* He couldn't turn round properly! It was like a plastic bucket thing and no matter how hard he pawed at it he just couldn't get it off. He also couldn't see a damned thing so bumped into everything on his wibbly, wobbly way to Dad. "It's a lamp shade! I've got a bloody lamp shade on me head!" he screamed. "They're turning me into a standard lamp! Help me!" But Dad just smiled, a guilty, secret smile at that! "Dad, Dad, I've died and gone to hell!" he barked. "Help me!"

Simon just calmly stroked his head and then picked him up (yes, actually picked him up), and carried him to the car to take him home. He must be dying if Dad was carrying him! The next thing Fred remembered was dreaming about the duck pond again and then he didn't remember any more.

He came to, drowsily, raising his head as an argument went on next to him. The thing on his head, the bucket-lamp-shade thing, had thankfully been removed temporarily in order for him to get some proper rest. Fred began to pick at the white bandage thing between his legs that had mysteriously appeared when he was sleeping, but he was being terribly distracted by the argument.

"No, I can't wait another four weeks, I just can't! You'll have to catch up!"

It was a girl's voice and a very insistent girl's voice at that!

"But Angelica, I won't be ready in two weeks' time!" said the boy. "My hair hasn't grown yet! Give me a bit longer, please? Bad enough that us boys have to die bald without being born bald too!" he implored.

"David, I will be overcooked if I have to stay in here for another four weeks! I will start peeling and that could damage my skin for life! You'll just have to live with it! Hair isn't everything! The rest of you is nearly done, so shut it! I'm the eldest and you have to do what I say, right?"

"Not all right!" came the sullen reply and he kicked her hard.

"Ow!" yelled Sarah, patting her stomach. "Calm down you two! I'm gonna be black and blue by the time you come out at this rate."

Fred wanted to tell the squabbling pair to shut up. His head hurt a lot and his balls were killing him. The last thing he needed was a row going on when he was clearly dying. He lifted his head up properly so that he could tell them to shush, but all he could see was Mum's tummy. *It truly was huge! Enormous in fact! So were her boobs and her chest was wet. Were they leaking? Were her boobs actually leaking? Jesus! They were!* Before he had time to process this juicy bit of gossip, the argument continued. *Yes, the*

voices really were coming from inside her lardy stomach!
There were people in there? Yes, definitely people in there!
Mum has eaten some little people! Ah, that would explain
it! That was why she was so fat! But before he could figure
out why Mum had developed a taste for little people instead
of the usual pickled onions, he noticed that (now he'd
managed to get some of the bandage off so that he could
lick his sore balls), he found in horror that actually his balls
weren't killing him, his balls... his balls... WEREN'T
BLOODY THERE! "Oh, my Dog!" he howled, "My balls
have gone missing, someone's stolen my balls! I've been
butchered, decapitated, mangled, de-flowered!"

Sarah bent down and patted Fred's head. "It's alright,
Freddie, don't panic, you'll be alright. Go back to sleep."

"Go back to sleep? Go back to sleep? Are you in your
right mind, woman?" he yelled. "Someone's stolen my
bloody balls! Call the police! Call the police! Thief, murder,
fire, help!" he screamed, then passed out in total shock.

Fred skulked and sulked around the house for days. The
bandage had been put back on, as had the bucket-lamp-
shade thing around his head to stop him doing it again. As
if! What was the point now? He couldn't even look at Mum
and Dad he was so mad with them! All right so they hadn't
actually done the butchering themselves, but they'd been a
party to it, this *evil* thing! They'd collaborated with 'Terry-
The-Terrible' down at the vet's. They must have! Aunty
Clarabelle had given him lots of healing, which was nice,
but that wasn't the point! He'd lost all interest in humping
his bed *and* his toy rabbit and life just wasn't the same
anymore. And he still hadn't asked Mum why she had eaten

little people or if they tasted nice, but as he wasn't talking to her he couldn't really now, could he? Fred let out his three-hundredth sigh of the day and lay down on the rug by the door as best he could with a bucket-lamp-shade thing on his head. "I'm not here to guard it, mind you!" he announced with a determined bark. "I'm on strike! Just so you know, I'm on bloody strike for the foreseeable, so there!"

Sarah just smiled and patted his head. "Good boy, Fred. You rest now."

"Boy? Bloody Eunuch, more like! Humph!" he woofed in absolute disgust.

Chapter 11

Sarah had just finished reading her latest book about Angels and Angelic Law, on her mission to sort out the 'ridiculous rule,' when all of a sudden out of the blue she had a new priority. A priority most unlike her. All she wanted to do, day and night, was clean! She cleaned the kitchen cupboards, she cleaned the cooker, and she even cleaned *behind* the cooker! She couldn't find enough things to clean! Clarabelle said she was 'nesting' and left her to get on with it.

The nursery was ready. One of the two single rooms on the first floor of the old house now sported two cots, two baby-changing units, and had been decorated in a beautiful rainbow of colours. Stars hung from the ceiling, along with colourful mobiles of fairies and butterflies. Baby monitors were everywhere in the house from the kitchen right up to the second floor in the main bedroom. There were even monitors in the bathrooms! Angelica was due in three days, but Sarah wasn't sure what would happen with David not being due for another fortnight. Maybe they'd split the difference and come out in a week. Simon had moaned about not having a say about the names, but she'd simply told him that Clarabelle had said the names were chosen already and that was that! "If it's any consolation," she'd said to him a few weeks ago, "you got to name Fred."

"No, dear, not quite the same thing naming your dog as naming your son and daughter is it?" he had said, but he'd only sulked for a few days, which was really good according to Angie. When her Tom was sulking it went on for weeks apparently she'd said, so Sarah had got off lightly all in all.

***

It was three o'clock in the morning on the eleventh of March when she'd woken with an urgent need for the loo, and again at four and again at five. Really, she didn't know how her arse could hold so much crap; it really was quite amazing! She reached into the medicine cabinet for the haemorrhoid cream yet again. God, she should have bought shares in the stuff she'd gone through so many tubes! No one warns you about that one, she thought grimly. Bloody iron tablets! You take one thing and that causes another, so you take something for that and that causes another! Blimey! She plodded wearily back to bed just as Simon was waking up.

"What's wrong, Fire Girl? You look really cheesed off?" he asked kindly, seeing her discomfort. *God love her, she did look rough today!* "You look lovely today, darling!" he lied brightly.

"I look like a sack of shit and you know it!" she

grimaced. "But thanks for trying." She really did feel very strange this morning. A little surreal, different, but she couldn't put her finger on quite what it was. He patted her tummy gently, reassuringly and jumped out of bed and into the shower to get ready for work. He was just washing his hair when he heard her screams. Shampoo all over his head and threatening to make its way down and into his eyes, he ran out of the shower and into the bedroom, stark naked in panic, to find Sarah standing looking with horror at a large puddle beneath her feet. "My waters broke!" she cried. "Look, puddle!"

Simon looked at the puddle. *That's not a puddle! That's a bloody lake!* He looked at her clutching her stomach and he swore to God his heart had stopped.

Nathaniel thankfully appeared from nowhere, patting his shoulder reassuringly in an effort to calm him down. Simon stood frozen to the spot staring at the lake just as the shampoo slid down and into one eye spurring him out of his stupor. "Aw!" he yelled, rubbing his eye and making it even worse, jumping all around the room in pain.

"Aw!" yelled Sarah as the first contraction hit her hard.

"What's going on?" yelled Fred, running into the bedroom to find out what the commotion was all about. He looked at the lake between Mum's legs and he just couldn't believe his eyes! "You never?" he woofed, "No way! You puddled in the house? Oh, my word, lady, you'll be in trouble now! Someone get the newspaper and smack her nose, hard!"

The next half an hour was total chaos with Sarah ordering Simon back into the shower to rinse his hair, getting her overnight bag out of the cupboard where it had been laying for the last two weeks, telephoning the hospital to tell them they were on their way and then getting into the shower herself, much to Simon's dismay! He felt terrified and wanted to get them to the hospital straight away where the experts would be waiting and where he could hopefully stop feeling so vulnerable and scared. Eventually, they got out of the house after locking a disgusted Fred in the kitchen. Simon had never been as relieved in his life as he was at that moment when they finally got to the hospital and the midwife took over, taking Sarah into a room for an examination.

She was put into a gown and helped up and onto the hospital delivery bed. With her legs splayed up in the air, to the horror of a watching Simon, the midwife poked and prodded before announcing merrily, "Only three centimetres, you've got ages yet. Have you emptied your bowels yet, Sarah?"

"Have I!? I must have gone about five times last night!" Sarah admitted happily without any embarrassment or hesitation.

"Excellent, your body is preparing ready for the birth. Saves us doing an enema on you, much better to do it naturally!" she beamed, then disappeared with a wave of, "check on you again in half an hour, rest when you can," and was gone.

God, it really was horribly personal and graphic this baby-birthing thing, thought Simon! He would never have thought that she could have discussed piles and poo and intimate things like that with him. It was funny the way that all barriers of politeness seemed to have evaporated as soon as she had gone into labour! *Maybe she needs, for some strange reason, for me to know every intimate detail! Maybe it's so that I can share it with her, be part of this huge thing that was happening to her?* Simon couldn't figure it out, but he hoped that she'd return to her normal state of discretion once it was all over! He really wasn't comfortable discussing piles and poo and things like that with his normally sexy and discreet wife! *TMI, just TMI,* he decided, *definitely 'too much information!'*

He settled down with her and was shocked and then horrified when the contractions came in earnest. *God, she was in so much pain! Was that normal?*

Clarabelle, where are you, mate? he called in his mind. Not being able to see or hear her, he just assumed and hoped that she was there helping his wife through this agony!

"Of course I'm here, silly boy!" Clarabelle exclaimed. "Where in heavens did you think I'd be when my Sarah is in labour?"

Nathaniel shook his head. "He can't help it, Clar, he's just scared. I'll give him a bit of healing too, while you work on Sarah."

Whilst Sarah and Simon clung onto each other's hands, Angelica was having yet another row with David.

"I don't care if you're not ready! I am!" she said firmly.

"But I've only managed to grow a bit of hair and if you let me have another week I can triple that!" he begged.

"Tough!" she announced, pushing down even harder on him. He was squashed like a tomato against the doors, which were only open a crack, and with Angelica's bum pushing down on his knees he was really very uncomfortable!

"What can you see? Tell me!" she ordered. "Quickly!"

"Nothing much!" he said, trying to peer through the crack. "Just a load of white. Nothing else yet."

"Well, push harder!" she ordered. David did as he was told and pushed hard against the doors. They gave a little bit, but not much.

On the other side of the doors, Sarah was screaming.

"Breathe darling, breathe!" Simon encouraged, holding the plastic tube between her teeth as she took another long drag on its gases. "Suck on this, babe. The nurse said that it'd help with the contractions. Suck hard!" Sarah sucked and breathed as deeply as she could. Slowly the pain subsided and then she started giggling. Everything suddenly seemed really funny! The clock, the equipment, Simon's face, everything! She giggled and giggled until she was in hysterics.

"Suck on this!" She screamed with laughter, "I know what I'd rather be sucking on!"

Simon's jaw dropped in complete shock. There was a time and a place and this wasn't it!

"Ah," said the midwife, popping her head around the corner, "bit too much gas and air by the look of it. They don't call it laughing gas for nothing, you know!" And then she was gone again.

The contractions came and went periodically over the next eight hours until finally it was time. Like it or not,

David was being pushed out by both Angelica from behind him and by Sarah's muscles, which were pulling and pushing all around him. It really hurt! He felt like he was being squeezed and squashed from every direction. He managed to get his head a bit through the doors, but there was this rope thing that was in the way. Every time he pushed it squashed against his throat and it hurt, it hurt a lot!

"Push harder!" ordered Angelica from behind him.

"I'm trying Anj, but I'm stuck!" he shouted in panic.

The next thing he knew there was this lovely really helpful chap moving the rope thing out of his way and helping to push open the stiff doors. He had a lovely air about him and seemed really kind, all glowing and soft and gentle he was.

"All right, mate?" the chap asked him. "We're nearly there, you just hang on my lovely. I'm Elijah by the way. Anytime you need me, you just shout, okay? We're gonna be great mates, promise. Off you go now, push, my friend." David pushed and wriggled a bit more.

"Who are you talking to? Who's there?" Angelica shouted from behind him.

"His name's Elijah, he's helping me," David shouted back.

"Well, tell him to get a move on, will you! I'm squashed!"

"You're squashed! You want to try it from where I am!" David replied indignantly, pushing against the doors even harder.

"Now, now, children," came a soft voice from besides Angelica's right ear. "You need to be helping each other not shouting at each other. Work as a team, aye?" Seraphina was pouring soothing light into Angelica, smiling sweetly at her as she continued. "I'm Seraphina by the way and I'm here to help. It won't be long now, child. Give David a minute and he'll soon be out of the way and then you can have your turn."

Angelica beamed at the pretty lady.

"Look on the bright side, my dear; he's the one doing all the hard work for you both, by the time you get to the doors, they'll be really easy to open!"

This made a lot of sense and Angelica relaxed. "Yes, good plan, let him get on with it. Let him do the hard work," she agreed sweetly.

On the other side of the stiff doors, a sweating, exhausted Sarah was holding onto Simon's hand in a vice tighter than any work-mate-bench known to man and was pushing as hard as she could. "I am ..." push pant push "never ..." push, scream, pant, "ever ... having sex ... " scream ... pant ... "again!" she yelled, as she gave the final push.

Kicking and screaming, David Brown came into the world, bemused, confused, and definitely not amused! Ten minutes later, a confident and assured Angelica was squeezed out to a waiting audience befitting her status, that of eldest child. *But apparently not! What was this? Was the woman in the white coat really saying that David was older? That couldn't be right?* She'd been in there two whole weeks longer than he had, so how come that he was the eldest? What, just cos he came out first? How ridiculous! Definitely not right at all! Angelica let out a wail of anger and disgust at the unfairness of this appalling injustice, but no one took any notice whatsoever!

Ten minutes later Sarah looked at her twins in both exhaustion and euphoria as they lay in her arms. *They looked incredibly similar!* The only obvious difference was that David was slightly smaller, which was to be expected as he wasn't quite full term, and whilst Angelica had a full head of blond curly hair, David had just a tuft of it, right in the centre of his head. *He looked like Tin-Tin bless him!*

Simon felt a sudden explosion of love in his chest as he looked down at them both in Sarah's arms followed by an equally strong surge of protection. They were both followed by an equally massive surge of fear and panic. "Oh my God, they're so tiny!" he whispered. "So fragile, so delicate!" He stared at his children in total amazement. He gazed at Angelica, a perfect miniature imitation of Sarah. She had managed to stop screaming and was looking up at her mother expectantly, as was David. Simon looked from one to the other trying to take it in. Their bright, blue eyes were wide open, perfect lips sucked on tiny chubby fists as they gazed up at him. He watched Sarah rapturously counting their fingers and then their toes, checking that it was all there and was totally overawed and humbled by the miracle of life that he had just been part of.

"Oh my God, Simon!" she whispered, "Aren't they just perfect!" Tears of pure joy were sliding down her face as she looked up at her husband, only to see that he too had tears spilling down over his cheeks with the emotion of the moment. He sat down on the side of the bed, holding her and the babies in a group hug.

"I will never, ever let anything happen to any of you, do

you hear me?" he said through his tears, holding onto them for dear life. Joining the hug, of course, were both Clarabelle and Nathaniel on their respective shoulders, whilst Seraphina and Elijah sat either side of the bed at Sarah's feet looking with amazement at the twins wondering what they'd let themselves in for! Clarence watched happily from the door. All nine of them said at exactly the same time,

"Wow!"

***

Two hours later, a euphoric, but exhausted Simon arrived home. Sarah had been washed and cleaned up, as had the babies, and all three were sleeping happily on the maternity ward. They would only be in for one night the midwife had said; all was fine, the babies were a good weight and Sarah could go home in the morning. Simon let himself into the house and grinned. "Fred, my boy!" he called as he made his way to a barking Fred in the kitchen, "We are a father! At last, we are a father!"

Fred had no idea what a father was, but whatever it was, it had made his dad happy. He was positively glowing! Fred jumped about in delight, forgetting that he'd been locked in since seven o'clock that morning and promptly pee'd all over the kitchen floor. *Ah well, if it's good enough for Mum to wet herself in the house, and on the bedroom carpet no less, it was good enough for me,* he thought with relish! *And where is she anyway?* Fred looked in the hall, but there was no Sarah at all. He padded back to Simon, placing a paw on his knee, he looked up at him with concern. "What have you done with her?" he woofed. "Is she locked in the garden too, for being naughty with her puddling?"

But Dad just patted his head and said no more.

Despite being totally exhausted, on instruction from Nathaniel, instructions that somehow got through to his tired mind, Simon felt compelled to scrub the bedroom carpet till the stain from Sarah's waters had been removed. Then he changed the bed. *Sarah would like that, to come home to nice clean sheets*, he thought, and then he poured himself the largest whisky ever and plonked himself on the sofa before ringing around the family to tell them the news. "Yes, Mum, they're both perfect and yes, Mum, Sarah's fine," he said to his delighted parents, listening to his dad chipping in every now and then from the extension phone. "Yes, good weights for twins. Angelica was three kilos and David was two and half so all good, Mum."

"Kilos? Simon, give me pounds and ounces love, I don't do kilos!" Linda pleaded. Saving the day from Simon having to do maths in his exhausted mind, James was now chipping in, "It's about a kilo for every two point two pounds love, so that's around six pounds six ounces for our Angelica and five pounds five ounces for our David, or something like that," he announced happily. "I can go and get a calculator if you like."

"Never mind a calculator," shrieked an excited Linda, "Go and book a flight! I want to see my grandchildren!" and then she burst into tears.

"Yes, dear, quite, dear, on it, dear!" agreed a delighted James, turning on the computer to arrange the flights home and the first sight of their grandchildren. "Well done,

Son," he said, smiling to a happy Simon down the phone. "You've made your mother and me very proud!"

After his mum and dad, Simon rang Ben and then Margaret, and finally Angie and Frieda until the job was done and all the family and friends had been informed. With a smile on his lips a happy, but knackered, Simon Brown fell asleep just where he was sitting, on the sofa with his celebratory whisky still in its glass barely touched.

Nathaniel smiled happily. "A good job done all round," he said to himself, and popped off upstairs to report in with the news.

***

Fred was quietly minding his own business the next day when Dad came home with Mum and the 'little people.' Clearly she had managed to cough them up or spit them out or something, cos her enormous lardy tummy was almost gone! They were laying in their little car seats and, bless 'em, they were so sweet! "Yippee!" he barked, "New little people to play with!" And he jumped around the house in delight, but for some silly reason the little people were now screaming and Mum was telling him off for scaring them with his bark. "I was talking to them!" he said in disgust, "Talking! Saying hello, you know, being polite!" And funny enough, she seemed to understand, did Mum! *Maybe she's finally learned to speak dog?* he wondered. Cos here she was now, sitting him down in front of the little people and explaining that this was Angelica (I know, I've heard her! Right little mouth on her!), and this was David (I know him too, though how he puts up with madam there I don't know!), and then she was taking them upstairs and putting them in the new nursery and saying to Fred that he had to guard them with his life! "Smashing!" he barked, "I love guarding! It's in the bones, it's in the blood! Say no more, Mum, I'm on it!" And Fred took 'the stance,' sitting rigidly on guard in front of the nursery door like a beefeater guarding Buckingham Palace. "I, Fred the Fantastic, shall guard them with my life!" he declared majestically. "With my life!"

Life was chaotic for the new parents for the first few weeks but gradually it all seemed to settle down. Linda and James returned to Spain and Simon returned to work after his paternity leave, to a relieved Sarah's delight. He really was an old fusspot, getting involved with everything and fussing over this and that until he drove her demented, bless him. She was glad to have the house back to herself after all the commotion and get on with things at last. Fred now lived permanently outside the nursery door or wherever the twins happened to be, never leaving their side except to eat and have a quick run around the garden. Life had settled into a new and nice routine.

"Time to get back to my studies, definitely time!" she said for the third time that day, watching her twins Guardian Angels again as they sat at the end of their cots. She had been aware of Seraphina and Elijah many times over the last few weeks as they hovered near her babies, but she hadn't been able to make any real connection with them. She could see them both, but she couldn't seem to communicate with them and it really was most annoying! She'd also been aware of her deceased dad popping in and out for visits, but hadn't been able to communicate with him either. "Yes, definitely time to learn a bit more," she decided, "and get this communication understanding thing sorted out!"

Chapter 12

Metatron had really been sooo busy that he just hadn't found the time to finish his investigations into the anomalies that had been occurring periodically throughout The Realms. Whilst they weren't as bad or as often as they had been, there was still the occasional rumble and it tended to be whenever he'd called a meeting and all the staff were present. It was possible, just possible, he considered, that it was coming from one of them, but until he knew what the energy was he just couldn't go confronting anyone; that would be most unacceptable! He may look stupid for a start! He was the 'All Seeing All Knowing' (or meant to be), and to confront his staff without fully knowing was just totally not okay, not okay at all! But he was getting close, he knew that! He couldn't possibly be seen to be getting it wrong, so no, he wasn't going to confront anyone until he was absolutely sure with what it was that he would be confronting them.

He had reluctantly called a senior management team meeting a while back with the Archangels to ask them if they had any ideas or knowledge, but no one had anything to say or add. Even Archangel Michael was in the dark about it and if 'The Warrior for Light' didn't know, then no one knew! It was definitely time to pick up the pace and get this sorted once and for all; that was definite. He considered for a moment asking Michael to come with him on this last tour, see if he felt anything, but then again, same thing, he - the 'Mighty Metatron' should know, not be using one of his senior managers to find out for him! *No, perhaps not.*

Metatron leaned over his map of the universes once again, checking his list of planets left to visit and there was only twelve left, the ones in the Milky Way. All the other universes and galaxies had been done and there was definitely nothing there that felt wrong or out of place. With a sigh, he set off for his tour having left strict instructions with his secretary not to be disturbed unless it was an absolute emergency. "Unless" he had boomed, "the Demonic angels try to overrun the heavens again or something equally rare, do *not* call me back! I have something *very* important to do!" And off he went.

***

Michael sat on Cloud 967 with Clarabelle. Not their usual Cloud 932, but one nearby. (Their usual one was being repaired so they'd had to make do with this one, but it wasn't their preferred choice.) "He's going to catch us sooner or later, Clar. It really was very awkward at the SMT when he was grilling all of us Archangels for information and I couldn't say a word - goes so much against the grain, for us both, my dear. I don't know what the answer is, have you had any thoughts?"

Clarabelle looked at her hands in despair, wringing them over and over as she shook her head sadly. "None, none at all, Mickey. Our only hope is my Sarah, but she's been slowed down such a lot because of the birth of her twins. She just hasn't had the time to study as much as she needs to, to be able to put a decent defence together. She's learned a lot, of course, but she still has so much more to understand. She can't even meditate yet and how she thinks she's going to take on Metatron when she can't even access The Realms I just don't know!" Clarabelle stared at her hands once again. She really was getting very nervous about it all. It was all well and good for her Sarah to tell her to 'leave it with me,' but they were running out of time, and time was one thing that Sarah just didn't have much of, not with newborn twins to look after.

"Well, she can't!" he agreed. "There's no way she can call a hearing up here until she's learned how to get up here, now is there? It's just impossible!"

"It is, I know!" Clarabelle nodded sadly.

"And what about her heart, is it open fully yet? Once that's open everything will follow, the third eye and then the crown, but none of it will work till her heart is open anyway. That should be the priority, Clar, that and teaching her to meditate."

"Yes, dear, I know. I'll get on to it as soon as possible, I promise."

They gazed at each other with such love, such warmth, and such tenderness that the cloud nearly took off, but they managed to rein it in, just!

Michael took Clarabelle in his arms and held her closely, whispering in to her ear, "My darling, no matter what happens, we will be together, of that I feel assured. We must have faith, my dear, faith and trust that a way will be found, no matter how unlikely or impossible it appears to be. Real love always finds a way, my darling Clarabelle, and ours will find its way too. Trust in love and it will guide you."

Clarabelle nodded, smiling up at him she simply said, "But of course, my dear, but of course."

***

Sarah was studying hard, learning as much and as fast as she could. She could feel the urgency somehow like it was almost in the air. The twins were sleeping and Fred was guarding the door as always, leaving her some peace to focus. She was learning about the planets at the moment, trying to understand how the experts says that there are ten in our solar system when Clarabelle says there are twelve. She was also trying to get her head around the fact that each planet had its own energy and that the energy influenced the earth and the people of the earth very significantly.

"Simple, my dear," piped up Clarabelle, who had suddenly appeared on the top of the sofa. "Some of the outer planets have not yet come into your orbit, or rather the orbit of your telescopes yet. Just because you cannot see them, does not mean that they are not there."

"I guess that makes sense," agreed Sarah.

"Ah, but there is plenty of evidence, dear, it's just that your scientists are resistant to it. Always been the same throughout your history, man rejects what he doesn't understand. Silly really, but it's the way humans are, bless. Anyway, ready? Let the lesson begin. ... In South American caves there are maps of the solar system dating back ten thousand years which show clearly the twelve planets all moving around your Sun. The drawings are in exact and correct alignment, order and to scale. Neither the Incas nor the Mayans had telescopes dear. They knew, as many before did. There have been many peoples through your ages that have known what is there, out there in your solar system. It does make me laugh how your scientists pooh-pooh the facts when there is clear evidence to show the contrary. That being said, the day is not far off now when Earth will be aware of all twelve planets - you have discovered two new ones this century alone and there will soon be evidence to show the last ones."

Sarah was amazed. *Wow, that's incredible!* "So how far out are these others then?" she asked, "And what do you mean we will see them soon?"

"Well," Clarabelle was definitely on a roll, relishing these lessons on the cosmos, "They have their own orbit you see, kind of goes in and out again, close to Earth - far from Earth. For example, your Saturn takes 28 years to come into full orbit of the earth, but that is nothing compared to the outer ones. The furthest one away only comes into the earth's orbit every 12,500 years. Each time it comes round some of the folk there come and settle on Earth for a while, bringing their knowledge with them for the benefit of humanity."

Sarah was gobsmacked! "Oh my God! Really? Wow! What are they called then, these aliens?" she asked excitedly.

"You have in your history called them Lemurians; that was 25,000 years ago. And then, of course, there were the Atlantians; 12,500 years ago. You must have heard of them?" Clarabelle was nodding to herself, recalling how it was back then. She herself was only 3000 years old, but she'd read the records and covered it in her training.

"Atlantis was real?" a shocked Sarah exclaimed. "Wow!"

"Oh yes, dear, smack in the middle of the Atlantic Ocean, hence its name, of course, and many of the occupants chose to remain after the others left. Some of your scientists think Atlantis, of course, was in the middle of the Mediterranean, near Greece, but really, dear, why on earth did they think it was called Atlantis? If it was in the Mediterranean Sea it would have been called 'Mediteris' now wouldn't it! Anyway, where was I? Oh yes, the Atlantians; well, they went far and wide, taking their knowledge with them across the globe, teaching and helping. Some of them mated with earth people and as that went on through the generations, the knowledge got diffused, watered down so to speak. It is they who showed you all how to build pyramids and the like. Of course, the knowledge of why the pyramids are there got lost over time, which was a shame, but anyway, the reason they are there is that they all align with the planets like a grid, a kind of energy line. The pyramids help to ground the universal energies that come down from the planets; very important they are, very important! Now then, what else did the Atlantians do, let me see? Ah, yes, they also showed people the map of the universe, hence the cave drawings I referred to earlier. Now then, let me think, what else did they give you?" Clarabelle trawled her memory banks, "Ah, yes, standing stones, stone circles, crystals, stuff like that."

Sarah needed a break to try to take it all in, but Clarabelle was continuing with her roll.

"And the planets, now then. Well, of course, it all revolves around the Sun, the giver of life. Nearest to the Sun is Mercury; he or she is the thinker, the analyst. I say 'he or she,' as Mercury is androgynous, both male and female energy, perfectly balanced. Then there's Venus, you know her, lovely energy of love and romance. I just love Venus! Don't you?" she beamed. Sarah nodded emphatically. "Then there is, of course, Gaia, that's planet Earth's real name, feminine energy again like Venus. Then there's Mars; he's the one with the masculine power and passion, to compliment Venus, you see. All the planets are so in harmony with each other, lovely it is, just lovely!" she beamed.

"So do Mars and Venus have more influence on us cos they're closer to us?" Sarah asked.

"Oh, good question, my dear! Lovely, smashing, in fact! Yes, dear, the closer they are the stronger the effect on you. It's why you have such strong love and passion in you as a race you see; because of those two, so you could blame them if you like, but I'd thank them if I were you, yes indeed I would!" Clarabelle grinned. And while she was thinking about those two planets she must ask Nathaniel about his extra training on Mars and Venus, maybe she could learn something new too! Her thoughts turned to her and Mickey and she smiled sadly. If there was going to be any 'her and Mickey' she'd better focus on getting her Sarah up to speed and smart quick! She continued in earnest. "Now then, who's left, let me think now, let me think." Clarabelle stared into space, a look of shear concentration on her face. "Ah yes, Pluto, Saturn, Jupiter, Uranus, Neptune and Chiron; oh yes, and we mustn't forget your moon. Very important is she, very important indeed!"

Sarah nodded, reaching for her pad and pen again. Her head ached and she really couldn't remember any more. She'd have to write the rest down and try to remember it all later, once her tired brain had processed this lot so far!

"Right then, pay attention, Sarah! Your moon - essential, just essential!" Clarabelle declared emphatically. "Controls the water on your planet, all of it. Not just the oceans, Sarah, but people too! Your planet is exactly 71.11 percent water, you see, more or less the same as you humans. You know that, don't you? Well, your human bodies are made up of around seventy percent fluid too! Water and blood make up the same ratio within your body as the water does on your planet."

Sarah looked blank, again!

"Your planet is seventy percent water, your bodies are seventy percent water, see? All aligned, all aligned! Anyway whilst Venus controls your love and Mars your passion, the moon, controls the flow and ebb of emotions. It's why you get more sensitive, more *emotional* around a full moon, you see?" She looked closely at Sarah to check that she was keeping up. Peering at her even closer she reached over until they were nose to nose. "Do you see?" Sarah did not see and stared at Clarabelle blankly. "Okay, let me slow down. Right, each planet has its own energy, you get that bit?" Sarah nodded. "Good," Clarabelle continued, "and the moon's primary energy is 'emotions,' so when she is in full flow, full moon, your emotions are at the surface. When she is not, your emotions subside, just like the tides; in and out, ebb and flow! Full moon - emotions up; waning moon - emotions down, get it?"

Sarah got it, hallelujah!

"It's why you get cranky around a full moon. You do you know!"

Sarah smiled. She did know! "So what about the other planets? If the moon does emotions and Mars does power and passion and Venus does love, what do the others do?" she asked, scribbling away with her pen. "And have I got this right, the planets are boys or girls?"

"Yes, dear, well male or female energy rather than boys or girls!" Clarabelle giggled then explained. "The universe works on polarities, balance; for every male energy there is a female. For love there is fear. For positivity there is negativity. See?"

"Yep."

"Good, excellent, smashing in fact! Well, after Mars comes Jupiter; he's the biggest, of course, and is the planet of good luck and good fortune, oh, and also philosophy. He gives the answer to the seeker too, very clever he is. After him comes Saturn, the second biggest and he is the taskmaster. His job is to get us to work hard and he will push you to expand and to grow. He can be a bit unkind at times, but he means well, bless him. Uranus is next and brings expanded consciousness, a new way of looking at things, helps to broaden your horizons so to speak; another feminine energy. She'll be working with you now, will Uranus, helping you to understand all of this. Neptune is the planet of illusion and change, feminine energy again, of course. Pluto is the tiny baby and is called a dwarf planet. He doesn't mind being called a dwarf bless him, small and mighty he is, small and mighty!"

"Well, yes, if he's good enough for Snow White," Sarah chipped in, "then he's good enough for me. I don't care if he is a dwarf!"

"Aye?" Clarabelle looked confused. She turned to Sarah and gently said, "She wasn't real you know, dear, Snow White."

Sarah laughed. "I know, hun, I was making a funny. Never mind, carry on. Tell me about this dwarf then, this Pluto."

"Well, dear, his energy is transformation, regeneration and rebirth. Then there's Chiron. He's really an asteroid rather than a planet but don't tell him I said so. Gets very uppity about it I can tell you! Anyway, Chiron generally shows you where you are wounded. He's called the Wounded Healer because he shows you what you need to heal and release. That's about all of them for now Sarah. I think you need a break dear, you look tired."

"Tired? I'm bloody knackered!" Sarah proclaimed earnestly. "But I've learned loads, thanks, hun."

"Smashing!" Clarabelle beamed. "Now don't forget to use them, work with them, call on them, and ask them for help, that's what they are all there for; it's what the entire universe is for! Everything is connected, you see, Sarah, so use that connection, like an old friend and use that friendship to lean on. Go and rest now, child. The twins will be awake soon and you could use ten minutes."

Clarabelle was delighted with the progress. It was coming along nicely. Whether it would come in enough time mind you, that was a different matter! She left Sarah snoozing and popped off to meet Mickey. He'd be pleased with progress, pleased as punch!

***

Metatron had checked out Pluto, Neptune, and Uranus and was currently making his way in towards Universe number thirty-four's Sun. He was just about to stop off at Saturn when he began to feel a strange vibration, a rumbling familiar vibration at that! *Ah ha!* he thought to himself. *I'm getting close, I can feel it in my wings!* Delighted, he continued onto Saturn to check it out. It was huge so it would take a while, but he had all the time in the heavens to discover the truth. After Saturn was Neptune, the largest in this particular universe so these two planets alone were going to take an absolute age! *Ah well, getting closer all the time. Won't be long now and I'll have my answer!* he thought to himself with immense pleasure. "The Mighty, 'All Seeing All Knowing' Metatron is nearly back!"

***

Lessons resumed the following day and this time Clarabelle was helping Sarah to understand everything that she had learned so far and begin to pull it all together.

"It's a bit like a jigsaw, you see, dear," she explained. "You need to have all the pieces and put them all together and then the picture starts to form."

"Yep, got that too. Doing well, am I?"

"Oh yes, indeed you are, my dear, yes indeed! Now, the next step is to understand how to meditate and how to open your heart. Once that is in place, all limitations cease to be!"

Clarabelle worked with Sarah for the rest of the day showing her the different types of meditation. There was going in and there was going out, and then there was how to meditate by closing down her conscious mind and going into her subconscious mind, where apparently she could access all things. The first type, 'going in,' involved closing down all thoughts and just going into a total stillness within yourself. This was a kind of Buddhist meditation. The second type involved going outside yourself, sort of leaving yourself with all of your energy being elsewhere from your body. Clarabelle described this as soul travel and, through this, Sarah could access the other Realms, other worlds and other times. This was more of the new age meditation she had said and that people also did this in their sleep, their 'dreamtime.' Sarah thought this particular one was brill! Clarabelle though, was a bit strict and said she was to practice the first one and get the hang of that before trying anything else.

"The trick, child," she had said, "is to quiet that busy mind of yours. Very difficult, very difficult indeed! How can you listen to the universe if your mind is too loud? You cannot, it drowns it out, simply drowns it out! You must learn to still the mind so that you can begin to listen to the universe's voice. It speaks to you through your heart, you know, but when your mind is so loud the heart cannot hear."

Sarah tried hard. She tried very hard. She practiced

every day trying to listen with her heart, but it was easier said than done. She wouldn't give up though, no matter how hard it was. She had to save Clarabelle, her best friend, her mentor, her guide, her Angel, Clarabelle who, day by day, hour by hour was getting increasingly anxious as an increasingly determined Metatron grew closer day by day, hour by hour, to the truth; a truth that would see her Clarabelle probably banished from the Angelic Realms forever!

***

As April showers turned into May sunshine, the garden blossomed, bursting into life, its colour filling every corner with new wonder and vitality. The twins began to sleep through the night and as the weeks went by Sarah had more time to practice her twice-daily meditations. She eventually began to get the hang of it, managing to quiet down her noisy and busy mind and just told it to shut up. "I am in charge of my thoughts" she repeated to herself, "I control my thoughts they do not control me!"

With practice, she succeeded in pushing out the thoughts that repeatedly tried to intrude and on each meditation, it became easier and easier. She was able to go deeper and higher, she was gaining confidence and trust, and she was getting stronger. The hardest part was trying to stay awake! Many times, when she went into that still, quiet place within her and allowed herself to fully relax, her body thought it was bedtime and insisted on going to sleep, whatever time of the day it was! Clarabelle helped her with this by poking or prodding her whenever she was just about to doze off and eventually her body got the hang of it, even if she was covered in bruises from all the pokes! By the end of June she'd done it! After two months of daily practice, she could finally meditate, and meditate well! She was getting closer to being able to help her friend and sort out this stupid damned law. She just hoped that it wasn't too late!

There was just this business left about the heart that she had to master. She really didn't get that one at all! Not yet, but it was next on Clarabelle's list and Sarah was confident that she'd master that the same way that she had mastered everything else. It really was a lot easier than she'd thought it would be. Once she'd accepted that there was a whole heap of help out there from the universe and once she had become comfortable with drawing on it, everything seemed to flow. The main thing was to trust and to be fair she did have a head-start with that one, what with Clarabelle and everything! Sarah wondered how normal people managed! People who couldn't see angels and stuff, how did they trust? If you couldn't trust what you were learning, then you couldn't take it in, but for Sarah that hadn't been a problem and it was all coming along nicely. Just as she was thinking how lucky she was to have all this help, she heard Fred let off a small bark. That meant the twins were awake, so lessons were over for now. Fred always seemed to know when they were awake long before their first noise hit the baby monitor, allowing Sarah time to get to them before they began to cry. The house really was very peaceful most of the time considering she had two babies! Good old Fred!

"How did it go?" barked Fred seeing Sarah coming up

the stairs to the nursery. "Getting the hang of it now, are we?"

"Shush, Fred, don't bark!" Sarah said sternly.

"Oh well, that's bloody charming isn't it! Only asked, I did! I won't bloody bother next time!" He woofed in annoyance at the rebuttal and went out to the garden for a wee and a sulk. The sulk, though, didn't last long at all when he spotted Aunty Clarabelle and Uncle Mickey under the tree having a cuddle and a chat. "Smashing!" he woofed.

But it turned out it wasn't smashing at all! Aunty Clarabelle was upset and Uncle Mickey was very quiet. Apparently, some bloke called Metatron had finished on Saturn and was just about to start Neptune, whatever they were, but whatever it was, they were running out of time and it was a disaster! "What's a disaster?" Fred barked, worrying.

"It means, Fred, my dear, that things are about to go very, very wrong indeed!" proclaimed Aunty Clarabelle and then she burst into tears!

"Oh, my Dog!" Fred thought in major alarm, *"This is a disaster! Oh, my Dog, oh, my bloody Dog!"*

"Fred," Uncle Michael was saying, trying to cheer his darling Clarabelle up, "Tell Aunty Clarabelle what this 'Oh, My Dog' thing is that you say."

Fred noticed how Uncle Mickey wiped Aunty Clarabelle's tears dry with his feathers as he said this and thought that was really sweet, bless him! "Oh, My Dog?" he woofed, "Simples! Them lot in there say, 'Oh my God' a lot, so I borrowed it. Did you know that 'God' is just 'Dog' backwards! I just swapped around the letters to suit me. Okay?"

Aunty Clarabelle was smiling now. *That's nice. At least she's cheered up a bit now.* He was sooo glad that he'd been able to help, even a tiny bit.

Fred worried for the rest of the day about Aunty Clarabelle's tears. He'd have to have a word upstairs himself and see what could be done. He'd have a chat with his mate Frank to see if he could help Aunty Clarabelle at all. Fred liked Frank a lot. He was really, really nice to him. He was to all the animals apparently, even the birds! Fred hated birds, but Frank said that all creatures were equal and should be loved the same, though Fred didn't see the point in that one at all! Anyway, Frank was quite high up so he may be able to help. He said they'd given him something called a Sainthood after he'd gone back upstairs to live (apparently that's good, quite important), as a sort of thank you for all his nice work with animals. 'Saint Francis of Assisi' was his proper name and apparently he was quite well regarded 'upstairs,' but Fred just called him Frank. It was much easier! "Yes indeedy!" Fred barked, "I'll have a word with Frank. He'll help, even if Aunty Clarabelle isn't a dog, I'm sure he'll make an exception and put a word in. Smashing!"

Chapter 13

The July sun shone low in the evening sky filling it with hues of pinks and purples as Sarah was getting herself ready for a rare night with the girls. Simon was going to babysit so that she could have a break and she couldn't wait! She'd prepared enough breast milk to see him through the evening, left the nappies and everything else out for him, and trusted that he'd be fine. She knew he'd fuss, of course, old fusspot that he was where the babies were concerned, but Clarabelle had said that she and Nat would keep an eye on him, and Seraphina and Elijah were there too so it would all be okay. She was just putting the finishing touches to her nail varnish as she half watched television in the living room, when Fred started woofing and prancing around excitedly in front of it. "Whatever's the matter with you, Fred? What you getting all het up about?" she asked.

"Simples, simples, simples!" he woofed, though try as he may he just couldn't get the click sound that those damned meercats made. He loved this advert! It was his absolute favourite!

"Oh, you like the advert do you, Fred?" Sarah was saying. "I do too. Funny little things, though I can't get the click thing myself."

Good Dog alive! Does she finally understand me? he wondered in amazement. *Quick, let's try something else. ...* "Aunty Clarabelle was crying in the garden," he woofed, as clearly and as slowly as possible. He waited, he waited, he waited some more.

"Mmm, Fred, shush now, aye?" Mum said as she carried on painting her nails.

"Well? Did you get it? Did you understand me? Did you? Did you?" He barked.

"Mmm," said Sarah absently, concentrating on her nails and trying not to get any on her skin, "I'm worried about her too."

"Bugger me!" said Fred in shock. "She did get it, she can finally understand me!" and promptly fainted!

***

An hour later, Sarah was sitting with an unexciting orange juice on Frieda's sofa looking with amazement at her two friends.

"Now I know you're jealous that we're drinking wine and you can't have any, mate, but there's no need to look so shocked, we always drink wine, nothing new there!" Frieda said, noticing Sarah's expression.

But it wasn't the wine that was making Sarah so surprised. It was the coloured lights! There was a yellow glow around Angie and a purplish one around Frieda. It was all over and around them and she could see it clearly. *This was a first! What the hell was it?*

"Ah well, dear, that'll be their aura that you're seeing," piped up Clarabelle.

"What's an aura?" Sarah questioned silently.

"It's their soul energy, dear. I'll tell you all about it tomorrow, all right? Just enjoy the evening for now; you've worked hard and you need a break and some fun."

Clarabelle was delighted! If Sarah was seeing aura's they really were doing extraordinarily well!

"And what's that dark shadow around Frieda's chest?" she asked.

"Negative energy, but don't worry about it. It's nothing sinister, just old emotional hurts that got stuck in her heart wall."

"What's a heart wall?"

"Will you just forget about it for now, please? I shall tell you all tomorrow. Now have fun!" Clarabelle ordered in one of her firm, authoritative voices. Sarah obeyed and focused on the girls. *Clarabelle was right; I do need some fun. All this coloured lights and the rest can wait.* She focused and successfully spent the rest of the evening enjoying herself with the girls.

Frieda noticed that Sarah was distracted again. She'd been like it all her life, as long as she'd known her anyway. It was as if she was having a separate conversation going on in her head half the time. She tried to pull her friend's focus back but before she had a chance to, Angie jumped in and did the trick.

"How's Granny Smith, Sarah?" smiled Angie, "Turned

into an apple yet?"

"Ah, the MFH could so easily turn herself into anything she liked, being a witch an all!" declared Frieda with a huge grin on her face.

"Actually," Sarah admitted, "MFH is now no more."

"What?" both girls screeched. "Really? What happened? Did she get a personality transplant?"

"Heart transplant, I think," laughed Sarah. "Well, she seems to have finally found one, for me, a little bit. Things are much better, much, much better! She hasn't been 'Mother from Hell' since last summer when I had a go at her. Come round a lot actually, really trying, she is."

"Yes," both girls agreed, "*Really trying* are the right words for your mother!" they grinned.

"She'll never be the perfect mother, I know, but she's actually behaving quite well these days," Sarah was saying.

"Bloody Nora! Is that our Sarah actually defending her mother?" both girls shrieked simultaneously? "Blimey, that's a first!"

Usually the three of them spent their girlie times together slating MFH, who was often the object of the laughter and brought much mirth to the proceedings. The girls had always been horrified by how badly Margaret treated her only daughter and were more than happy to criticise her whenever possible, to show their solidarity for their friend, but here was Sarah now defending MFH! Unheard of!

Sarah changed the subject as best she could, much to Angie and Frieda's amazement. It just didn't seem right to Sarah anymore to slag her mother off, not since Clarabelle had shown her why her mother was so hard, so damaged, and especially since she'd been trying so hard to mend fences, which Sarah knew was really difficult for her mum. No, she didn't want her mother to be poked at, not anymore. Those days were over. She was even beginning to like her, a bit. She loved her, of course she did. She was her mother, she couldn't help but love her, but she'd never *liked* her. There hadn't been anything to like! Not for a long time, but these days it was different. Margaret was softer, kinder, and nicer, and she'd actually been really quite supportive of Sarah for the first time ever! She regularly babysat the twins, seeming to really enjoy her time as the doting granny, cooing and ahhhing over them, talking baby talk, tickling and playing with them. She even liked Fred! Sarah often caught her mother chatting to Fred, stroking his head and patting him lovingly. Sarah had never imagined that her mother was a dog person, but surprise, surprise, her and Fred seemed to be really good friends. She wouldn't walk him though, saying that he pulled on the lead too hard for her - after one particular trip to the park when Fred had gone berserk when he'd seen a duck, but apart from that, her mother had actually been a tower of strength and support to Sarah over the last year. Yes, her mother really was a surprise, a good one, and Sarah wouldn't have her poked at any more.

Sitting quietly watching from the sofa Clarabelle beamed. *Her heart is opening more and more*, she thought, *I think we are ready. Smashing, just smashing!*

***

The following week Fred was pacing around his favourite apple tree in the front garden waiting for Frank to arrive, pawing at his bone distractedly with every pace. July had turned into August and Aunty Clarabelle was cuddled up with Uncle Mickey in the back garden sitting on the bench there, hidden from view, being all lovey-dovey as usual. They'd only just arrived and Fred had been a bit nervous that Frank may spot them so he'd chosen this tree at the front of the house especially. He knew Frank wouldn't be able to see them from the front. *Dog, he was so clever!*

"Hope he can help, he must help, has to help!" he woofed at the bone.

"Help with what, Frederick?" came the soft, gentle voice from his left.

"Yay Frank! How are you buddy? How's tricks? What's occurring upstairs, my man?" Fred barked noisily, jumping around St Francis of Assisi who stood quietly and calmly smiling at the dog. "Did you bring any birds? Can I have one? Can I? Can I? Just one, pleeeeeeeze?" he barked excitedly.

"Now, Frederick, what have I told you? No you cannot have one! Birds like all creatures are to be loved and respected," he replied with a smile.

"Respected! You're having me on! Don't be daft, Frank! Respected my arse, as if! They're for chasing, catching, ripping their heads off, and shaking them till they break!" barked Fred happily, shaking his head back and forth in his efforts to show Frank what he meant and get him to understand the essential art that was 'duck-head ripping.'

"Yes, well we shall have to agree to disagree on that one,

my dearest Fred," he smiled. "Now what is so urgent that you need my help with, dear one?"

"Oh, Frank, do I need your help! I need it big time, buddy! It's a love problem - not that I get it at all, this love thing, not since they made me a bloody eunuch, mind you, but a friend of mine, a good friend, well she loves someone and it's not allowed, forbidden, in fact, and she's gonna get in deep, deep shit apparently, and I dunno what to do?"

"Forbidden love? Mmm, an interesting problem, my dear Frederick, interesting indeed," Francis said, scratching his beard, "and why is this love forbidden, do you know?" he enquired politely.

"Nope, not a bloody clue, mate! All I know is it's not allowed where they come from and they're gonna be thrown out, sacked, banned, sent away - if they get caught and that's just not bloody right!" he barked in disgust, "not right at all!"

"Ah, that is a problem indeed, a sad problem," he nodded. "Love is grand, love is pure, and love heals all. It is the glue that holds all together, gives life, transmutes and heals, it is the wonder, the WONDER I tell you, of ALL. Real love flows, grows and 'IS' and has a power like nothing else, nothing else at all!" he declared emphatically.

"Well?" barked Fred, "Never mind all that namby-pamby stuff! What can they do, my friends?"

"They can pray to the Almighty for help with this love, Frederick, my dear. They must pray to The Almighty, the 'All That Is'! Love always finds a way and I feel," he smiled, "that this love will find its way too."

"Really? That's it? Ask the 'All That Is'? Is that it? Is that all they got to do? Jeeeez, well that's easy! Yay! Cheers,

Frank, my mate, I knew you'd know, ta buddy, ta heaps, you the man! Hugs n hugs!" Fred barked, jumping on Francis doing his best impression of a bear hug as he wrapped his paws around him, licking his face with gusto, tail wagging at ninety miles an hour.

"Thank you, Frederick, that's quite enough washing for now," Francis laughed, pulling the excited Fred from his face. "Now do you think you might be able to find some love in your heart for our friends the birds, now that you know how important love is?" he enquired kindly.

"Don't be daft, Frank! Birds are for chasing, especially ducks! Ducks is the 'bestest best'! I LOVE chasing ducks!" Fred barked, "As if! Give up chasing ducks? I'd rather die!" he said dramatically, rolling onto his back, all four paws in the air for effect, doing his best impression of being dead.

"Yes, well," Frank laughed, "if there's nothing else, I must be off. Take care Frederick, blessings to you, dear one." And Francis was gone.

"Cheers, mate, ta a lot," Fred barked at the empty space where Francis had been standing just a second ago, "I'll tell 'em, sort it, fix it! Fred the Fantastic to the rescue!" and ran in the house to find Mum and tell her he'd fixed it for Aunty Clarabelle. Maybe he'd even get some doggy chocs as a reward, smashing! Yes indeedy, doggie chocs, yay!

***

Metatron was just approaching Mars when he felt the rumblings in his feathers. It was strong here the energy, very strong. He stopped mid-flight, pausing for a moment. He stretched his wings out fully and stayed very still, floating in the weightlessness of pure space, feeling the sensations of the energy that pulsed around him. This strange energy, a powerful energy, was now radiating throughout his being. His feathers absorbed the atoms within the energy particle by particle, sending signals into every spec of Metatron's energy field ... and suddenly he knew ... he could feel it ... he could sense it ... he could name it! It was, and he had to take a breath to register the shock, it was ... this energy, it was ... romantic love ... *and* it was *mixed in* with Angelic Love! *NO! This can't be right! Angelic-unconditional-pure-love ... mixed in with human romantic love? It cannot be so!* Metatron rocked with the shock. He felt the energy again, to check, double check, triple check! But it was so, he knew it, he could feel it - there was no doubt, no doubt at all! It was radiating out from Gaia, planet Earth, pulsing like a beacon, a homing device, out into the cosmos. It stretched out as far as Mars and Venus! It stretched all around Metatron as he floated, beaming out for all to see. *Oh, the shame! The embarrassment! The shame that one of my angels could fall prey to this human weakness they call 'Romantic Love' is just horrific! Incomprehensible!*

Metatron's feathers darkened as his energy filled with horror at the realisation. He looked down, focusing his attention at the bright light he could now see, and see clearly far below on planet Earth. "I can feel you!" he boomed down across the darkness of space towards the light, "I KNOW!"

The whole cosmos shook, vibrating across the multiverses. It was time. It had run out. ...

In Sarah and Simon's garden far below, Clarabelle and

Mickey froze. Turning to each other in horror, they wrapped their arms and wings around each other in protection from the energy that was now falling all around them. The sky darkened, thunder roared, lightning bolted across the sky, and suddenly the heavens opened with the heaviest, almighty downpour that Redfields had ever seen. The sky was crying, sobbing, and along with it, both angels. Tears rolled down Clarabelle's cheeks unchecked, unstoppable, and uncontrollable. Michael too, wept, sadness engulfing every atom of his being.

"Oh, Mickey!" she sobbed. "He knows!"

"He does indeed, my love, he does indeed," Michael replied softly. "It is time."

***

"Mum, Mum! I fixed it, I fixed it!" Fred barked as he ran into the house, bounding up the stairs to Mum's room with his exciting news. "I, Fred the Fantastic, the Amazing, the Wonderful, have fixed it!"

"Fixed what, Fred?" called Sarah.

"Bugger me, she can hear me again! Woohooooo!" he barked excitedly. "Fixed it for Aunty Clarabelle!" he yelled, running into her room and jumping on her bed without thinking.

"Down, Fred! Down!" Sarah screeched, seeing his muddy pawmarks from his recent trip to the garden all over her cream duvet. The heavens had suddenly opened just as Fred had run in from the garden and he was soaked. He hadn't even noticed. Shaking himself dry automatically, he splashed muddy water without a care across the entire bedroom, splattering every wall. Flicks of mud flew onto the ceiling stretching into every corner.

Suddenly Sarah froze. The mud didn't matter, the mess didn't matter. Nothing mattered. Standing stock still, she stared out of the window. Fred stared too. A look of horror on both faces, they turned simultaneously towards the window, then to each other.

"Too late!" they both yelled. ... "It's too late!"

The sky had darkened, the energy was heavy; the thunder clapped and the lightning streaked. Both ran down the stairs two at a time and out into the garden, stopping dead in their tracks. Clarabelle was hunched over, being held up by Michael. Both were drenched and crying. She turned to Sarah with utter despair.

"He knows, Sarah, he knows!"

"I know, hun, I know," she said sadly.

"But we can fix it, we can fix it!" Fred barked. "Frank told me what to do!"

All three looked at Fred in amazement.

"We've just got to ask God. That's all. That's what Frank says, just ask God!"

"Oh, Fred dear, if only it were that simple!" Clarabelle and Michael said together. "But sadly it is not. We must go now, Fred. We are being recalled."

Their feathers heavy, their hearts heavy, their faces ravaged with fear and grief, they held hands for one last time as they prepared to fly home. Standing side by side in the garden they turned to each slowly.

"Ready?" Michael asked quietly.

"Ready," Clarabelle replied heavily.

And then they were gone.

Fred turned to Sarah with shock.

"What the hell. ...!"

"I know, Fred, I know," she said sadly. "I'd better prepare for the biggest meditation I've ever done in my life. I have to do it now, right now. I have to go with them, I have to be there, I have to help, I have to save them!" she cried, and ran into the house.

Angelica woke with a start, David too. They looked at each other and began to scream; a scream that only babies of five months old can scream.

"WA Wawa!" they both yelled. "Waaaaaaa!" They didn't know why they were crying, they just cried. Sarah ran into the nursery flustered and upset.

"Not now, please?" she soothed, picking up the screaming infants and holding them close. "Not now, darlings, please? I have to help Aunty Clarabelle and I can't do it if you two are crying!"

But the crying went on, and on, and on. The twins were inconsolable, as if they knew that something was terribly wrong and nothing that Sarah could do would calm them, nothing at all.

For the next two hours, Sarah tried to feed, cajole and quiet the crying twins, but nothing she said or did made any difference. Fred tried to calm them down too but he couldn't help either. The twins just cried and cried, and cried some more. Sarah stared desperately out of the window looking up to the heavens. Dark and ominous they glared back. "Clarabelle, honey, oh my God, I'm so sorry, I can't get there!" she called. "I can't help you, I can't do it!

I'm so sorry!" *All the months of learning, all the weeks of meditating, all that work, so that I could be there, at Clarabelle's side, to argue for her, to help her! And all for nothing! Will I ever see Clarabelle again? Oh, God, what's happening up there? The not knowing is just awful!*

As the time ticked on relentlessly, a defeated and desperate Sarah sat on the bed with the crying infants in her own despair and anguish, and cried with them.

***

Clarabelle and Mickey walked silently up the steps to the Angelic Hall. The huge doors swung open as they approached. Side by side they walked through the open doors, descending down the wide sweeping steps into the magnificence of the hall that opened up below them. An enormous amphitheatre, pillars and posts stood tall around the sides of the angelic temple; carved exquisitely, they dominated the perimeter of the temple as far as the eye could see, holding up the high domed ceiling. White mist swirled around hundreds of gathered angels, standing silently on the many tiered rows as they walked in. On the circular stage in the centre of the room below them, at the very bottom of the many steps stood Metatron, his regal wings open to their full and powerful thirty feet span. He stood majestically, commanding everyone's attention.

"Be seated," Metatron boomed, his voice reverberating around the room, bouncing off the ceilings and cylindrical walls. Everyone sat. "Archangel Michael," he shouted furiously, "Join me now!" Michael walked heavily down the steps towards Metatron. "Second Level Angel, Class 1, Clarabelle, join me now!" Metatron shouted again, glaring at Clarabelle as she walked slowly towards them down the steps with shaking legs. Her heart beat heavy in her chest, her breathing tight, her halo dim as she stood, head bowed in front of the Mighty Metatron, an angry, cold Metatron. "Angels of The Realms," he boomed, addressing the crowd. "These two angels have breached Angelic Law."

The silent room seemed to become more silent still. Every angel in the temple stood in shock as Metatron continued, "They have broken the most basic angelic laws and have been ..." Drumroll ... "Deceitful, dishonest, deceptive ... and ..." dramatic pause ... "they have allowed themselves to be contaminated by human weakness!" Metatron glared at them in disgust. They both quivered. Turning to the crowd again, Metatron spread his mighty wings. "They have ... they have ... fallen in love!"

The crowd went nuts.

"No!" shouted one.

"How can this be?" shouted another.

"It's impossible!" shouted a third.

Clarence looked at the floor. His little sister stood shaking and trembling, tears in her eyes and he could take it no more. "If I may, Sir," he shouted, "I would like to speak for my sister." Clarence stood up determinedly.

"What? Who speaks?" glared Metatron. Seeing Clarence standing, a lone angel standing amongst thousands who sat, Metatron glared some more. Clarence could feel his bravado fading fast. He looked at Clarabelle and finding some courage inside him, he took a step forward.

"It is I, Clarence, First Level Angel, Class 2, brother of Clarabelle. I wish to speak for her," Clarence called out, in a voice much stronger than he felt.

"You may speak!" Metatron barked. "Come down."

Clarence descended the stairs carefully, joining the drama and hoping he was doing the right thing. "It is not their fault, Sir," he said. "They can't help it. They have spent too long on the earth plain, working with the humans. Archangel Michael is, of all the angels, the one who spends the most time with them. Clarabelle too. It is not their fault that the earthly energy of romantic love contaminated their purity. They should be pitied, not punished, helped, and not banished." Clarence implored. "I ask you to forgive their indiscretion, to understand, to have compassion! We are angels, compassion is in our atoms." Then he turned to the crowd. "I implore you!"

Metatron looked at Clarence and scowled. He had a point, even he could see that. Metatron hesitated, then turned to the crowd. "Angels of The Realms, what would you have us do with this unclean pair?" he asked. No one spoke. Everyone loved Michael and no one was prepared to speak out against him, but at the same time, no one wanted to argue with the Mighty Metatron either, especially when he was in *this* mood! And poor Clarabelle, she was after all only a Second Level Angel!

"Mercy!" someone suddenly shouted from the back.

"Stand, you who call for mercy, stand and speak!" ordered Metatron.

"It is I, Francis of Assisi."

A quiet murmur went through the temple. Everyone turned to stare, shocked! Saints were allowed into the hall, but they never spoke. All they ever did was sit quietly at the back, never speaking!

"Speak!" boomed Metatron.

"Love is the centre of all things. It is the giver of all life, of all energy, it is the force of the 'All That Is' and is open to all, free to all!" declared Francis, understanding now his little chat with Fred earlier. "Surely even angels are allowed to love?" he asked quietly.

"Love?" boomed Metatron, "LOVE? This is not love! This is romance!"

"But love has many forms," declared Francis, defending strongly now. "Angels know only unconditional love, but romantic love can be as powerful, as pure, as... Perfect?" His voice wavered slightly. Deciding he'd said enough, Francis sat.

Metatron considered this opinion. He looked up, he looked across, and he looked down. Finally, he looked at Clarabelle and Michael. He spoke slowly. "I have decided to give you a choice," he declared. "You can chose to be cleansed from this *contamination* that you hold within you, or ... you can choose to keep it!" he said firmly. "As this romantic love is clearly so important to you, I have decided to allow it," he boomed.

Clarabelle and Michael gave a visible sigh of relief, but it was short lived as Metatron continued, "But ... I cannot allow this *thing*, this *love*, within my Realms! It is contagious, it is contaminating, and it is not angelic! Therefore, should you choose *not* to remove it, *not* to cleanse it, *not* to clear it away ... *you*, Archangel Michael and *you*, Second Level Angel Clarabelle, will be banished forthwith to Gaia, planet Earth, where your love can do no harm. You will not return to these Realms, now or ever! Decide now!" he boomed.

The room was silent, Clarabelle was silent. Michael was silent. Metatron looked at them both expectantly.

Clarabelle burst into tears, Michael shook, and the crowd rumbled, but no one argued. Metatron had spoken and Metatron's word was final. That was it!

There was no way either of them were going to go into the healing temple and have their love removed so ... there was simply no choice, no option, no alternative - they would have to be banished ... forever ... and ever ... amen.

As one, they lifted their heads from their bowed position and slowly stood up straight. Reaching their hands out to each other, their fingers entwined around each other's. Metatron stared disbelievingly at their joined hands and glared. They looked up, bowing slowly and deeply to Metatron, then turned and bowed to the crowd. Lifting their heads up high, they turned to each other, smiled, and walked slowly up the stairs together - out of the Angelic Temple and out of the Angelic Realms, for the very last time.

Chapter 14

Sarah woke with a start. At some point the babies had stopped crying, she had stopped crying, Fred had stopped stomping and all four had fallen asleep on the bed - the mud-splattered bed, still dirty from Fred's shake-dry earlier, before the commotion, before time ran out.

Clarabelle and Michael were standing at the foot of the bed holding hands and looking incredibly, desperately sad.

"Oh my God, what happened?" Sarah blurted, "I'm so sorry, I couldn't meditate, the babies wouldn't stop crying, I couldn't get there. Oh, God, Clar, I let you down, I'm so, so sorry!"

"It is not your fault, Sarah, dear, there was nothing you could do," she sighed. Her voice was small, her halo so dim that Sarah could hardly see it. There was a tinge to Clarabelle's normally white feathers, feathers which had turned a shade of grey and they were getting darker by the minute.

"So what happened, what did he say, this Metatron?"

Sarah exclaimed. "What did he do?"

"We are both sacked, Sarah, sacked from The Realms anyway. And not only that, but we are banned, banished from The Realms, from our home! And," she added in a whisper, "we are banished forever!" She stated it simply, quietly, effectively, sadly.

"No! What do you mean banished? What happened?"

"We are banished to planet Earth. We were given a choice, a choice to love or leave. We left! We are never to return home, never to ..." and Clarabelle burst into tears once more.

"So are you still my Guardian Angel? You're still here so that's good, isn't it?" Sarah asked. She was trying to get her head around it all. *Banned? Banished? What the hell!* Sarah was fuming. *It was appalling, disgusting, unfair and definitely not okay!* "Well, I'm not bloody having it and that's that! I'm just not bloody having it, do you hear!" steamed Sarah, "It's not right. It's wrong. It's not fair. It's pathetic, it's, it's ..." she ranted on.

"Yes, dear, I just wanted to let you know. Now if you'll excuse me ... I ... I need a moment; a moment to compose myself. I'm sorry, my dear, I must go." and Clarabelle, hand in hand with Michael, disappeared suddenly, leaving a trail of tears behind her on the floor, blending beautifully with the dried mud-splattered cream carpet.

***

Sarah lay in Simon's arms in their freshly cleaned and changed bed much later that night, trying to find a solution. Hours went by, her eyes grew heavy, and slowly, eventually, finally, she drifted into sleep and found herself floating in a sea of white mist. In the mist, coming slowly towards here were her dad and her gran, arms outstretched they walked up to her and held her, pouring love into her.

She heard her father's warm, rich baritone voice speak to her - "Sarah, my child, ask God for help. Use the power and the learning you have gained. Link with others to help you - you are not alone. Use Ben, the angels and Fred. Do not underestimate Fred. And, Sarah, I have to warn you that a time is coming of great pain, of great loss. You will get through this, my child, you will get through it. We will be close, we will be there, of this I promise ..." and then he and the mist were gone.

Sarah woke with a start! *Was that my father I just saw? Heard?* It was his deep Scottish voice, his love, she knew that, she recognised it. In all the years since he'd been gone, she'd never seen him, but now, instead of being uplifted by this amazing dream, all she could feel was fear. *A time of great pain, great loss he had said? Oh my God, I'm going to lose Clarabelle!* she thought frantically. *What else had he said; ask God? And use Ben? Fred? How?* Sarah's semi-conscious exhausted body and mind gave up and she fell back into sleep. She dreamed dreams of Clarabelle being gone from her life forever, to never see her or hear her again and woke at dawn with tears dried on her face and fear hard in her heart.

***

The days passed by in a blurry haze. It was late August, the summer sun sat high in the sky. The garden was ablaze with beauty, but Sarah could not feel it. Clarabelle was nowhere to be seen. Since being banished to Earth, Clarabelle had disappeared regularly for days at a time, not wanting to be around Sarah when she felt so sad. She didn't want to pass on her sadness, she had said. The house felt empty, void, and heavy. Everyone felt it and everyone knew it. Even Simon was aware of something. Fred lay guard at the nursery door, sighing regularly, in between farts (having demolished a week's supply of doggie chocs in his need to comfort eat!), still trying to figure out how to fix the mess they were all in. He sighed again, farted again, sighed some more, and suddenly in a Eureka moment, he had it! Frank had said ask God, so why the bloody hell weren't they asking Him? "We got to ask God!" he barked, jumping up with new zest. "We got to do that praying thing! Mum, Mum, where are you?" he shouted, running around the house trying to find her.

Sarah was sitting in the garden under the apple tree. She'd been there for hours! She had risen early and gone outside as she often did to watch the dawn break across the garden, in an attempt to lift her low spirits. The early morning sun shone down gently lighting up the garden as Sarah sat pondering.

"Mum, Mum!" Fred barked, "I got it! We got to do that prayer thingy and ask God!"

"Hi, Fred, you're up early!" Sarah smiled. "Prayer thingy? I pray all the time, hun."

"Oh, my Dog, you can really understand me at last, yay!" he barked, "Smashing!"

"Yes, it's rather interesting being able to understand you, Fred. I never realised just how bad your language is before! Do the twins understand you too?" she asked, with her 'concerned' voice on. Fred nodded solemnly.

"Well, then it's got to change, Fred, do you hear me? All this swearing, it's got to stop!" she said sternly. "Your language is appalling, just appalling!"

"Yeah, yeah, nag bloody nag!" he woofed in disgust. "Anyway, Mrs., this prayer thing, you got to get Ben and Clarence the Spy, and Simon and Nat, and Aunty Clarabelle and Uncle Mickey. Get 'em all together and do the prayer thingy. Right?" Fred ran around in circles as he barked instructions to a surprised Sarah. "And you got to all hold hands and link your energy and you got to go to God and tell him to change that bloody stupid law! Okay, Mum? Got it? I mean even you can manage that, yeah?"

"Got it, and what do you mean 'even you'? Cheeky thing!" Sarah retorted. "At least I don't go around farting all day, Fred, nor do I lick my behind! Bloody disgusting!"

"Show me another way to wipe my bum, lady, and I'll happily oblige!" Fred replied huffily. "It's not like I got a choice now is it and it don't taste pretty, trust me on that one!" he grimaced. "Especially after a week's worth of doggie chocs! Anyway, you gonna sort out this prayer thing then? Get 'em all together?"

"Yes, Fred, of course I am. I was thinking the same thing myself, actually," Sarah said thoughtfully, planning in her mind how and where to do this.

"Yeah, right, course you were, lady, course you were! Take all the bloody credit, that's right! Typical bloody woman!" and Fred was gone, back to guard duty outside the nursery door. The twins would be awake soon and if he got there soon, before they woke up, he could manage to stop that awful screeching thing they did with a few woofs to shut them up. Worked every time, bless 'em. A stern word from him (okay, bark then), and they shut it! Loved 'em to bits he did, would gladly die for them, but the noise - man, it was gruesome! *I just wish Dad had the know-how! Didn't have a clue he did, not a bloody clue! They wrapped him around their tiny little chubby fingers they did! Terrible it was, just terrible! He was putty in their little tiny hands! And the lungs! How little people have such huge lungs on them I don't know, scream the bloody house down they would if I wasn't there to shush them. Thank Dog for Fred - 'Fred the Incredible,' 'Fred the Diligent,' 'Fred the Magnificent,' - Dog they are sooo lucky to have me!*

Fred lay down heavily at the nursery door, one ear cocked waiting for the screech, and sure as eggs is eggs, Angelica awoke, stretched and opened her mouth to start yelling, as she did every morning! No sooner had she taken the big breath ready to blow and the first decibel of screeching commenced, Fred stepped in with his words of wisdom (or fatherly threats, he wasn't sure which), but it worked every time and that was all that mattered. "Mum's coming now," he woofed menacingly at Angelica, in his sternest, firmest voice, "with boobs at the ready, so shut the hell up, you noisy little madam!" he ordered, and Angelica shushed. She knew better than to argue with Fred! David looked at his sister's angry red face and grinned.

"You know Fred doesn't like us crying, Anj. Just play like me, look," he said, pointing at his toes which were in the air trying to poke the mobile hanging over his cot and make it twirl, "I can nearly reach it now, yay!"

"Yes, well, David," she scorned sarcastically, "not all of us are interested in our toes! I'm *far* more interested in my stomach at this precise moment in time thank you very much!"

David just laughed, trying even harder to reach the multi-coloured twinkling toy that dangled teasingly just out of reach of his fully stretched, air-born toes. "Elijah, do us a favour, mate, lift me higher, would you please?" He asked and sure enough, his toes stretched that little bit higher and the mobile twirled as his toes made contact. "Yay, cheers, buddy!" David yelled, poking the mobile harder.

"Elijah, really, should you be doing that?" came Seraphina's gentle voice from the top of Angelica's cot. "You may hurt him!"

"Don't be daft, Sephi, he's fine. He's just playing," he grinned. "Shush now," he motioned them all. "Your mummy's coming. Let's all be happy and nice today, okay people. She's got a lot on her plate right now, so let's all be good little girls and boys, alright?"

Sarah opened the door to the nursery and was happy to note that both children were wide awake and playing nicely in their cots. God, she was so lucky. They hardly ever cried! She had just perfect children!

I think not, lady! thought Fred from the door, but said nothing, managing for once to keep his thoughts to himself - for two whole seconds! "Perfect!" he scoffed. "It's the bloody army of happy police that do it! Hard bloody work it is too I'll have you know, lady!" That army of 'happy police' was, of course, himself, 'Fred the Magnificent,' with a tiny bit of help from Sephi and Elijah, who between them all were responsible for the calm, happy children that hardly ever cried. "Nout to do with perfect, lady, nout!" he woofed.

Simon joined the scene of perfection a few minutes later, fresh from his morning shower, towel wrapped around his waist, he kissed the top of Sarah's head as he came into the room; lifting David into his arms, he smiled at his children with delight. "Good morning, my little people!" he grinned, "and how are we on this fine morning?"

David smiled up into his father's loving eyes and grabbed his finger, squeezing it hard. Simon felt his heart melt, again, as it always did. The rush of love poured through him and he smiled the biggest smile that reached deep into his blue eyes, making them sparkle and water with emotion and pride. Angelica took in this tender scene between father and son and wailed as loudly as possible, hating being left out, always needing to be the centre of attention, and it worked a treat. Simon smiled at her wailing angry face, immediately handing David to Sarah and reached over for 'his little princess,' picking her up and pulling her up to his face to kiss her nose.

"Sucker!" yelled Fred from the door. "She gets you every time! Grow a pair, man! Stand up to the little vixen! Show her who's boss!"

"Shush, Fred, I'm Daddy's little princess and I will not be left out!" Angelica shrilled (in baby language, but Fred understood, genius that he was), grabbing Simon's finger and sucking it hard. "Yuck! Tastes of soap!" she spat in disgust, but gazed up in adoration at her father anyway.

Sarah smiled at this interaction, knowing Fred was right. Simon was a total sucker for both his children and she knew he'd have to toughen up with them before long or the 'wondrous ones' and the 'terrible twos' were going to be a living hell! He may be a sucker for his children, but she loved him beyond belief. He was her world, her night and day, her heart and soul, and she adored him with every inch of her being, just as he did her. Sarah reached for her husband and suddenly held him tight. *I am sooo blessed!* she thought, pushing away firmly, the sense of impending dread that had been with her for days. *Blessed! It's all going to be fine! Just fine!*

Chapter 15

Sarah fingered the top of the mug distractedly as she sat in Ben's kitchen the following day. Her tea, long cold, had formed a film at its surface and looked most unappetising!

"Fresh one, Sis?" Ben asked, noting her expression of concentration, the cold tea and her hunched shoulders.

"Mmm," she replied, half aware of her brother's presence, her mind so filled with the problem that was her Clarabelle. "So, Fred reckons we need to ask God," she blurted, "but really? Is that possible?"

"Well, it's worth a try, hun, don't you think?" he replied gently. "Nothing to lose is there?"

"I guess not; so how's tomorrow for you? It's the weekend, Mum's got the twins, and Gina's going shopping with Joe for new shoes ready for when he starts school next week, so we should have some peace. It's the first of September tomorrow Ben, that's a good day to do it. Clarabelle says that number one signifies new beginnings, fresh starts, change, and stuff, so numerologically speaking it's a good day to try to get laws changed. Come over to mine after lunch, we'll sit in my lounge and I'll have a go at this meditation thing, see if I can get an audience with the man at the top, change this ridiculous law. I mean, it is a ridiculous law, isn't it?" she asked, feeling nervous at the thought of the task ahead.

"I guess so," Ben agreed, "but I've got to be honest, Sarah, I'm not sure. Not at all sure! I mean, all these laws they have up there, there must be a reason for them, don't you think? I mean, they must know what they're doing, don't they?" Ben wasn't at all sure about this whole plan, but he was willing to give it a try to help his sister.

"I guess all I can do is ask," she said firmly. "Ask and ye shall receive, isn't that how it goes?"

"Well, we'll give it a bash, Sis, do our best, aye?" Ben ruffled her hair fondly, putting the kettle on to make her a fresh cup. She looked quite strained bless her, over-tired and heavy, like the weight of the world was on her shoulders, poor thing. Ben didn't have a clue if they could sort this 'angel marriage rule' thing out or not, but if Sarah wanted to try it, he was happy to oblige. He knew if it was his Clarence in trouble, he'd move heaven and earth to help him, though he couldn't imagine Clarence ever being in trouble with 'upstairs'! Far too 'Angel First Class' perfection was Clarence!

"Yes, tomorrow," they said. "We'll do it tomorrow."

***

Metatron sat at his desk in his office, pondering. Which one of the Archangels could possibly replace Michael? Someone needed to step up, but I really don't know who to pick. The gap in The Realms since I banished Michael is palpable. He is missed, much missed! Metatron briefly considered his actions. There had been no other choice, he'd simply had to banish him! Regrettable, of course, but necessary. Michael is still working down there, of course, helping the Earth people where needed, but there is a gap up here, and one that needs to be filled. Metatron looked at his list of candidates again, shook his head, and put the list to one side. He'd come back to it later, when the dust had settled, sort it out then.

***

The afternoon sun hung high in the late summer sky, shining its rays across Sarah's garden and onto her old Victorian home with a plethora of colour and brightness as August turned to September in the Brown household. The rich, golden, heavy drapes were drawn against its brightness in front of the tall French doors in the lounge, in their attempt to block out the sun's light and dim the room. Candles were lit in every corner twinkling gently, casting a soft glow all around them. Larger candles burned more brightly on the marble fireplace and yet more in the hearth. Incense was burning on its stand, wafting gentle aromas of Nag Champa into the room. Soft gentle meditation music was playing and Sarah was finally ready.

She had cleansed her living area just as Clarabelle had shown her to do long ago, creating a perfect sacred space for this important group meditation session. The candles, incense, and music were part of that cleansing ritual, 'raising the vibration' so Clarabelle said.

"Elements, Sarah, elements!" she had chirped. "Earth, air, fire, and water, nice sounds and nice smells, easy!"

There were plants in the room creating the earth element, the French doors were open slightly to allow a flow of air, candles were, of course, for the fire element and a vase of flowers provided the water element. The incense created the 'nice smells,' whilst the calming meditation music provided the 'nice sounds.' Clarabelle was happy.

The room was ready, Sarah was ready, Ben was ready, and the angels were ready. Simon on the other hand, was not ready, not ready at all, bless him! He sat on the corner of the sofa next to Sarah, bemused by it all, but willing to help in any way that he could. He didn't have a clue what he was meant to do! He only knew that Sarah needed him and that was good enough for him. Nathaniel perched on Simon's shoulder, trying his best to reassure him.

"It'll be fine, mate, fine, promise! Just give her your love, that'll be enough, that's all you got to do, matey, easy!" he piped up confidently, although his hair betrayed the confidence, spiked up as it was, Gonk style, to its full six glorious, bright orange inches - always a sign of stress with Nat! "No one's expecting you to travel up there to The Realms, Simon, mate. Just focus on your love for your Sarah and send it her way. It'll help lift her as she meditates, that's all she needs," he grinned.

Simon relaxed, although he didn't know why, not being aware of Nat at all, but he followed his instincts and began to focus on Sarah. He loved her so much, so very much. His Sarah; his love, his life, his heart, his wife. She was his world, his night and day, and he'd give his life for her, willingly. If she thought she could help Clarabelle, then he would do whatever he could do to help her make it happen.

Clarabelle sat, not on Sarah's shoulder, as usual, but next to her, cuddled up in her full size against Mickey, who sat patiently waiting on the other corner of the sofa next to her. Their halos shone brightly, energy radiating out all around them, pulsing, both of them energising the room with their love, their light, and their incredible power. The two of them alone generated enough power to light up a small city!

Ben was sitting in the chair opposite Sarah, Clarence perched behind him on the top of the chair.

"You ready, laddie?" Clarence asked Ben, pouring as much light into him as he could muster. He'd spent all morning preparing in the Angelic Temple, charging up his light and powering up his halo so that he could, in turn, 'power up' Ben for this meditation.

Ben glowed, grinned, and nodded. "Yeah, mate, I'm ready! Ready as I'll ever be!" he confirmed. "Let's do this thing!"

Fred sat on the floor between the sofa and the chair in his guard-dog-stance, doing his best impression of watching a tennis match. He looked from Ben to Sarah, from Clarence to Clarabelle, from Nathaniel to Mickey and nodded his approval. "Yay, baby, let's do this 'thing!' " he woofed. "I'm ready, I'm ready!" He really wasn't sure if Mum could pull this off, but with his help, she may just manage it. He was, after all, 'Fred the Incredible!'

Sarah took a deep breath. "Can we please all hold hands?" she asked. Ben, on the other side of the room, stretched out his right arm, putting his hand on top of

Fred's head. Mickey did the same from the left, and everyone held hands, joining their energy as one.

"That's right, use me as a bloody stool! No respect, no respect at all!" moaned Fred to himself, but managed to keep his mouth shut, for once.

It had begun!

***

Metatron looked at his candidate list again. No really, there just wasn't anyone who could replace Michael. *What to do, what to do?* he wondered.

"METATRON ... THE MIGHTY METATRON ..." he heard dimly across The Realms, "I NEED TO TALK TO YOU!"

Who in heaven? he thought, looking up from his list in surprise.

"It is I, Sarah Brown. I humbly request an audience with you, 'Mighty Metatron.' " The voice was clear, insistent, firm, and getting firmer. Not just that, but it was getting louder, getting closer. Metatron rose, turning his head to one side to hear more clearly where this strange voice was coming from. Suddenly, the huge double doors to his office opened and there stood Sarah Brown. And not just Sarah Brown but a whole posse of helpers to boot!

Sarah took in the large room; she took in the image stood behind the desk and she felt really quite faint! A huge, massive, enormous angel stood in front of her, head cocked to one side and was looking at her in shock. She pulled herself together, straightened her weak and wobbly knees as best she could, and opened her mouth. "Mighty

Metatron, I humbly ask that you reconsider your decision to banish angels Clarabelle and Michael from the Angelic Realms, and ask that you reinstate them," she declared firmly.

Metatron's mouth dropped open in complete shock.

"Immediately and forthwith, straightaway, please!" Sarah continued.

Metatron's dropped mouth closed in annoyance. An eyebrow raised, he walked slowly from the behind the desk, took a step forward to examine the party sceptically. *Immediately, forthwith? Who is this bit of a girl to question me! To question my decisions? And is that a dog I can see? A dog? Really? In the Angelic Realms? And this upstart Sarah Brown had a man with her, another human! Who was that?* He quickly searched the identity bank within his inner-knowing and came up with the answer. *Ben Smith, ah! Brother and sister had joined to do battle, had they? How very interesting!* Metatron smiled. Behind them, hovering by the door, behind the dog who seemed to be guarding them, stood Archangel Michael, along with angels Clarabelle, Clarence, and Nathaniel. Nat shuffled his feet nervously, watching the floor intently. Clarabelle's knees were knocking, but she was holding it together, supported, of course, by Mickey who had his arm, firmly around her. Fred put on his meanest look and puffed himself up, glaring at Metatron.

"Yeah, that's right, buddy, a dog! And I'm watching you, pal!" he declared. "Lay a bloody feather on any of them and I'll bite your wing off, right, got it!"

Clarence jumped with alarm, cleared his throat, and stepped forward quickly. "I think, what Sarah is trying to say, is that..." he hesitated, looked at Metatron and took another step into the room, "She is asking for help, for us all to be able to resolve this unpleasantness, to bring back equilibrium, peace, and harmony to the Angelic Realms and to each and every one of us. To find a resolution." Clarence took another step forward. "It is written that humans ask us angels for help, and it is our job to help when it is asked for. She is asking, as a human, for angelic help. You are 'The Mighty Metatron'! You are the only one who *can* help." Clarence stepped back, sure that he had overstepped the mark, but determined to at least try to help his little sister. He'd done his best. He watched Metatron intently for his reaction to this mutiny.

"I admit there is a bond between these two ..." Metatron waved theatrically at Clarabelle and Michael, "lovebirds!" He practically spat the words, "which is, unfortunately, quite strong and powerful."

"And yet that bond is love! And love is good, isn't it?" Sarah chipped in. "I mean, does it matter that they are angels? Should it matter? Should it count and if so, why?" she asked. "Isn't love what makes the world go round, heals all things? It brings joy and happiness, so why can't they, just because they're angels, be allowed to love?"

"Mmm," Metatron scratched his head, thinking, considering, hesitating, just briefly. Briefly enough for Sarah to throw in a bit more.

"I mean," she continued, "if it's a law, this 'angels can't marry thing,' and it's God's law, can we ask Him? To change it, I mean? Laws get changed on earth all the time, they have to! Things change, don't they? Why can't this law be changed? It's outdated! In fact, I think it's racist against angels; its 'angel-ist'! It's wrong!"

Metatron looked at Sarah like she'd gone mad! Ask the boss? Don't be ridiculous! But Sarah ploughed on,

"And another thing! If this law of 'Free Will' really exists, and I'm told it does," she stared hard at him, "why are angels exempt from it? I mean, why can't they have free will too, to love who they want to love and be with who they want to be with? If it's good enough for us humans, I don't see why it's not good enough for angels! And it's their will to be allowed back upstairs, I mean here, to The Realms, where they live! It's their home, and what kind of free will is it that doesn't let them come home? It's ridiculous!"

"Good point!" came the mutterings from the door. Mutterings not only from the posse but also from a growing group of angels who had gathered nearby, drawn by the spectacle that was unfolding at Metatron's door of these uninvited visitors to The Realms.

Metatron hesitated. This human, this upstart, she had a point!

"And we humans, we aren't very good at it most of the time, love, I mean. We get it wrong loads. We mix up love with need and stuff, but you lot, you lot *know* love, unconditional perfect love, pure love. You lot are *experts* at it! So why can't you allow love between these two? It's beautiful you know, if you'd only see, if you'd only look! Their love, just beautiful, I tell you! It won't hurt anyone up here, not one angel, I just know it! You lot may even learn something! Human love, romantic love, I mean, it may be different to angelic love, but it's still love!"

Metatron scratched his head even harder. This was really very alarming. *Oh dear, what to do? Questioned like this, argued with, and disagreed with! And in front of my staff! Not good, not good at all! Not good for my street cred, my kudos, not to mention my authority!*

Suddenly the room was filled with an energy like none that Sarah could ever even begin to imagine, comprehend, or compute in her limited human mind. A wave of pure power washed through the room like a tsunami, practically blowing each and every one of them off their feet and then it stilled. A silence filled the space and then a voice spoke. It spoke into their hearts, it spoke into their minds and it reached within their very being, at every level, from the very cells to the surface of the skin within the humans, from the bones to the tips of the fur within the dog and from the atoms in the centre of their being to the tips of their feathers within the angels.

"Free will is My Law," The Voice said, "it is *the* law, it is *absolute*, it has *no* exceptions." And then The Voice was gone. Just like that!

Wow! thought Sarah. *Did I just meet God?*

"Unreal!" said Ben

"Oh my!" said Clarence

"Crikey!" added Nat

"Thank you," said Clarabelle and Michael in unison.

"Yes, sir!" said Metatron

And that was that!

***

Sarah came around from her deep meditation and glowed. She had a huge, serene smile plastered all over her face, her eyes shone brightly and she felt rather high.

"Wow!" she exclaimed, looking at the others in wonderment as they opened their eyes too.

"Wow indeed!" Ben agreed, "Bloody hell, Sis!"

"Wow what?" asked Simon, not having a clue as to what they were on about, having not been privy to the shared experience of the others. He wasn't sure if he'd fallen asleep or what had happened, but looking at the clock on the mantelpiece he was gobsmacked to see that it had been over an hour since they'd all held hands and began this thing.

"It worked!" screeched Clarabelle, in absolute delight. "It really worked! Oh my! Oh Mickey!" and she flung her arms around Michael in unadulterated delight. He smiled serenely. Turning to Sarah, he thanked her for all she had done, stood up, and motioned Clarabelle to follow him.

"Yes, dear, yes!" she beamed. "We must return and sort everything out. Get Mickey reinstated, of course, and then the wedding to plan! Oh my goodness, what shall I wear?" she gabbled happily, "My halo! Must get it polished! And the venue! The Angelic Temple will make a super venue for the wedding, don't you think, Mickey? Simply super!"

"What?" almost shouted Simon in frustration, not being able to hear the conversation around him.

"It worked!" announced Sarah happily, hugging her husband. "We won! They can be together, it's all sorted!"

"Really? It worked? You did it?" he asked in astonishment, "What happened?"

Sarah relayed the events to a bemused Simon who was more than a little blown away at the thought that his wife had just met God! Not only that, but she had caused this law that she disagreed with so much to be overturned.

"Wow, wife of mine, you really did it!" he grinned, hugging her with delight. He was practically bursting with pride and surprise at the same time, not to mention a huge amount of shock.

"Yo, people! Anyone remember me?" shouted Fred amongst the commotion. "I helped too, you know! If it wasn't for me guarding everybody that Metatron chap would have chopped your bloody heads off! Yeah, that's right, I saved the day, me, Fred the Fantastic!" he barked, but no one was listening, they were all too busy celebrating and jumping around and everyone was hugging Mum, argh! "That's right, lady, take all the bloody credit, typical!" he moaned, but he couldn't help but be happy; after all, Aunty Clarabelle and Uncle Mickey could get married now, just like Mum and Dad. He was surprised at The Spy though, hadn't seen that one coming, no not at all! *Fancy that, 'The Spy' helping! Maybe I'll be a little nicer to him from now on*, he decided.

"Thank you, Frederick," smiled Clarence, from Ben's shoulder. "I always had my sister's best interests at heart, you know."

Fred cocked his head to one side and looked at Clarence in new light, woofing quietly, acquiescing just a tiny bit towards the former enemy. "Mmm maybe, but I'm watching you, pal!" he muttered.

"Let's crack open a bottle and celebrate then, Sis," shouted Ben over the racket, "I think we've earned it, don't you?" He grinned at Sarah. Blimey, she really did it!

"She did indeed," smiled Clarabelle from the door just before she flew off with Mickey. "She did indeed! Smashing!"

Chapter 16

Fred had had enough of the chaos, what with Mum taking all the credit an' all, and looking at the state of Dad, decided that he had too! It was time for some normality after all this excitement! He trotted into the kitchen, picked up his lead between his teeth, pulling it from its hanger by the back door and trotted back to Dad, who was standing in the middle of the lounge amongst all the chaos looking bemused and confused. "Yeah, I know, Dad, right out of your depth aren't you, pal, aye?" Fred barked. "Don't you worry about a thing, mate, I'll save you! I, Fred the Incredible, will save the day, *again!* Come on, mate, let's go." He dropped the lead at Dad's feet and pawed his knee insistently. Simon looked at Fred, he looked at the lead, and then he looked relieved, Dog love him! "Smashing! Let's go!" he barked again. With any luck there'd be some ducks today and maybe, just *maybe*, Dad would let him off the lead and he could chase them all round the pond again. He *loved* chasing ducks, just *loved* it!

Simon patted Fred's head, clipped the lead to his collar and headed towards the door. "Taking Fred out, hun, won't be long," he called, and then he legged it. His head was all over the place and he felt really, really uncomfortable! He couldn't put his finger on what or why exactly, all he knew was that whilst he was extraordinarily proud of his Sarah, he was also a little scared. In fact, he admitted as he walked down the lane, he was a lot scared! "Come on, Fred," he smiled, "let's go and chase some ducks, buddy."

"REALLY! Oh my Dog, no way! Yay! Ducks, here I come!" Fred barked in delight, "I LOVE you, Dad!" and pulled on his lead harder, heading for the village centre and the duck pond. Fred loved Redfields, loved it to pigging bits! It was absolutely *the* best place to grow up. There were hardly any cars, being a sleepy village, so was nice and quiet. Fred didn't like cars, noisy smelly things, and he liked trucks and lorries even less. They scared him, although he'd never admit it to anyone, not even Dad, being 'Fred the Incredible' an' all. Thankfully, there weren't many of them in Redfields, apart from the deliveries to the shops on the high street, but they usually went round the back of the shops, so he didn't have to see them very often. *Dog, they stank!* The fumes off those things nearly knocked him out! *It's alright for the grownup humans, being a lot taller than me. They get away with just a whiff from up there, but from down here on the pavement it's just bloody awful! God knows how little people managed?* Fred wondered. Those noisy, wailing lot in the prams, pushchairs and strollers! *No wonder they yelled!*

Fred spotted the duck pond up ahead and pulled on his lead. "Come on!" he yelled, "Come *on!*" He pulled even harder in his haste to get there. Fred loved the duck pond, surrounded as it was by fields and trees. Perfection, just perfection! There was one part of the park he wasn't allowed in mind, the play area. Cordoned off, it was, to keep him out so the little people could play safe. Fred didn't know what that was about at all! "My tree, my tree!" he yelled, as they came around the corner and in through the gates.

The park spread out majestically before him, tantalising him with its promise. *So many trees to sniff, so many to pee on, so many ducks to chase, and maybe even catch one and rip its head off! Yay!* Fred had a favourite tree, of course, the one he always loved to pee on, cocking his leg and aiming perfectly, just high up enough to tell other dogs to stay away. This was his tree, *only his*, and his wee was a warning sign to all other dogs to stay away. "Mine!" it said. "Piss off!" And then it came, that special moment, the best, most *perfect* moment, the removal of the lead! "Fan-bloody-tastic!" he barked in absolute delight.

Fred bolted off, doing at least two hundred miles an hour, he reckoned, although admittedly that may be a small exaggeration. "My tree, my tree!" he barked with delight, running around it several times working out which angle he'd direct his pee at today. "Acute or obtuse today, I wonder?" he barked, and went for it. "Yep, that's definitely an acute angle today, forty-three degrees, I reckon," he woofed proudly, running to the next tree to do the same.

Simon watched Fred and smiled. *God, I love that dog! Mad as a hatter, he is, but he's my best friend, apart from Sarah, of course, and I do love him to bits!* Simon strolled through the park smiling, keeping an eye on Fred as he walked, watching him running and playing, sniffing and peeing periodically, depending on which tree he fancied today. *Life was so simple for dogs,* he decided; *playful, loyal, fun and easy.* Simon pondered being a dog. "Maybe I'll come back next time as a dog, but then I guess it depends who your owner is. Nah, bit risky," he decided. Simon walked past the cricket grounds, the tennis courts, the childrens' play area, and the picnic area, doing a full circuit of the park before coming to the pond.

"Yeah that's right, leave the best till last!" shouted Fred, running up suddenly from behind him. "Teasing me again, Dad, you naughty, naughty boy!" and threw himself in with a huge splash. "Ducks, ducks!" he yelled, "I'm gonna get you, I'm gonna rip your scrawny, bloody necks off!"

"Fred, leave the ducks alone!" shouted Simon from the bank of the pond, laughing as he watched Fred splash about. Graceful he was not! He had no chance of ever catching one, Simon knew, but he tried anyway. As soon as he got close, the duck would simply fly off, leaving Fred jumping about in the water to turn his attention to the next duck, splash after that one, who would do exactly the same. On and on the cycle would go until eventually Fred had enough and gave up. Still, it wore him out, and Fred was always at his happiest after a walk with Dad and the obligatory duck chasing.

"One day, you bastards!" screamed Fred in frustration, watching the last duck fly away leaving the pond empty of all wildlife, the previously clear water now muddy from his chasing and jumping, and Fred along with it. "One day!"

"Come on, Fred," called Simon gently, "give it up, buddy, it's never gonna happen, not unless you grow feathers and learn to fly, mate," he grinned. Seeing the state of him, he took the stance, the boss stance. Dad didn't do that very often, but when he did, Fred obeyed. "Shake!" Simon commanded, standing firm and authoritarian. "Time to dry off now, bud, you can't go home like that. Mum will kill us both if I take you home in that state," he grinned.

Fred obliged and began the long, slow shake from the end of his nose to the tip of his tail as Simon backed off so that he wouldn't get caught in the cross fire. Fred did his best to remove the mud and water from his fur and did a pretty good job of it too, after all, if he didn't, he had to have that Dog awful *bath* thing! He *hated* baths, absolutely bloody *hated* them! "You don't have to tell me, mate, I know!" he yelled at Simon, shaking again, and again, and again. "No bloody bath for me!" he woofed happily, "I, Fred the Fantastic, can wash-and-go!"

He looked around from his last shake just to make sure there were no ducks left to chase and noticed Simon had wandered off, strolling ahead in an anti-clockwise direction around the park to give Fred a chance to dry off properly before the short walk home down the lane. "Wait, Dad!" he yelled, bolting after him. "Wait for me!"

Simon walked slowly through the park smiling. *God, I'm so lucky!* The walk had calmed him down from the scary stuff earlier and he decided not to be scared anymore. So okay, his wife was able to talk to angels, fly up to heaven, meet with God and get universal laws overturned. Okay, so it was weird, it was definitely not normal, but it was who she was. And she was his wife, the mother of his children and the best thing that had ever, ever happened to him! It was her birthday next week, early September, the third birthday he'd had with her and he wanted to make it special. The first year, when he'd first fallen for her and fancied her like mad, trying his best to woo her, he'd bought her the angel necklace. Ben had said she liked angels - little did he know then what he knows now! No wonder she liked angels!

The second year for her birthday, three months after they had married, he had bought her a bracelet; a delicate, gold beautifully embellished bracelet with diamonds cut into it. She'd loved that too, thank God! This year, her fortieth, he wanted to make it extra special. He wanted to give her the best birthday ever! After all, not only would she be turning forty, a special birthday in anyone's book, this year she had also given him the most precious thing any human being can give another, a child, two children at that! He smiled; pride, love and joy all mixed up together at the thought of his children. His beautiful, amazing, fantastic children! The twins were coming on just beautifully. Nearly six months old now and they were sitting up and trying to crawl. Each had their own little personalities, little idiosyncrasies, and little individualities, despite being twins. Angelica was his little princess and David his pride and joy. *What to get my Sarah that could possibly even begin to show how much I love her?*

"Birthday, birthday!" Fred barked. "Did anyone even *notice* my birthday, aye, aye? It's today actually, first of September you know, not that anyone cares!" he moaned, but it didn't matter really, *not really*. After all, Dad *had* brought him to the park and he'd had a *super* time on his birthday, absolutely super, so he magnanimously decided to let it go.

"What to get her, aye, Fred?" Simon pondered,

muttering to himself as he walked. "Maybe another necklace? What about a ring, eternity ring, or is that for anniversaries?"

Fred was just about to chip in with some helpful suggestions like chocolate and stuff when he noticed the duck. It was waddling along, pecking at the grass just at the edge of the park. Way out of its territory, the duck was oblivious to the looming danger. Fred stared. He couldn't believe it! He didn't even have his lead on yet! There was nothing holding him back *and* it was his birthday! "Oh my Dog, there is a God!" he yelled, and he was off. Fred ran faster than he'd ever run before in his whole, entire life! His tail, pointed like a rudder for stability, his body, strong and athletic, muscles rippling, he was a guided missile aiming for his target, the duck, at extraordinary pace. He took off like a bat out of hell, yanking Simon unceremoniously from his intense contemplation and concentration of birthday gifts with a start.

"Fred, Fred, *no!*" shouted Simon, watching Fred heading full speed ahead for the exit to the park and the lone duck that waddled happily through its gates.

"Ducks, ducks!" screamed Fred in delight.

"Fred *no, no!*" screamed Simon at full pelt behind him.

Fred was oblivious to Simon, totally focused on catching the duck, ripping its head off, and finally having his prize. He ran harder and faster, his tongue hanging out in anticipation of the kill, his ears bouncing and flying in the wind. He ran like his life depended on it. He ran out through the gates of the park, he ran over the pavement and he ran across the road. "Ducks, ducks!" he yelled.

Fred didn't see the lorry. Fred didn't see Simon. All he saw was the duck that was now flying at full speed ahead of him.

The lorry driver was lost. He was not looking at the road ahead of him as he drove down the high street of the sleepy village, his focus and all his attention at that particular moment on his map, trying to figure out where he had gone wrong. He looked up and saw the dog ahead of him too late. "Jesus!" he yelled, slamming on the brakes, but knowing it would not be enough to stop his seventy-two tonne truck in time to avoid the dog. He grabbed the steering wheel, pushed his foot down on the brake as hard as he could and prayed. Tyres screeching, smoke pouring off the offending brakes, the scene went into slow motion before his eyes as the lorry skidded down Redfields' high street trying in vain to stop in time.

Simon saw the lorry. Simon saw Fred.

Fred saw only the duck, now just inches from his open jaws.

Simon's brain did not press the stop button as it should have in its instinct for survival. Instead, it pressed the 'run faster' button automatically to save his dog, his best friend, his buddy. Simon got to Fred just in time, pushing him out of the way of the impending truck a split second before it hit. Simon did not feel the lorry hit him with its full seventy-two tonne weight. Simon did not feel anything at all...

***

Clarabelle and Michael had had a wonderful time. They'd been welcomed back home to The Realms like the proverbial prodigal son. There were hundreds there to welcome them home, hundreds! Even Metatron showed his face, briefly, poking his head out of his office door for a moment to see the commotion as Michael and Clarabelle walked up the enormous staircase and back into The Realms jubilantly. He had nodded to them both, but then went back to work. Sitting at his desk, he had looked at his candidate list and ripped it up, smiling. As long as the Boss said it was okay, then he guessed it was okay, although he wasn't sure what effect the lovebirds' romance and behaviour would have on the others. At least he didn't have to sort out a replacement for Michael now; that was a relief! Really there was no one who could have replaced him anyway, not really.

Clarabelle was twirling around happily, examining the Angelic Temple in detail as the venue for her special day. She was glowing and floating, her feathers back to their normal pure whiteness now that everything was sorted. She floated up each of the four aisles that swept down and into the temple from all four corners of The Realms. They spread from the south wing to the north wing, from east to west. Clarabelle whooshed left and right, up and down looking for the best angle to approach the stage at its centre for her bridal walk. She imagined herself gleefully gliding down the staircase in her bridal outfit, halo polished, and shinning like it had never shone before. Not that she had a bridal outfit, of course, having never been married, and there were certainly no bridal outfitters up here to order one from, but she could 'miracle' one up. *Oh yes indeed, I can miracle one up!*

"Oh my, oh my!" she chirped happily as she sent her order for her gown telepathically out across The Realms. "Tomorrow, yes, tomorrow, I think. Our wedding will be tomorrow!" she beamed.

***

Redfields was just a big village really: a pretty high street with a few shops, a chapel and an old pub, the cricket ground and pavilion, the small school, the duck pond in the centre with its willow trees, set amid open parkland; the whole thing wrapped up and parcelled by fields of rolling countryside. It was a quiet village, a small population, the sort of place where everyone knows everyone. The sounds of children's laughter could be heard across the village as they played, the noise of dogs barking travelled easily through the quietness, windows open to the summer breeze in most homes and offices.

As Clarabelle was twirling around the angelic temple ecstatically, Sarah was preparing the evening meal, ready for when Simon got back from the park with Fred. She heard the squeal of the tyres in the distance as they skidded to a screaming halt on the main road just a few hundred yards from their home. She heard the dog barking frantically. She heard the blood rush to her head. She felt her heart stop. She dropped the frying pan in her hand and she ran. She ran like she'd never run before. She flew down the lane on legs that were weak and then she saw him lying there; her love, her soul mate, her husband. Laying sprawled in front of the lorry, his body twisted and turned at a strange angle. She saw Fred laying across him, guarding her husband's broken and bleeding body, keeping him warm, instinctively protecting.

"Dad, Dad," he howled, "I'm sorry, I'm sorry, please don't die, Dad. I'll never chase ducks again, Dad, I promise. Just be okay, please be okay!" Fred begged, crying and howling like the world had come to an end, and for Fred it had. If Dad died it was absolutely the *end* of the entire *world*.

"Mum, Mum," he cried, seeing Sarah running towards them, "I've hurt Dad! I think I've killed Dad! I think he's dead! Oh my Dog, no!" he howled.

Sarah threw herself on the ground in front of her husband and screamed for Clarabelle. Putting her hands on her husband's broken, lifeless body, she begged for healing, for help, for a miracle. Clarabelle appeared out of nowhere, suddenly taking over, shining a light straight into Simon's heart and with a jump, it sprang back into life. It beat weakly, irregularly, but it was beating.

The tears streamed unchecked down Sarah's cheeks as the paramedics arrived, pushing her gently out of the way as they took over. Time had stopped for Sarah. It was standing still, as still as her heart, which she swore had stopped beating. She hadn't heard the ambulance arrive, despite its screaming sirens. Since the screeching of the tyres, Sarah had heard nothing but the silence in her head, which was deafening. She looked up at the people around her. A large crowd had gathered and the police were there taking statements, but she hadn't seen them arrive either. A man in a bright yellow safety jacket, clearly the lorry driver, was being interviewed and breathalysed, standard procedure in an accident of this kind, as he stood shaking, trembling, and crying. She could see his head shaking as he repeated over and over, no he hadn't seen him, he'd come out of nowhere, no he hadn't been drinking, no he hadn't been speeding. Their mouths were moving she noted, but she heard nothing.

She could see people motioning to her, speaking to her, but she heard nothing except silence. She was aware of being helped into the ambulance and she was aware of holding his hand as they sped to the large hospital in the nearby town of Redville eight miles away. She was aware of being helped out of the ambulance and she was aware of running beside the trolley down the hospital corridor as they all sped with it to the emergency trauma unit. She was not aware of anything else.

***

Ben arrived quickly. Someone had called him, Sarah didn't know who or when, nor did she care. She was too numb to care. Ben held Sarah close, stroking her hair with one hand, he wiped the tears away which silently fell with the other. He saw the blood on her hands and chin, Simon's blood, transferred to her face and body as she'd kissed his lips softly and held his bleeding hand gently in the ambulance. "He's in surgery now, Sarah. They're doing all they can," he said quietly. "Mum's got the kids, you're not to worry. We're all here for you, darling."

Sarah looked at her brother in surprise. *When had he arrived? How long had he been here? How long have I been here?* "My babies! I have to fetch my babies!" she exclaimed, pulling away to stand up.

Ben pulled her back down, repeating himself quietly he reassured her, explaining that Tim had called him within seconds of Simon being hit by the truck. Tim knew Ben well, ever since he'd taken over as Manager of Sarah's shop and at some point, Sarah had given him emergency numbers just in case. He'd always hoped he would never need them, but he had today, this awful, awful day. He'd rung Ben immediately, and Ben, having taken in the shocking news relayed quickly and calmly by a shaking Tim, had told Gina to drop everything, get his mother, and go to Sarah's house to look after the twins. Mum was there now, he explained to a shaking Sarah, looking after the twins and Joe, keeping it together for them all, whilst Gina was at the vets with Fred. Gina had picked Fred up from Tim at the store who was convinced that the dog was hurt because there was so much blood on him. No one was sure if it was Simon's or Fred's blood on the dog or both, but they'd know soon enough as he was presently being checked over.

Sarah simply nodded as Ben talked and took control, calmer in the knowledge that her twins were safe with her mum. She'd not even thought about them since it had happened, she realised, her babies! *Did I really just run out of the house and leave my two six month old babies on their own? How long had they been on their own?* she wondered, but her brain wouldn't seem to let her think about it, almost knowing that she couldn't take any more things to worry about other than her husband and his condition. "Critical," they had said. "Swelling on the brain," they had said. "Urgent operation needed," they had said, "neuro-surgery," they had said Sarah stared at the flowers in the picture on the wall in a daze. *This cannot be happening*, her mind said. *I am dreaming*, her mind said, *I am going to wake up from this nightmare any minute*.

But she did not wake up. It was not a dream. It was real. Her husband was in there, fighting for his life, right now, this very minute. "Fight, Simon," she called in her head, "Fight, my darling! Fight with everything you have!" But she heard no reply. She felt no reply. She heard only silence. She felt nothing but aloneness and a great, engulfing fear.

***

Simon gazed down in surprise at the people below him. He was floating somehow, weightless, free, light; as light as a feather! It felt amazing! He smiled, a quiet, unassuming smile as he watched them operate on the man below. It looked familiar, the face, he knew it from somewhere, and he wondered how he'd been allowed to be in here, in this operating room watching the surgeon perform the delicate operation on the man's brain. *Wow, I can't wait to tell Sarah about this! And what are those?* he wondered, noticing two bright figures, transparent figures, hovering either side of the man. *Are they angels? I think they're angels, yes, there's two of them, standing over the man. Yes, definitely angels, I can see the wings. How strange!* And was that a third angel, up here floating with him? A black one, a dark one, and he was calling him, approaching him. He was reaching out his hand to him, up here on the ceiling. Simon took his hand, this dark angel, he just wanted to, had to, and then everything went black.

Chapter 17

For the first time in his young life, Fred did not struggle, writhe, or wriggle as he sat in the bath. He watched the soapy water run red, blood red, away from his body and into the plug hole, and he cried. His tears went unnoticed by the vet, hidden by the gentle flow of the warm water from the shower head as he was cleaned down of Simon's blood. He did not struggle as they dried him, examined him, poked, and prodded him. He did not pull on his lead as Gina took him gently home afterwards. He did not jump all over everyone when he got in as he always did. He simply lay down in the hall by the front door, on Simon's slippers and he cried some more.

Granny Smith tried to coax him into the lounge, but he wouldn't budge. She even lit the log fire in the hearth for him to lay in front of, which he usually loved, but Fred wasn't interested. She made his favourite dinner, but he couldn't eat. He didn't argue, he didn't speak, he didn't mutter, and he didn't moan. The world had stopped for Fred the minute Dad got hit by the truck and he had stopped with it. He wasn't going to move until Dad came home and if Dad, God forbid, didn't come home, well then, he would die with him, it was as simple as that. His place was by Dad's side, in life or death. End of.

***

Clarabelle and Nathaniel watched the operation unaware of Simon floating above them. They poured healing light into his body, they poured calmness and perfection into the surgeon to make sure he did the best job he could possibly do. They filled Simon's body with light and power until their energy was gone and their halos grew dim. They'd moved silently to his head, standing either side of the surgeon. Holding their hands together over the damaged brain they had poured their power into it, rebooting it, reorganising it, restructuring it, and doing what they could to repair it. They had moved down silently, working on either side of the operating table pouring energy into his broken, bruised and battered body. They had directed healing into his broken bones; ribs, wrists, and pelvis and watched as the cells slowly started the process of knitting back together gently. After what seemed an age, when there was no more light to give, their power spent, Nathaniel turned to Clarabelle solemnly and nodded to the door.

"We've done what we can do now, Clar, it's up to him now. You go to your Sarah, hun. She needs you, my friend."

Clarabelle nodded quietly, slipping silently from the room she floated down the corridor slowly with what little energy she had left, leaving Nathaniel behind to watch over

Simon.

Clarence stood over Ben and Sarah in the family waiting room, focusing his energy and power onto both as he shone healing light into the brother and sister. He looked up and smiled sadly as Clarabelle came into the room, reaching out his hand he held hers tight.

"Oh, Clarence!" she wailed, "I didn't see this coming! None of us did! Not even Nat knew. He will be alright, won't he?" she asked, her voice trembling.

"I'm afraid I don't know, my dear." His gentle, very sad reply, spoke volumes and Clarabelle clutched his hand tighter.

"But we know, we always know, when it's their time, when something big happens, don't we?" she asked, confusion on her face. "I just don't understand how we missed this! And poor Freddie!" she exclaimed, "He's never going to forgive himself for this!"

"Clarabelle, my dear, we know what we need to know. Some things are kept from even us. Some things, sometimes, just occasionally, are best even for us not to know. We just have to trust, my dear, trust that there is a purpose in this." Clarence shook his head sadly. He truly didn't know if Simon was going to make it or not. It wasn't looking good, that much was clear, despite the help of the angels, he'd seen the signs too many times over the eons not to recognise it. The Grim Reapers were waiting, he'd noticed one earlier but had said nothing to Clarabelle. She didn't need to know, not yet anyway.

It was such a shame, huge shame, enormous shame, if Simon did have to go now. He and Sarah had only had two years of happiness together, not much really in the scheme of things. Clarence hoped that he was wrong, goodness how he hoped that he was wrong, but he had a feeling, an inkling that Simon's time was up. *Poor Sarah! Poor, poor, darling Sarah. And the twins! Those poor children, left without a father at such an early age. And poor old Fred! It was his fault this had happened and he knew it. He'd never get over it, poor dog, the guilt would probably kill him and even if it didn't, he'd never be the same.* Clarence scratched his head. There must be something he could do? Was there, anything, anything at all that he could do? He would try, he'd simply have to! He would ask, ask if there was any chance, any possibility, if there was anything at all that could save Simon, and if there was, he would find it, he would do it, or see to it that it was done.

***

"Mrs. Brown," the surgeon spoke in a grave but gentle tone to the silent, shaking Sarah. "We've done all that we can. The next forty-eight hours are critical."

Sarah heard the words, watching them coming out of the doctor's mouth almost in slow motion, but she wasn't taking it in. Her mind seemed to accept a few words here and there and yet reject others, so that the sentences were all broken up and disjointed. 'Twenty-four ... hours ... particular ... coma ... safe ... breathing for him ... swelling ... reduce ... time ... forty-eight hours ...' and then she was being led to her husband's side, a chair waiting for her body to collapse into just as her knees gave out. She took Simon's hand, she stroked it, she held it against her face, and she prayed. She prayed like she'd never prayed before.

"Thank you for pulling him through the operation …" she prayed, "Thank you for helping him … Dear God, please … please don't take him away from me … Please bring him back to me … I need him, God, I need him so much, please …" she begged, and then she felt it. The dread in her heart. Heavily, cloying, suffocating dread. She could feel it hard inside her, twisting unmercifully as it deepened, locking into her very soul. And she wept.

Ben stood by her side, a supportive, compassionate, understanding hand on her shoulder watching sadly, helplessly as his sister wept into Simon's hand. Her tears fell onto his broken skin, sliding down them and onto the crisp, white sheets below. He knew instinctively to say nothing. Just be there for her, be her strength, that was all he could do, and Ben wiped away his own tears quickly.

***

Sarah sat in vigil at her husband's bedside; not sleeping, not eating, not moving for the next two days. Her hand did not leave his. Ben came and went, Margaret came and went, Gina came and went, and Angie and Frieda came and went. No one could get her to move, to leave, or to eat. On day three, Linda and James arrived. His mother's face was gaunt, strained and terrified! The first flight they could get, she'd said. I'm so sorry, she'd said. James just stared at his son as he lay unmoving, watching the machines breathe life into his son; his poor, broken, battered son! And he wept.

None of them left the room for days. None of them ate. The best any of them could manage was water, but even that was a few sips here and there. The consultants came and went, the nurses came and went, and the registrars came and went, but still Sarah would not move. At some point, James led the silent Linda from the room and took her to the hotel that had been hastily booked from the airport. It was the closest one to the hospital that they could find, needing to be near their son for when he woke. If he woke. He *would* wake, he simply had to!

Back in Rose Cottage, Fred was exactly the same. He hadn't left Simon's slippers which were sitting in the hall near the front door. He could not be moved, would not be moved, would not eat, and would not sleep. Life had stopped for both him and for Sarah until Simon woke up.

David and Angelica somehow knew. They sensed it, they felt it. They were strangely quiet, strangely still. They drank their bottles silently, they ate their mashed up food silently, they gazed at their angels quietly, and they waited. The entire Brown household waited. The Smith family waited. The angels waited.

***

The doctors waited five days following the operation before starting the process of bringing Simon round, allowing his brain time to heal from the swelling of the accident and the surgery. They reduced the sedation gradually, monitoring it closely and by day eight it was out of his system, the swelling on his brain now gone.

"He is still critical, Sarah," they said. "It's just a matter of time now. If he starts breathing for himself, we can have more hope. That will be the beginning of the road home, but it may be a long road, Sarah. You know that, don't you?" Sarah nodded. They had explained to her over the past few days that there may be extensive damage to Simon's brain following the accident, that's if he woke up at all! He had died twice on the operating table they said, but they had managed to get him back. His coma was deep, allowing him to heal. They had said it was a good thing.

Over the last few days, the surgeon had patiently explained to the terrified Sarah and Linda that both Simon's frontal lobe and the cortex or something had been compromised by the swelling and that they would only know the extent of the damage once he came to and woke up. Sarah had been terrified that he wouldn't know her, wouldn't know the children and wouldn't remember their life together. The doctor had reassured them as best that he could, without giving any guarantees. He had explained that if the amygdala was intact then Simon's memory should be okay, not that she knew what the hell an amygdala was! He'd gone on about the basil ganglia seeming to be solid, so they think his motor functions are fine, meaning he should be okay to walk, but really, until he woke up, they just wouldn't know what damage was there. Only then could the tests begin. For now, though, Simon was still not breathing unaided despite the lack of sedation, the ventilation machine doing the work of his lungs, breathing oxygen and life into his still and silent body, a body that seemed determined not to wake up!

***

Simon floated through the black mist weightlessly. He was in a tunnel, a long dark tunnel and it was quiet, it was silent, it was still. The silence engulfed him, the stillness engulfed him, but he was not afraid. He felt an all-consuming peace that reached into the very core of him, its stillness seemed to permeate into his very being. The dark, misty angel floated with him, smiling at him now and again, guiding him and leading him towards the light. It was a long way off, the light, but there was no rush, no rush at all. They moved towards it gently as if they were on a slowly moving conveyer belt. There was no rush, they'd get there in the end. After all, they had all eternity. ...

***

Fred had finally fallen asleep. Exhaustion had taken over and he slept deeply, fitfully. He yelped out in his dreams, his paws twitching, crying out for Simon as he searched for him in the darkness. "I can't see him, I can't find him, where are you, Dad?" he called, but there was no reply.

Sarah too was dreaming from her chair at the hospital next to Simon's bed, refusing to leave his side even for a second. She slept fitfully, dreaming dark, lonely dreams. She wandered in the dark, calling, calling, but she could hear nothing, see nothing. "Simon, Simon, where are you?" she called, but only the silence answered back. "Come back to me, my love, come back!" she called.

The silence answered her with its stillness.

Margaret Smith walked purposefully down the hospital corridor to her son-in-law's room. Her shoulders held back, a determined look on her face, she pushed open the door and glared at her daughter. "That's quite enough, Sarah!" she said to her. Sarah was, as usual, sitting, hunched over Simon's bedside holding his hand tightly. Margaret took in her daughter's pale face, the dirty unwashed hair, the sallow cheeks, and the hollow eyes as she raised her eyebrows in alarm at her clothes which were all but hanging from her daughter's bony shoulders, evidencing the enormous weight loss of the past ten days. She knew that Sarah was still not eating, just bits here and there. She was as worried for her as Ben was. Someone had to snap her out of this and if she couldn't do it, then no one could. Margaret decided that everyone was being far too nice to Sarah, too sympathetic. They were letting her wallow, letting her give up, letting her fade in her grief, her panic, her despair, and it wasn't doing her any good, no good at all! Someone needed to be firm with her, someone needed to be tough, and if it was one thing that she was good at, it was being tough! "Your children need you, Sarah, your dog needs you, *and your life* needs you!" she said firmly to her daughter. Margaret wasn't just concerned now, she was downright scared! Sarah was a shadow of her former self, a shadow!

Sarah just sat, unmoving, continuing to stare at Simon's chest, watching him breathe, watching the machine breath. She barely moved and barely acknowledged her mother's presence, so intent was she on watching the machine keep her beloved Simon alive.

"Sarah!" her mother shrilled. "You are no good to him half dead, no good at all! Not to mention being a mother to your children!" Sarah sighed, half registering her mother's words.

"My babies? Are they alright?" she asked, her voice frail and weak.

"Yes, yes, of course, they are alright!" Margaret replied, "They are alright in that they are being fed, watered, loved, and looked after, but it is not me that they need, Sarah, it is you! You've not seen them, you've not held them and you've not been home. You have not been home for ten days, Sarah! Ten days! They are not just losing their father, Sarah, they are losing their mother as well!"

Somewhere in Sarah's foggy, frightened mind a light came into the darkness. A light that was her children; her love for her children and her maternal instincts reared up from the fog and began to kick in.

"And poor Fred," Margaret continued, "I just don't know what to do with him, Sarah!" There was fear in her voice, Sarah noted sadly. "He is not eating, fading away he is, fading away! I do believe that he will die, die, Sarah!" Margaret insisted. "But he may eat for you, Sarah. Please come home for a while, dear, just a few hours, aye?" she asked, kindly now, almost begging, a pleading tone in her normally strong, firm voice. "I shall drive you and I promise to bring you back later, after you have eaten. Spend some time with your children, Sarah, get some proper rest, and then come back later. You will be stronger for it, Sarah, more able to help Simon, what do you say, dear?"

Sarah sighed, a resigned sigh, but she knew that her mother was right. She needed to go home, just for a while. It had been ten days now and she'd refused to leave his side, believing he'd wake up at any moment, and wanting, no *needing* to be there for him when he did. But he hadn't woken up, and Sarah had to begin to allow for the possibility that he may not wake up for days, even weeks. She could not comprehend him not waking up ever, that could not register, could not be a possibility, and yet it was. She could feel that it was, but yes, her mother was right. It was time to go home, just for a while and be with her babies, just for a while. She stood up slowly, realising as she did so just how weak her body had become since the accident. "Yes, Mum, you're right," she smiled weakly, "let's go home."

Margaret's face gave away her relief, and her surprise. No one had been able to get through to Sarah, not even Ben, and it was a small miracle that Margaret had achieved what the others couldn't. She smiled with relief, taking her daughter's hand, she led her gently from the room.

Some time later, bathed and with freshly washed hair, a slightly stronger Sarah held her babies in her arms, Fred at her feet, all four of them having finally been properly fed and watered. Margaret sat quietly watching them from the chair by the fire, the relief evident on her face. The twins had eaten more for their mother than she'd been able to get them to eat in days, and even Fred had managed a bit of chicken, but only when Sarah had coaxed him to eat. She'd talked to him, like a proper person, had Sarah! Margaret had heard her tell him that she loved him, that it was not his fault, that she forgave him, and that she needed him. He'd eaten a bit then, like he'd really understood her or something! And then Sarah had told him he had to stay strong to help her get Dad back, and then Fred had eaten some more.

The four slept as Margaret watched, making sure the babies didn't fall from their mother's embrace as she slept. She didn't want to move either of the sleeping infants, somehow knowing that they needed their mother's touch in that moment. They needed her warmth and her love, that it would somehow make up for all that they had missed and gone through over the past ten days, and in turn, their mother needed them. They all needed each other. Margaret watched the scene and her eyes filled up. She began to cry, softly, quietly, feeling the loss for her daughter of her beloved Simon, knowing that he was fighting for his life as his family lay sleeping. For the first time in her life, Margaret Smith prayed. She asked God to help her daughter, her grandchildren, and her son-in-law, then she wiped her eyes, gazed into the fire and she slept too.

***

Sarah returned to the hospital much later that night. The corridors were still, quiet, her footsteps echoing as she walked, more strongly now, back to her place at his bedside. She entered Simon's room silently, returning to her chair she took his hand, "Baby, I'm back," she whispered softly. The door opened moments later as the consultant came in to the room. He had watched her from his office as she'd walked down the corridor back to her husband, and he knew that he couldn't put it off any longer.

"Ah, Sarah," he said, "I'm glad you're back." He noticed that she looked stronger, brighter and fresher. Now was the right time to tell her. "Sarah, my dear, I've been running some tests on Simon," he hesitated, watching her face for signs that this was not the time, but Sarah smiled at him encouragingly, so he took a deep breath and quietly, gently, in the softest voice he could possibly muster continued. "It's not good news I'm afraid, my dear. There is no activity in the brain; he has gone, Sarah, I'm sorry but he has gone."

Sarah's shock was palpable. It reverberated through her body like an electric volt. "No!" she exclaimed, "He can't be gone! I've only been gone a few hours! He's still breathing, look!" she said, pointing to Simon's chest as it moved gently up and down.

"That's the ventilator, Sarah, my dear, just the ventilator, I'm so sorry. He can't breathe for himself; his brain is showing no signs of activity. There are no instructions from it going to the body, to the heart to pump, to any part of him."

Sarah stared at him in horror.

"I would like you to discuss with your family, Sarah, and consider that the best course of action for Simon would be to turn off the machines and let him slip away quietly, but there is no rush, take as long as you need, my dear." Sarah just stared at him in even more horror.

"Turn off the machine, turn off the machine? *Kill* my husband!" she cried. "No! NO, NO!" she shouted. "He is coming back, he is waking up, he is, he *is!*"

Clarabelle rushed into the room, holding Sarah tight,

trying to calm her rising hysteria, to help her, to somehow give her what she needed, but she couldn't, and she knew that she couldn't. The only thing that Sarah needed was Simon.

The doctor patted Sarah's shoulder gently, "Just give it some thought, my dear. We can talk again tomorrow," he said and then he was gone.

"Oh, Clarabelle," Sarah screamed, "No, no, no, please God no." She sunk to the floor, holding her stomach in agony, collapsing into a broken heap. She lay there sobbing on the floor and Clarabelle could not comfort her in her pain, in her grief, in her shock. Sarah howled like a wounded animal, lamenting, wailing, and grieving; grieving for her love, grieving for her loss, grieving for their broken lives, and grieving for their children as she sobbed and sobbed until the sun rose with the early morning dawn.

***

At some point in that following day, that fateful horrible day, the hospital transplant coordinator had turned up and explained to the broken Sarah that if she wanted Simon to be able to offer his organs for transplant, it would need to be within the next twenty-four hours as they were beginning to fail and would be of no use after that time. He asked her to think about it and left quietly. It was always a difficult conversation to have, asking the next of kin to turn off the machine and let their loved ones go, but it was a necessary conversation. One that he had had many, many times.

Sarah watched the man leave quietly and shook her

head. *Could I possibly do that, let him go?* She knew that if there was no hope, Simon would want his organs to be used, they both would. She needed to think, and think clearly. *What to do? What on earth to do? Where is Clarabelle when I need her?* There was no way she was doing anything until she'd checked with Clarabelle that there was *really* no hope! In the meantime, she needed to think about her babies. If she was going to do this awful thing, this dreadful thing, then David and Angelica needed to say goodbye to their father. They all did.

She walked slowly down the hospital corridor to the phone on the nurse's station. "I need to phone my family," she said quietly in a voice that seemed far, far away. The nurse, having seen the transplant coordinator leave some minutes before, handed her the phone without question and left her to have some privacy for what would, without doubt, be the most difficult conversation she would ever have.

Sarah rang home, let it ring for a few minutes then put the phone down again. She couldn't, she just couldn't! She walked back to Simon's room distraught. She just didn't know what to do for the best! She looked at her husband as he lay, the machine breathing for him. He was still, lifeless, and empty. He was gone! She could feel it, she had felt it since that night when he was in surgery. He hadn't been there, just his body, an empty shell. His energy, his love, his WILL, that will that she knew and loved, that will that she felt every second of every day, it was gone.

She sat for hours, watching him. The more she watched him, the more she knew that he was gone. They were right. She knew what she had to do. She had to let go, she just had to. Something, somewhere deep inside Sarah clicked into place and she knew she was ready. Not for her, but for Simon. She'd never be ready for her, but she could do it for him. He'd hate it if she let all his organs die with him when there were so many others that could be helped with them. Dying children saved with lung transplants, blind people able to see again, heart damaged people given a second chance at life, those with liver failure on dialysis for days and hours able to live fully again. Yes, she had to do it, there was no choice. Seconds later, Ben walked in. *Thank God for Ben!* Sarah found a strength deep inside her that she didn't know she had. She sat her brother down gently and relayed what the consultant had told her, what the transplant coordinator had told her and asked him quietly if he would please fetch her children so that they could say goodbye to their father. Ben was horrified, mortified, and burst into tears. He sobbed shamelessly for his friend, for Sarah, for their children, and he sobbed for himself. He sobbed until his tears were spent and then he looked up from his tears and nodded quietly. Sarah handed him a tissue and, blowing his nose, Ben walked quietly out of the room, out of the hospital, and to his car. He didn't know how he was going to drive, but he'd manage it. He needed to find some strength and do what was needed now to help Sarah, to help Simon, and to help their children.

Sarah watched Ben walk away. She stood up straight, looked up at the sky, swallowed and took a deep breath. She walked back with heavy steps to the nurse's station and picked up the phone once again. Pulling the tattered piece of paper from her pocket with their hotel number on it she slowly dialled the number. Linda and James, Simon's parents, were told. They were told that their only son was gone. He was gone. She didn't know how she told them, but she told them. Sarah heard the phone fall from Linda's hand as she collapsed onto the floor sobbing cries which could be heard across many floors of the hotel; cries of despair, of anguish, and of agony, and she heard James' weak, defeated voice say quietly into the phone that they were on their way and then the phone was hung up, James putting it gently back on its receiver as he bent to pick up his broken, sobbing wife from the hotel floor.

Clarence sat quietly on Ben's shoulder, patting it gently as he drove to Sarah's house. "I know, laddie, I know," he said sadly. "But we'll get ye through it, I promise ye that. Somehow, we'll get you all through it."

***

The whole family were gathered to say goodbye to Simon. The 'only two visitors at a time' hospital rule was waived as the entire family stood around Simon's bed saying their goodbyes. One by one, they stepped forward, each saying what they wanted to say to their friend, their son, their son-in-law, each then stepping back, letting the others have their turn. Linda had been the longest, holding her son, stroking his hair, talking and reminiscing over his childhood. "Such a sweet boy," she'd said. "Always such a good boy. You did so well, we were always so proud of you … I love you, son; my only, dear son. I love you." Finally, she had stepped away and into her husband's arms. James hung onto his wife like his own life depended on it. He seemed to have aged ten years over night; they all had.

Sarah stepped forward, holding Angelica close to Simon's peaceful face, allowing her to stroke her father's cheek for one last time. "Kiss goodbye to Daddy, darling," she said with a trembling voice and tears in her eyes, bending the infant closer to Simon's face. Angelica put her chubby hands onto Simon's cheeks and kissed his lips, then let out an almighty wail.

She knew and Sarah knew that she knew.

"Take her out, Mum, would you, please?" she asked, handing her to a shaking Margaret. She turned to Gina, taking David from her sister-in-law's arms.

"Your turn, sweetheart," she said to the silent infant, holding him to Simon's face just as she had Angelica. David leaned over, held his father's face and kissed him with a huge smack, then he, too, let out an almighty wail. Sarah handed him back to Gina with a sigh. She turned and smiled weakly at her family, their family. "Thank you all for being here, with me, at this time. Thank you for everything that you've all done," she said, her voice raspy. "But I'd like to be alone with my husband now, if you don't mind. I need to do this by myself."

Everyone nodded silently, never doubting for a moment that Sarah should be the last one to say goodbye to 'her' Simon, and to be alone to do it. Each came to her, slowly holding her, trying to give her strength in any small way that they could, and then they filed slowly out with heavy hearts.

Sarah turned to her husband, smiling she said simply, "Let's have one last night together, aye, my darling? I'll let you go with the dawn, I promise. You can fly away on the wings of the angels in the morning, alright, my love? I need you this one last night, this one last time, okay, sweetheart?"

And Sarah climbed into the bed with Simon, wrapping her arms tightly around the love of her life, her soul-mate, her best friend. She spent the entire night watching him, stroking him, loving him, and dreading the sight of the dawn rising as it inevitably would, but she was ready now, as ready as she would ever be. She was ready to let go.

Chapter 18

Clarence stood before Metatron's door and knocked firmly.

"Come in," called the 'All Seeing, All Knowing' Metatron. Clarence entered the room and took a deep breath.

"Ah, Clarence, my dear, what can I do for you?" he asked, watching a nervous Clarence with interest.

"I need an audience with the 'All That Is' please, Sir," he asked respectfully, "and I need it urgently," he added.

"Well, I don't know about that," Metatron said in surprise. "He is rather busy!"

"I know, Sir, I'm sorry, but it is urgent that I speak with Him," Clarence insisted.

"This is the second time that you have made such a request, is it not?" pointed out Metatron, "First Class angels do not normally see the 'All That Is,' Clarence. I shall ask, of course, but it is most out of keeping you understand?"

Clarence nodded his agreement. He knew it was out of keeping, he knew that, but he just *had* to do something, anything!

"Very well then, give me a minute," Metatron replied. "You may wait outside."

Clarence walked out gratefully, focusing on what he was going to say, how he was going to say it, but he didn't need to. Before he'd even closed the door to Metatron's majestic office, The Voice called, "Enter, Clarence! With what do you require MY help?"

Clarence spun round, pushing open the huge double doors, he stumbled back into the room and held his hand up to his eyes immediately to shield himself from the brilliant light. "Can we save Simon, Sir?" he asked the light. His knees were shaking, along with his wings and halo. "Is there anything that we can do to bring him back? Anything at all?"

The Voice replied quietly, softly, lovingly, "Only love can bring Simon Brown back, Clarence. The mighty, the *almighty* power of love that can heal all, that can bring about miraculous transformation that can bring about life and bring about hope! Only love." He said.

"But there is love! There is *much* love for Simon!" Clarence stated.

"Yes there is love, Clarence, my dear. But your Simon Brown is gravely ill, critically ill, so very damaged, my dear one. He is damaged right down to the cellular structure of his being. It would take an almighty love, a special love, a love like none that has ever existed before in all time. A love so pure, so powerful, so supreme, so unconditional, so perfect. That is the only love that could possibly bring him back. A love so powerful it transcends all else, even death!" The Voice said.

"Does this love exist?" asked Clarence hopefully. "Does it exist anywhere, anywhere at all?"

"But of course!" He said, "Of course it does. And you know where it does, Clarence, and you know who."

"Do I?" Clarence blurted, wondering what love could possibly exist that could cheat even death. "Where? What love?"

"The love that I speak of... It is the love that is the purity and the power between two *'Beings of Light,'* Clarence. A love that rocks and shakes the multiverses themselves it is so strong, so powerful, and so beautiful that it shines above all others. It is the love between two *angels* that can save Simon Brown, and *only* that." He said.

Clarence's draw dropped. Clarabelle and Mickey? Oh my goodness!

"But know this," The Voice warned, "they will need to use *ALL* of their love, every atom of it, every molecule of it; that love which they hold so dear for each other, in order to bring about enough force to heal the cells within Simon Brown's brain. They will be sacrificing their love, giving it to another, giving it to Simon in order to save him. They will no longer feel that love, that bond, that connection between them. It will be gone from them and into Simon Brown's cells. It will be gone from them forever! And," He continued, "they can only do it if they do it willingly, freely. It is *their* love to give or not to give. It is their choice - their *free will choice!*"

And then The Voice was gone.

Clarence fell down onto the floor in shock. Even Metatron looked shaken. *Could he do it?* Clarence wondered. Could he ask Clarabelle and Mickey to give up their love to save Simon? They'd only just had it agreed a little while ago and poor Clarabelle had been busy planning her and Mickey's wedding! The Angelic Temple was booked and everything! Mind you, that was all before Simon's accident. All the wedding plans were on hold at the moment and nothing was going to change that until Simon recovered, or didn't!

Metatron watched Clarence's confusion and smiled the biggest smile he had smiled in eons. His smile reached into every part of his being. *Now* it made sense, now it *all* made sense.

***

Simon floated through the dark tunnel, drawn to the light at its end like a moth to a flame, a flame of brightness so powerful, so beautiful, so incredible that he could not resist. The light was closer now, closer than it was before. The dark angel floated with him, holding him warmly, safely, gently; and he smiled.

Simon passed others on his journey through the tunnel, many others. They, too, were each held gently by a dark angel, a force, a protector, as they journeyed towards the light. Each had a smile of serenity on their faces; serenity and acceptance, peace, and tranquillity. There was a rightness about it somehow, a perfection, a purity that he could not comprehend. He just knew that he had to follow the light, and follow it he did. Without question, without hesitation, without regret. The power of the light was so strong in its draw he could do nothing but surrender to it;

willingly, happily, completely, and totally. There was a sense of reality to it somehow, like it was all meant to be, like he was coming home, and he felt an excitement within him, a sense of celebration, perfection, beauty - and he smiled. "Home," he said simply, "I'm coming home."

***

"Don't you leave me, Simon Brown!" Sarah cried. "Don't you *dare* leave me, do you hear me? I *need* you! You get back here right now, mister!" she ordered, staring at Simon's peaceful face as she willed him to return, forced him to return. The dawn was beginning to rise and with it, her strength to let him go had faded with the night. Deep inside, she hoped and prayed, that somewhere, somehow, in his dark and damaged brain there was a spark of light, of hope; that somehow her love could draw him back, bring him home, back to her, to her children, to *their* children. "Please come back," she begged. "Please!" She looked at the clock on the wall, it was seven fifteen. The transplant coordinator was coming at eight am. The machines would be switched off and her Simon would be gone forever. "Please come back, baby," she called. "Please, please come back."

But Simon could not hear her pleas, he could not feel her love. All he could feel was the pull of the light as he moved closer and closer towards it.

Suddenly Sarah heard a voice, a familiar voice, a warm rich Scottish voice.

"My darling girl, we are with you, supporting you, helping you, me and Gran. Lean on us, child, we are here with you, for you, always," said her father's voice.

"Dad?" Sarah asked in surprise, "Dad?"

"Yes, child, of course, yes! Did you think we would not be here for you now, at this crucial time? At this time of pain, of suffering, of loss! We tried to warn you, Sarah, to prepare you. We knew this was coming, we could see it, from here in this place of seeing, this place of knowing. We tried to warn you. You are strong Sarah, you *will* get through this, of this I promise you."

"Oh, Dad, I thought that warning was about losing Clarabelle, not my Simon!" she cried. "Is there no hope? Is there nothing anyone can do? Anything at all?"

"No, my dear, there is not. It is his time," her father's voice gently said, although there was some hesitation, some doubt, she was sure of it. Or ... *is this just my imagination? Is this just hope?*

"Only a miracle can save him now, Sarah, and we know not of any miracle powerful enough to cheat death, my dear, not once it has gone this far, not when it is written. He is on his journey home now, and, Sarah, please know that we are waiting. We are waiting with his family, his ancestors, and his forefathers. We are all here, gathered, to welcome him home. He will not be alone, of this I promise you."

"But I want that miracle," she cried, "I *need* that miracle! I can't lose him, I just *cannot lose him!*"

Clarabelle stood back and let the family help for a moment. She'd been by Sarah's side day and night for thirteen days now, trying to help, but this next hour was going to be the hardest. She tried to put more light into

Sarah, more love, but she knew it wouldn't be enough, not nearly enough. Clarabelle stood up straight and sent out the distress signal, a signal that flew half way around the globe and back again in milliseconds. Moments later, Mickey arrived, flushed and flustered.

"You called, my dearest?" he smiled.

"Oh, Mickey, I need your light, my love, to help my Sarah through this," she cried. "So much pain, so much pain, God, bless her. It's nearly time, nearly time to switch off the machine and let him go, as she must!"

Michael shone his light into Sarah's heart, but it would not glow. Her heart was closing down, retreating, withdrawing, and running, in a vain attempt to save her from the immense pain that would come soon, the pain that she would feel as the machine beeped its last beep and her Simon finally let go and was freed.

They gathered around her, those that had gone before, as the morning dawn chorus rang out across the sky. They held her and loved her, trying as best they could from the other side to help her, but they could not. No one could. They knew that only a miracle could save him and save Sarah from the pain. They had heard that there was a small possibility, that there was such a miracle in existence, a tiny possibility, but they had not wanted to give her false hope, not when they were so unsure. They had heard, across the cosmos that there was possibly a love so huge, a love that normally does not exist, not anywhere in all the multiverses, but possibly, just possibly did exist, at this exact moment in time, and could possibly save him. They did not know where, they did not know how. It was just a rumour.

***

As Sarah was trying to regain the strength that she had had the evening before, trying to prepare herself for what she knew she must do, Clarence was rushing back from his audience with the 'All That Is,' heading straight for the hospital. The transplant coordinator was on his way and the ventilator was due to be switched off at eight am. Clarence checked his time, looking at the sun's angle and sped even faster. *Seven-thirty, only thirty minutes left!* He was speeding almost as badly as the Grim Reapers regularly did, but he didn't care. *If I get a ticket, then I get a ticket! Time was of the essence! Simon was more than half way down the tunnel of light and they didn't have long if they were going to save him.* He flew faster, more urgently towards his goal. He knew that at that very moment, Clarabelle and Michael would be sitting there, together, helping to get Sarah through this agonising ordeal. Sure enough, he could see the light radiating out in the distance from Simon's hospital room, pulsing out into the cosmos, this very bright light that was their very special love, their very incredible love.

"Clarabelle, Clarabelle, I've seen the 'All That Is,' " he yelled, "I've seen Him, I've seen Him!" Landing with a bump beside them he rushed on. He was panting, flushed and hot, he wiped his brow quickly. "There is something, there *is* something! *You* can save him, you can save him!" he ranted. "You and Mickey!"

"What? How?" she exclaimed with a start, looking at

Clarence as if he'd gone completely bonkers.

"It's *you!* It's *you* and *him!*" he grinned, "It's your love! That's what can save him!"

"But how? I don't understand! How could I possibly save Simon? Me, an angel Second Class! I don't have that power, Clarence, don't be ridiculous!" She shook her head at her crazy brother in surprise at this mad suggestion.

"Not you on your own, Clar! You and Michael!" he insisted, "The two of you together, you can do it, you can do it together!"

Sarah looked at all three with amazement, then shock, then disbelief, then joy. She shook her head. "Am I dreaming?" she asked. "Is this possible?"

Clarence nodded emphatically, and then he explained, relaying the message from the 'All That Is,' watching the dawning shock register on Clarabelle's face, Sarah's face and lastly, Michael's face.

"You are kidding me!" Clarabelle beamed. "We can save Simon? Bring him back from the tunnel? Give him back to my Sarah? Oh my, oh my! How very, very wonderful!" she squealed in absolute delight. She spun around to Michael, grabbing his arm she grinned, "Oh Mickey! My darling, wonderful Mickey, what a gift! To be able to save Simon! To use our love to save Simon! What an incredible gift!" she screeched, totally excited now, completely blown away by the very thought of it. She was jumping up and down like a demented rabbit in her excitement.

"But Clar, your love will be gone then, you know that don't you?" Clarence asked gently. "You can't keep it, you'll be gifting it to Simon. You understand that don't you, my dear, it will be gone from you and Mickey, gone forever!"

"Yes, dear, yes, of course I understand. Of course I do!" she beamed.

"But there will be no wedding, no celebration, it will be gone, vamoose, disappeared, as if it never existed!" he said with concern. "No wedding, no celebration!"

"Of course there will be a celebration, my dear, of course there will!" she grinned. "How could there not be! My Sarah's Simon will be back, back from the dead! How is that not a cause for celebration you silly angel?" She was smiling. Happily and joyously smiling, beaming in fact!

"Aren't you bothered?" Clarence asked in amazement. "To give up your love? Isn't that going to kill you?"

"Bothered? Why in heavens would I be bothered?" she asked in surprise, equally amazed at such a daft question, as she saw it.

"Oh my God, Clarabelle," Sarah cried, "I can't ask you to do that, darling, to give up your own love to save mine! I just couldn't, I couldn't do it!"

"Don't be silly, child, of course we'll do it! There really is no question! If *our* love, our magical, wonderful, amazing love can save Simon, *save* him, mind you," she squealed. "How could we not!"

It really was very simple to Clarabelle. She really didn't know what the fuss was all about! She was an angel, Mickey was an angel; their love was unconditional, pure, and gifted. Now it was time to gift it to someone else! After all, that's what angels do; they love, they give, and they help! She turned to Archangel Michael, her 'Mickey,' who was smiling happily back at her, nodding his agreement without any whiff of hesitation or regret. "Ready, Mickey?" she asked merrily. "Let's do some 'miracle-ing,' my dear!"

They stood side by side holding hands for one last time, unified in their task. Michael squeezed her hand gently, then let go, moving around to the other side of Simon's hospital bed. Second Level First Class Angel Clarabelle and Archangel Michael stood over Simon's bed, gazing at each other with complete adoration and both smiled deeply. They looked at Simon, concentration evident on their beautiful faces, and began.

The light of their love shone from both of their hearts directly into each other's as they stood smiling serenely at each other from either side of Simon, pulsing between them like a laser show. Clarabelle nodded, reaching into the light at its centre with both her hands. Michael did the same. They held the light briefly in their hands for a millisecond; gazing at it with rapture, they looked up from it and smiled at each other - '*their* smile,' '*that* smile,' the smile that says, 'I love you,' - for one last time. Then they turned their hands over, pointing the light downwards, they beamed the laser-light brightness of their love, *their* wondrous, joyous love into Simon's broken brain.

Sarah stood back and watched the incredible events that were being displayed right before her very eyes. She watched with humbleness this extraordinary sacrifice that was unfolding before her and she rejoiced. She had never known such gratitude, such incredible thankfulness as she felt in that very moment. She held her hands to her mouth, her breath held as tight as her hands as she prayed, "Please let this work. Please don't let their *huge* sacrifice be in vain, be for nothing, please!" she begged. She turned to Simon and whispered, "Please come back, Si, please come back to me."

The light beamed from Clarabelle and Michael for what seemed like an eternity, and then suddenly it was gone. Every ounce of it, every speck of it, every part of it, spent! Simon's damaged, dying body had absorbed it, absorbed all of it.

***

Simon was happily heading towards the light, getting closer, getting nearer, when all of a sudden he felt himself being sucked backwards, away from the light. He was being pulled back, harder and harder, stronger and stronger. It was like a giant vacuum cleaner was sucking him up, pulling him back, reversing him down the tunnel. He pulled against its force trying to go forward towards the light. It pulled harder. He pulled against it some more. It pulled harder still.

The dark angel too felt the pull, the vacuum, the suction, and whipped his arms out, suddenly creating a net behind them, magically sticking it against the walls of the tunnel to stop them from being pulled back any further. Simon felt the net around him and felt himself stop. He couldn't go forward, he couldn't go backwards. He surrendered to the net, looking longingly at the light. He reached out his hand towards it but could not reach it. He waited.

"Well, Mrs. Brown, it's nothing short of a miracle!" the doctor exclaimed. "A miracle, I tell you! I have never known brain activity to return like this, not ever, not in all my thirty years!" The doctor scratched his head in bemusement. He just couldn't understand it, could not understand it at all! The machines had started bleeping, 'out of the blue' early this morning just before the transplant coordinator had arrived; bleeps that evidenced clearly the brain activity that was getting stronger and stronger in Simon Brown. There was no doubt, no doubt at all, that somehow Simon's brain had suddenly decided to work again! The transplant coordinator had been sent packing, with a 'sorry, but he's staying with us'!

The doctor reached over to the ventilator and gently reduced the switch, allowing Simon to begin to try to breathe for himself, and breathe he did! He couldn't quite believe this, but sure enough, Simon Brown was definitely beginning to breathe for himself. He looked at Sarah in shock, the disbelief clear on his face. "We just have to wait for him to wake up now, Sarah," he said, "and we shall take it from there."

Sarah beamed at the doctor. Her eyes shining, her face a picture, she just grinned, and grinned some more.

"Well, my dear, I do believe we did it!" chirped up Clarabelle happily from her shoulder. "Smashing! Just smashing!"

"Clarabelle. ..." Sarah turned slowly to her best friend, her saviour, her miracle, and she burst into relieved and grateful tears. "How can I ever thank you? How can I even begin to thank you?" she sobbed. "What you did, what you've done, how can I ever thank you?"

"No thanks needed, my dear, not a single one, it was a pleasure, my dear, my *absolute* pleasure!" she beamed. "Always happy to help, always!"

***

Fred could not believe his ears when Mum came home with the news. She was jumping, Aunty Clarabelle was jumping, Uncle Nat was jumping, but there was no sign whatsoever of Uncle Mickey. None at all! *How very strange!* thought Fred. *I'd have thought he'd have been here to celebrate! But no, there was no sign of him, and Aunty Clarabelle hasn't even noticed that Uncle Mickey is gone and if she has, she doesn't seem to care! Weird or what! She just kept jumping and squealing and hugging Mum and laughing and being really happy.*

Fred jumped too, joining in with joy and relief, happiness, and exhilaration. "Woohooooo, Dad's okay," he barked, "Dad's okay, he's okay!" he yelled. "Thank Dog for that, oh, thank Dog!" Fred spun round in delight, chasing his tail at least ten times and didn't even fall over from the dizziness! *Dog, he was clever! Woohooooo!* They were all joining in. Even 'The Spy' was jumping!

Clarence was indeed bouncing up and down along with Clarabelle and Nat, *all three jumping like demented rabbits on speed*, Fred decided. Mum was hugging Ben, the twins were squealing and gurgling, kicking their legs up in delight as Seraphina and Elijah jumped for joy too. Gina was dancing, and even Granny Smith was dancing! *Blimey!*

"So where is he then? Where's Dad? When's Dad coming home?" barked Fred excitedly. "When, when, when?" he woofed happily, the relief pouring through him like a steam train.

"He has to wake up first, Fred, when he wakes up!" Sarah shouted, grinning happily, then burst into tears all over again.

"Why hasn't he woken up yet then?" Fred barked. "If Aunty Clarabelle and Uncle Mickey's fixed him, why hasn't he woken up then?" he yelled. *No one was listening, again!* They were too busy celebrating to pay any attention to Fred. "Dad should be here, joining in, jumping up and down with us!" barked Fred insistently, but he wasn't, he wasn't here! And Fred wanted him here, he wanted him here very much! "Celebrate? How the bloody hell can I celebrate without Dad?" he barked. "Are you mad, woman? No way!"

Fred couldn't celebrate, not properly, not till he'd seen Dad and he *knew* he was okay.

"He'll wake up soon, Fred," Sarah smiled. "And then he can come home, promise."

"Soon, soon? Why isn't he awake now?" he barked.

"I'm not sure, Fred, I don't know why he hasn't woken up yet, but he will! He'll be back, I just know it!" Sarah beamed happily.

"Right then!" Fred decided. "If he isn't awake I'll just have to wake him up myself! I'll go get him! I'll fetch him myself! After all, it's what dogs do! Fetch!" And Fred went back to Dad's slippers by the door, thinking up a plan about how he could get past the hospital guards and go and wake Dad up, but before he knew where he was he was nodding off after all the excitement. And 'Fred the Fantastic' forgot all about fetching Dad and fell into a deep, happy sleep.

Chapter 19

Fred's nose was to the floor; sniffing, sniffing, sniffing. He could follow a trail anywhere could Fred, being 'Fred the Fantastic' an' all! He'd been following Dad's trail for mile after mile down this long, long tunnel. He'd know Dad's scent anywhere and he'd picked it up ages ago! On and on Fred went, following the scent; sniffing, sniffing, sniffing. It was getting stronger, the scent, it was getting closer, and it was getting easier! The tunnel wasn't so dark now, there seemed to be light coming from the other end and Fred could see much better. Not that his eyes didn't work perfectly well in the dark mind you, but it was easier now that he had a bit of light!

Fred felt funny in the tunnel, he decided, strange funny! It was like he knew it, this weird tunnel, like he'd been here before. "What? Nah, can't be, never been here before!" he decided, then carried on sniffing; following the trail, mile after boring mile. Finally, up ahead he could make out a barrier, a net of some kind, and there seemed to be something trapped in the net. It wasn't struggling, it wasn't fighting and it wasn't moving. It was just hanging. *Maybe it's dead?* wondered Fred. *Maybe it's a big, fat fly caught in a spider's web and it's gonna be eaten by a big, huge, fat hairy spider?* Not that he liked flies, mind you, annoying horrible things they were, buzzing around your head and ears, determined to piss you off! He wasn't that fond of spiders either for that matter, but they definitely weren't as bad as flies! *They deserved to die!* decided Fred, looking at the hanging thing in the net as he kept sniffing, sniffing, sniffing, and getting closer, closer. "Death to all flies!" he barked happily as he sniffed. *But wait, what's this?* Fred stared at the net which was closer now. The thing trapped in it was big, really big! It must be a *giant* fly! "Bloody hell!" he gasped as he got closer still, "that's not a fly, that's ... that's my DAD!" he yelled, running down the tunnel at full speed towards his buddy. "Dad, Dad, it's me, it's Fred!" he yelled excitedly. "I'm here, Dad, I'm here! Don't you worry about a thing! I, 'Fred the Fantastic' will save you!" he barked, and Fred the Fabulous, the Extraordinary, the Magnificent, started biting at the net, breaking it apart with his teeth. Bit by bit he pulled, he twisted, he turned. Bit by bit the net broke away, finally freeing Simon and along with it, a dark, shadowy figure. "On your bike, pal!" Fred barked at it. "Piss off! You ain't welcome here no more!" He bared his teeth at the dark angel and began to growl. "Don't make me bite you!" he warned, baring his teeth even more. He put on his most menacing tone and barked as hard as he could at the shadow. "Be gone! Get away, go home, shoo!" he yelled again, then lunged forward to take a bite out of the hovering Grim Reaper, who, seeing fangs and a very scary looking Fred, clearly about to pounce, flew off at speed.

Fred watched him disappear down the tunnel towards the light, then grabbed Dad, but he didn't seem to be moving, despite being freed from the net. He was just floating there, all dreamy-like and funny. "What you been on then, you naughty boy?" Fred gently asked the dazed Simon. Simon just grinned. "Come on, snap out of it, man! Wake up, wake up!" he yelled forcefully.

Simon opened his eyes dreamily and smiled happily at Fred. "Freddie! Hiya buddy!" he grinned, slurring a bit. "I seen angels! They're real you know! Ssssssmashingggg. ..."

"You're bloody stoned, Dad!" Fred said in shock. "Jeez, Mum's gonna kill you! Come on! Let's get you home!"

And Fred pulled, pushed, dragged and yanked a stoned Simon all the way back down the tunnel. Inch by inch he dragged. Centimetre by centimetre they made progress slowly. Dad got heavier and heavier as they got nearer the beginning of the tunnel and Fred really didn't know if he had it in him to get him back, but he pressed on. He needed to get him back to bed before Mum saw the state of him. *She'd kill him, she'd absolutely kill him!* Fred saw the hospital bed in the distance, hovering tantalizingly at the entrance to the tunnel and found a bit more strength. With one last push he managed it, heaving Simon unceremoniously back onto the bed with a big, huge plop, and then 'Fred the Fabulous' collapsed in a heap on the floor underneath it.

"Ow!" moaned Simon, opening his eyes. "That hurt!"

The nurse, checking Simon's blood pressure at that

exact moment ran from the hospital room as fast as she could.

"Doctor, doctor, he's awake!" she called excitedly. "Mr. Brown's awake at last!"

***

Fred was just congratulating himself on a job well done when he was rudely awakened from his lovely dream by Mum absolutely *screaming* the house down! He tried to stand up to see what all the fuss was about but, God, he was tired, dog tired! And he ached, God how he ached! Every muscle ached, his jaw was the worst! He'd been carrying Dad, well dragging Dad, in his mouth for an absolute age in his dream. His lovely, lovely dream!

"That's fantastic news, doctor. Yes, doctor. On my way, doctor!" Mum was saying, crying and laughing at the same time. And then she was pushing Fred out of the way of the front door, *pushing* mind you, and she was running down the path and throwing herself into her car. Fred watched her do a wheel spin down the lane, smoke coming off her back tyres, but he was too tired to care. Granny Smith was crying, the twins were crying, everyone was bloody crying.

"Shut the hell up!" Fred moaned, barely semi-conscious. "Trying to sleep here!" and fell back into an exhausted sleep.

***

Sarah ran into Simon's room twenty minutes later to find him sitting up in bed sipping water through a straw.

"Hi, baby," he grinned. "I'm back!" His voice was

gravelly, croaky and weak, but he was talking and he was most definitely back! Sarah threw her arms around him and smothered him in a million kisses.

"Oh my God, Si," kiss ... "You gave me such," kiss ... "a," kiss ... "scare," kiss ... "I thought," kiss ... "I'd," kiss ... "lost you!"

"What happened?" he asked. "My head hurts!"

Sarah explained to her husband all about the accident, how he'd been in a coma for two weeks, and how ill he'd been. "Do you remember anything," she asked, "about it, the accident? And everything else, do you remember everything else?" Simon looked confused and for a moment Sarah's heart stopped. "I mean me, us, the children? Do you know who you are, Si?" she gabbled.

"You are my wife, Sarah, and you are the most beautiful thing on this entire planet and I love you to death!" he smiled. "Children, two - David and Angelica, mother, one - Linda, sister, one - Jane, father, one - James. Dog, one - Fred, Brother ..." he watched her face fall at that ... "Zero," he grinned. "Headache, one - ouch! Can I stop now please?"

"Oh thank you, God!' Sarah sighed an enormous sigh of relief. "Yes, yes, of course, you can stop now. Rest, darling, rest."

Nathaniel watched the pair from the rail over Simon's bed where he was perched happily. *Gosh that had been a close call, but Simon was back thanks to Clarabelle and Michael. They really should have a medal or something!* He may have a word with someone upstairs, see what could be organised; there should at least be a party. He loved parties, totally loved them!

"Fred's quiet, Anj," **David** pointed out thoughtfully. "I think he's sad, don't you?"

"Sad? Our Fred? Don't be ridiculous, David!" Angelica scorned. "Fred doesn't know the meaning of sad!" She shook her head at her brother in exasperation. *God, boys are sooo dumb!* She carried on examining her nail thoughtfully, wondering if she could wriggle from the high chair's straps and reach the rattle that Mum had put just out of reach. She stretched as far as her chubby arm would let her but no, damn it!

"No, Angelica, not until you've finished your breakfast," Sarah said, as she washed the dishes. "You can play once you've had that. Now eat up, there's a good girl."

"But, Anj," David implored, "Look!" He pointed at Fred, who was laying silently in the hall by the door on Dad's slippers again. "He's been there for days, Anj, days!" he insisted. "He doesn't play anymore, he doesn't even shout at us to shut up when we cry like he always used to! I think something's wrong."

"Oh, David, do shut up! So he doesn't bark at us anymore, so what? Just enjoy it would you! It's nice not being told off by him all the time. What *is* wrong with you today?"

David shook his head at his sister. *God, girls are just sooo selfish! Up her own arse again, as always.* He turned to watch Fred and called out to him (in baby gurgle, of course, but he knew Fred understood. Fred always understood!), "What's wrong, Freddie?" he asked worriedly. "Why are you sad?"

Fred raised his head slightly, looking at David through the open kitchen door and sighed loudly. "Oh, I dunno, buddy, just am," he woofed quietly, putting his head back on to Dad's slippers with another sigh.

"See! I told you he was sad, didn't I!" exclaimed David, "I told you, see I told you!"

"Oh, shut up, David, eat your rusk, you're getting on my nerves now!" Angelica moaned. She couldn't understand the concern, not one bit! *So what if Fred was sad? Everyone got sad sometimes! He'd get over it!*

"I think you're mean!" David humphed, wondering if he could reach the cupboard where Mum kept the doggie chocs and sneak one to Fred. That would cheer him up! Fred loved doggie chocs!

Sarah listened thoughtfully to the conversation that was going on between the siblings and had to agree with David. Fred really wasn't himself, not at all, and hadn't been since the accident, even though Simon was going to be okay now. He'd seemed initially happy once he knew Simon was going to be okay, but then he'd gone downhill. In the two weeks since Simon had awakened from his coma, Fred had deteriorated at almost the same rate as Simon had improved! She looked at Fred thoughtfully, wondering if dogs got depressed. *Perhaps it was post traumatic shock? Now that Simon was going to be okay, maybe it had all hit him?* Everyone else just felt incredible relief since Simon had woken up, but Fred seemed to have gone down quite badly. He barely moved and David was right, he definitely didn't play, didn't moan, and she hadn't heard him swear for days! That was bad!

She moved to the cupboard, reaching for the doggie chocs that were kept up high, way out of the reach of paws and teeth, taking a few out she walked into the hall. "Here you go, Fred," she smiled, putting a few in front of his nose on the floor. Fred lifted his head a fraction, looked at the doggie choc, sighed, and put his head back down on Dad's slipper ignoring them completely. *Jeez, this is bad!* thought Sarah. "Okay, Fred, what's wrong, hun? Tell Mum." She leaned down beside him and stroked his head gently, squeezing his ears softly just the way he liked it.

Fred looked up at her with tears in his eyes. His mouth downturned, he let out another sigh and closed his eyes.

"Talk to me, Freddie, tell me what's wrong, honey," she implored.

"It's my fault! It's all my fault!" he howled. "Look at what I've done! I'm a bad, bad dog!" and he let out a loud cry. A sad, long, lonely howl filled with anguish, pain and guilt. "I nearly killed Dad, I made everyone suffer, I hurt everyone, everyone! I made everyone cry!" he yelped. "I'm a bad, bad Fred!"

"Oh, darlin', no you're not, sweetheart!" Sarah reassured. "It was an accident, Fred, an accident! These things happen, honey, they just do. And anyway, he'll be home soon, I promise. Another few days and Dad will be home. He's going to be alright, sweetheart, he's gonna be fine."

Fred didn't move, just looked at her all sad.

"They're letting him out in a few days, babe. He's nearly all better, honest!"

Fred still didn't move, other than to repeat his lamented guilt.

"But it's my fault!" he cried. "It's all my fault!"

"Don't feel guilty, honey, it's not good for you, darling, not good at all. Have a doggie choc. Go on, Fred, you love doggie chocs. Look," she motioned, "watch Mum." Putting one up to her lips she pretending to eat it, "Yum, yum!" she grinned.

"Bloody hell, woman, are you for real!" he barked, standing up angrily. "Yum, yum? Yum bloody yum?" Fred could not believe his ears! "I can't think about doggie chocs when I've done this! I should be put down, put down, I tell you! I don't deserve to live! It should have been me, I should have been hit by that truck not Dad. It should have been me and all you can say is yum-bloody-yum!"

Before Sarah had a chance to reply Fred stomped out into the garden and lay under his tree in disgust. *Yum bloody yum? She had no idea, no idea at all!* He looked up at the tree sadly. "You get it, don't you, pal? You get that I'm a bad, bad dog don't you?"

Every muscle in his body hurt, his head hurt, his jaw hurt, and his heart hurt, as if his body itself were punishing him for the bad, bad thing that he had done. And he deserved it! He deserved it all! Fred laid down under the tree dramatically and prayed for death.

***

Fred was dreaming. He was back in the tunnel, Dad's tunnel. He was sniffing; searching, searching, searching! Not for Dad this time, he was searching for something else. He didn't know what, but he knew that it was in this tunnel. "Fred," a voice called suddenly from the darkness. "It is time to forgive yourself. The accident was planned, arranged, destined. It was known. It was right. You did nothing wrong."

A bright light suddenly appeared in front of him and Fred stopped sniffing and sat down in shock. He looked slowly around him in awe. *Where was that voice coming from? Whose voice was it! It seemed very commanding, knowing, and yet it was a gentle voice, a loving voice, a caring voice, a familiar voice! And it was coming from inside the light!*

"You, Fred, were destined to come with Simon into the light, to guide him and protect him on his journey home. To die with him," said the Voice.

"I knew it, I just bloody knew it! I should be dead, I deserve to die!" He howled at the light. "Who are you anyway?" he barked. "And why ain't I dead then, if I was meant to die?"

"Do not be alarmed, Fred, do not be afraid. It is I, 'The Mighty Metatron,' " the voice said. "We do not want you to suffer this blame, this guilt any further, Fred, so I have come to explain to you."

Fred sat bolt upright. *Metatron? The angel that I was going to bite the other week? Wow! And he's being nice to me? Why is he being nice to me?* Fred stared at the light in front of him. He couldn't see anything other than the light, but he trusted the voice that was coming from it, although he had no idea why.

Metatron continued, "The 'All That Is' chose not to inform me of that which was known to Him. In His mighty wisdom, He kept me in the dark, but I Metatron have now been briefed, fully briefed (he emphasised), and all is well."

Fred swore that Metatron was grinning at him, but as he couldn't see him, that couldn't be right!

"It was Simon's time to die that day, his time to come home, and you Fred had agreed to be a part of that plan, the plan to bring him home, but the plan was changed. Another way was found, a way to enable Simon to live. The unheard of and previously un-thought of plan was arranged; a miracle! A very large miracle! The romantic love between angels! It was permitted, nay encouraged to develop, in order to get ready the love, the power that *He* knew would be used to save Simon, the only thing that *could* save Simon. *He* knew about the romance, the 'All That Is.' He knew about it ages ago! It was planned, it was all planned! He watched their love growing knowing that it would be sacrificed to save Simon - and sacrificed willingly. That was always the plan."

"Bloody Nora!" shrieked Fred. "Blimey! So Aunty Clarabelle and Uncle Mickey was meant to fall in love and then give it to Dad to save him? Well, that's a shocker! But they thought they was doing something bad! But it was really good?" *Bugger me!* He couldn't get over this!

"Yes, Fred, that is correct," the Voice said, "and not only that but the romance needed also to be forbidden, to encourage Sarah to want to learn about her gifts so that she would fight for Clarabelle.'

"Really? But why?" he asked, confused now. *What had Mum got to do with all of this?*

"It is Sarah's path to further develop in her own way. She will help many others in time, but to do that, she needed to learn, and she needed a motivation in order to want to learn. Battling for Clarabelle to be allowed her forbidden love *was* that motivation. So you see, Fred, the angelic romance not only saved Simon, but it helped Sarah grow. So do not feel guilty, do not suffer. It was all as it was meant to be. Release this guilt to me now."

Fred grinned, positively beamed in fact! *Wow, so I haven't done anything wrong after all? I've been part of a great plan, a mighty plan all along? Double wow!*

With that, Metatron stretched his light into Fred (right into him mind!), and Fred suddenly felt extremely, extraordinarily free and happy!

"But why didn't I die instead of him being hurt?" he barked. "Why couldn't I go in his place? What's so special about me?"

"That is simple, Fred! Simon had travelled a long way down the tunnel towards death and needed help to get back. Your help! Your job was to find Simon in the tunnel and bring him back to his loved ones on earth. You are a dog, Fred, a golden retriever dog, a *retriever*. Only you could find him, only you could *retrieve* him and bring him back. You could not have done so if you had gone with him into the tunnel. Do you see now, Fred?"

"What, you mean it was planned that Dad would get hurt, and that I'd be the one to save him? No way!" barked a delighted Fred. "You are kidding me? You're telling me that if it wasn't for me, Dad would still be stuck in the tunnel? That I saved him?"

"Yes, Fred," Metatron confirmed, "that is so."

"Bugger me!" Fred woofed quietly. "Gobsmacked or what!"

The light was beginning to fade gently, retreating into the darkness of the tunnel, but he could still hear

Metatron's voice calling to him in the distance.

"One day soon you will remember many things, Fred, many things that you cannot know at the moment. One day soon your memory will be activated and then you will understand everything. Go now, Fred, go back, go home, go, go. ..." and then he was gone, the light was gone, and Fred woke up with a start.

He sat up with a jump. "Mum!" he yelled, jumping high into the air. "It wasn't my fault, well it was, but I saved him and everything's okay! Mum, Mum, I'm back! 'Fred the Fantastic' is back!" He ran into the house full of beans and bounce and as he ran, he realised that all of his aches had gone. He felt like a puppy again! Nothing hurt anymore, in fact he felt totally, fantastically, smashing! "Bloody hell!" he yelled, "I really did save Dad! Oh my Dog!"

***

Simon was getting stronger every day. His recovery was nothing short of a miracle and the doctors just couldn't get over it! Simon could though, *blimey could he!* He remembered floating over the operating table, he remembered seeing the angels, all three of them! He remembered floating down the tunnel with one of them and he remembered the light that he was following. Above all, he remembered the peace. It was almost a euphoric peace. The memories, the awareness, the understanding, the experience of it all, it had all come back to him gently, gradually, shockingly, in the first few days after he woke up. *There really was a tunnel, a tunnel that they went through when they died. There really were angels! Bloody hell!*

Simon reflected on his conversation with his wife the previous year when she'd first told him about her angel. He'd been so sceptical, so disbelieving, so. ... Simon couldn't think of the words! *Never again,* he vowed. Never again would he disbelieve his wife. Never again would he feel scared by her gift, her incredibly special gift!

Sarah had told him about Clarabelle and Michael, how they'd given up their love to save him and he just couldn't get over it. None of it! *It was just so miraculous, so unbelievable! So incredible!* And he remembered Fred; Fred coming to get him from the tunnel and drag him back. He'd talked to him, he'd understood him! Seeing angels, talking to his dog! *Wow, it was just all so surreal! Life is sure going to be different now. Weird different, good different, but different. ...*

***

The bells rang out all across the Angelic Realms. The celebrations had started!

The huge doors swung open as Clarabelle and Michael approached the grand hall of the Angelic Temple. Side by side they walked through the open doors, descending down the wide sweeping steps into the magnificence of the hall that opened up below them. Pillars and posts stood tall around the sides of the hall, adorned with thousands of candles and golden bells, even more than usual! White mist, as always, swirled around the hundreds of gathered angels who were standing on the many tiered rows applauding enthusiastically as they walked in. On the circular stage in the centre of the room below them, at the very bottom of the many steps stood Metatron, his regal wings open to their full and powerful thirty foot span. He stood majestically, commanding everyone's attention, and he was *smiling* a huge, happy smile!

Clarabelle and Michael took their places at the front in the seats that had been reserved for them and stood, waiting for the ceremony to commence.

"Be seated," Metatron boomed, his voice reverberating around the room, bouncing off the ceilings and cylindrical walls. Everyone sat. "Second Level Angel, Class 1 Clarabelle please step forward." Clarabelle walked nervously onto the stage. "Archangel Michael, Warrior for Light, please step forward." Michael followed Clarabelle onto the stage and stood in front of Metatron. Both angels had their heads bowed in deference to the Mighty Metatron.

"For services to mankind, please accept these golden feathers of honour with our love and thanks," he boomed, holding up two golden feathers. "You two have demonstrated without hesitation the love and giving nature of all angels - to serve and help others, to give selflessly with compassion and unconditional love. Your sacrificial act which saved Simon Brown's life was beautiful and we are all very proud of you. Well done, good job both." Metatron placed a feather on Michael's shoulder and then one on Clarabelle's.

She stared at the feather in delight and beamed, positively beamed! *That was two feathers now, TWO! Another golden feather and I'll be promoted up to a First Class Angel, blimey!* She turned to look at Michael and smiled shyly. *He's alright, as angels go, I suppose, but I really didn't know what all the fuss was about!* she thought to herself, realising that she'd gone right off him, didn't fancy him at all anymore! And as for love? Well, yes, she loved him, she loved everyone, but she was an angel, so, of course, she loved everyone! But anything else ... really? She really couldn't understand how she had thought for even one moment it was possibly anything more than just normal angelic love! And to call Archangel Michael, 'Mickey,' how ridiculous! She'd been behaving very oddly that much was clear, but it seems that it'd passed now, as if she'd woken up from a long and weird dream. How very strange!

"Now, where is that party? I do so love a party!" she grinned, "Smashing, just smashing!"

Chapter 20

Sarah and Simon's house was packed to the rafters! He'd been home for a week now and was back to his old self. He'd insisted on a party to celebrate, although he'd had to work some to persuade the overprotective Sarah that he was well enough for celebrations. He had persuaded her, of course, Sarah not being able to deny him a thing at the moment. He didn't know how long it would last, her giving him his every whim, but he was sure going to milk it for all it was worth!

The music played loudly, balloons, streamers, and decorations adorned the house from every ceiling, every corner, and every door. A huge banner hung across the hall with a 'Welcome Home Simon' sign in big, bold letters. Sarah had had it made after he'd woken up and whilst he was recovering, she had put it up so that it would be there for when he'd come home. It had been lovely, the homecoming. They'd celebrated with tea and biscuits, just them and the kids; quietly, safely, sensibly. Now that the antibiotics were out of his system and his energy was back to normal, he wanted to celebrate properly. He wanted a party! And what Simon wanted, Simon got, for now anyway!

It seemed that half the village had turned up for the celebratory party as well as all the family. In the living room were more banners declaring 'Happy Belated Birthday Sarah and Fred' (Simon had that one ordered and sorted when she'd been out shopping.)

Fred looked at the banner happily, although to be fair, he thought it really should have read 'Fred the Fantastic,' being as it was all down to him that Dad was here anyway! "No bloody credit, no credit at all!" he moaned, chewing on his two hundredth doggie choc of the day, then promptly threw up! "More doggie chocs, yay!" yelled Fred looking at the mashed up mess on the floor, he dove in and ate it all up. Well, he was nothing if not house proud!

"Oh, Fred dear, must you?" exclaimed Aunty Clarabelle from her perch on the mantelpiece. She was sitting with Uncle Nat and The Spy, as well as Sephi and Elijah.

"Oh, gross!" shrieked Seraphina in disgust. "That's just gross, Fred!"

"Waste not want not!" he woofed, licking up the last of his vomit happily.

"Where's Dad?" he yelled, having managed to take his eyes off him for five full seconds. "Where's my Dad?" Fred panicked, ran into the kitchen, ran into the garden and ran back into the house. "Dad, Dad, where are you?" he yelled frantically.

"It's alright, buddy, I'm here," shouted Simon over the din of the music to a distraught Fred.

"Oh Dog, I thought I'd lost you again!" Fred barked, jumping up and licking Simon's face madly with relief.

Simon ruffled Fred's fur and hugged him tight. "I didn't say thank you, did I, buddy?" he whispered quietly in Fred's ear. "Thank you for saving me, for bringing me back." he grinned.

"You remember? You remember me saving you? In the tunnel? No way!" exclaimed Fred excitedly. "It was dark you know, but I, 'Fred the Fantastic' saved you, Dad!" he barked.

"I know you did, buddy, I know. Thank you." And Simon smiled the biggest smile he'd ever smiled in his entire whole life. "I've seen some strange things, mate, I can tell you, very strange! But never mind that, come on, let's find Mum, I feel a dance coming on," Simon grinned, a secret funny grin. "Let's celebrate! Let's celebrate it all!" and he moved in from the kitchen to the lounge, a devoted Fred by his side, looking for his wife.

All five angels watched the partying going on around them; Nat, of course, bopping madly along with the music, nearly falling off the fireplace in his enthusiasm. Fred grinned, watching the goings-on around him. Mum was dancing with Dad, though Dad was limping a bit, his leg still a bit stiff from the accident, but he was jigging with the best of them, Dog-love-him! Ben was twirling Gina around, even Granny Smith was doing a jig! Linda and James were chatting to Dave, the landlord of the Crown, and the twins were bouncing up and down in their chairs, sucking on jelly and ice cream.

"I am not sucking, Freddie!" corrected Angelica

indignantly from her high chair. "I am biting! Look! I got a tooth!" she grinned proudly. Sure as eggs is eggs and bones is bones, a single tooth was poking out of Angelica's gum.

"Ha! I got two, look!" yelled David, pointing at his mouth. Angelica stared in horror at David's mouth.

"Not fair! Not fair!" she yelled. "Mum!" she screamed, "David's being nasty to me again!"

Then Dad was changing the CD from dance music to some other stuff that everyone knew (by some 70's Swedish people apparently), and the next thing Fred knew was they were all singing. Singing mind you! Every bloody one of them! Not that he could call that drunken screeching singing!

"Mind me ears, you're killing me!" barked Fred. "Sensitive you know!" But no one took a blind bit of notice.

"I believe in angels," they sang, the whole bloody lot of them! *The house shook, bloody shook mind you!*

"I have a dream, a fantasy ..."

"Yeah, pal, I have a dream, a dream you'll shut it!" barked Fred.

"To help me through reality ...

"And my destination makes it worth the while ...

"Pushing through the darkness still another mile ...

"I believe in angels ..." (they sang that bit *really* loud!)

"Something good in everything I see

"I believe in angels ..." (even bloody louder!)

"When I know the time is right for me

I'll cross the stream, I have a dream ..."

"Oh well," barked Fred, "if you can't beat 'em, join 'em!" And he joined in, howling along as best he could.

"I believe in *angels* ..." he howled, in his bestest, biggest voice. After all, it was a party and it was a *smashing* day, just SMASHING!

Epilogue

The celebrations had been exhausting. Fred was fast asleep, snoring happily on Dad's slippers. It had taken him three days to get over the excitement of it all, three days! It was a beautiful morning in the Brown household but Fred was oblivious to it as he snored noisily. He twitched periodically, snorting and dribbling and twitched some more.

Angelica laughed. "Look, David," she pointed, bobbing up and down in her bouncer, "Freddie's being funny!"

David peeked through the crack in the kitchen door and watched Fred as he twitched and jerked. He giggled. "He's dreaming, Anj. He's having a funny dream. Look, he's smiling. His teeth are bared. I think he's laughing!" he grinned, then went back to his bouncing.

Sarah smiled as she finished the ironing. She loved listening to her twins chatting to each other with their baby talk; just gurgles and burbles to everyone else, but they seemed to understand each other and that was all that mattered. She looked at Fred with almost the same love as she did when she looked at her children. He'd saved the day and she loved that dog to absolute bits! "God bless him," she smiled. "He is funny."

Fred was not funny! Fred was having a funny dream! A *really* funny dream; funny weird, mind you, not a funny 'ha-ha' type of dream! Fred dreamed he was back in the tunnel again, floating! Floating, mind you! He looked around him in surprise, then amazement, and then shock. "What the hell?" he barked. But it wasn't a bark. It wasn't a bark at all! "What the hell!" he exclaimed again, looking around him, noticing the long black cloak trailing behind. "What the bloody hell is that?" he yelped, confused and scared, nay, terrified! *What was going on!*

The long black cloak stretched far out behind him and seemed to be coming out of him, from his bloody arse no less! "Where's my tail?" he yelped. "Where's me bloody tail!" But it wasn't a yelp! It wasn't anything like a yelp! It was a thought, and not even thoughts, but words! Proper words, and they were coming out of his mouth. A real mouth, a human mouth! Well it looked like a human mouth! "Oh my Dog!" he cried, and then without warning, he was zooming down the tunnel at the speed of sound and the next thing he knew he was in a room. A huge room and it was light! Really, really light, like he was standing in the middle of the sun or something, it was *that* bright! Only he wasn't standing, and he wasn't sitting; he was bloody *floating!*

"Ah, Fred," said 'the Voice' gently. "Thank you for coming. I thought you and I should have a little chat."

Fred sat down with a bump. He could see a huge angel, a massive angel, clear as bloody day, right in front of him! And he could see a light behind it, a power. … And he *knew* this power, and he *knew* this angel, and he suddenly, he majestically *knew* where he was, and he knew *who* he was.

"Hello Metatron," Fred grinned, standing up to his full ten feet shadowy black height, "Long time no see, Boss! Thought I'd never get home, never! Great to see you!"

"It's good to see you too, Fred," smiled Metatron warmly. Fred had always been his favourite Grim Reaper and he'd missed him, they all had. "The 'All That Is' wants a word, Fred, check up on progress, see how you're doing, all right?" he smiled.

"Yeah, course, Boss," he grinned, looking behind Metatron at the light.

"So Frederick, how is the mission going?" asked the 'All That Is,' booming out from the centre of the light.

"Oh, very well, Sir! I get it now, I get it completely!" Fred assured, nodding emphatically. "They really love each other don't they, these humans? I mean, who'd have thought it! Never realised before, Sir, never realised!"

"They do indeed," He said. "So what have you learned from your visit to planet Earth then, Frederick? From this experience?" He asked.

"Well, Sir, I see now how hard it is, you know - when I come to fetch one of them, how hard it is for them to let go, Sir. Never realised it before, do now though!" he grinned. "Great idea making me a dog too, sir, fabulous idea if I may say so, sir!"

"Yes well, Fred, you Grim Reapers are by your very nature, 'Retrievers' are you not? Fetch, fetch!" The 'All-The-Is' laughed. "I thought it would be amusing to make you one, a real retriever, just for a while, a Retriever Dog, a golden retriever at that!" He grinned.

"He's got a great sense of humour, the 'All That Is,' doesn't he?" Fred grinned at Metatron, who was laughing richly at the joke.

"But, of course, He has, of course!" chuckled Metatron.

"And you changed my usual trailing black cloak to a tail so I wouldn't miss it hanging behind me didn't you, Sir? Very clever, very clever indeed!" grinned Fred.

"I do my best!" He chuckled. "So do you think when you come home and return to your post as Grim Reaper you will have more compassion now, Frederick? More care and love for those left behind when you collect them?" He asked.

"Oh yes indeed, Sir, yes indeed!" Fred exclaimed. "Never realised before, Sir, now I do. They find it really hard to let go you know, to say goodbye. Sad really. I never realised before just how painful it is for them when I turn up, bless 'em! I could have been gentler in my approach, Sir, a lot more in fact," he admitted guiltily. "Will now though, promise!" he grinned. "To be fair, I've become quite attached to them, these humans," he said in surprise. "They are really quite nice. Didn't much care for them before I must admit, but they're really rather sweet."

"Sweet!" Metatron could not keep the amazement from his voice. "Sweet?" *This was really quite worrying! Grim Reapers had to keep a distance in order to do their job! Sweet, indeed! Maybe they'd gone too far, letting Fred live amongst them like this? He'd gone soft! It was time Fred woke up and smelt the roses! It was time to reactive his memory.* Metatron waved his arm, pointing a light at Fred from the end of his fingers. Fred sat with a bump, suddenly feeling weakened by the touch of the light. Energy buzzed around him, through him and inside him, activating something deep inside and Fred immediately remembered everything!

He was 'Fred the Grim Reaper' from 'Down in Transport,' come to collect Simon and take him back upstairs. That had been the plan. In and out and no nonsense! He, in the form of 'Fred the Dog' was meant to live for one full year, get to know the humans, learn a thing or so in that year to make him a bit more sensitive, a bit kinder, and then he was meant to die at the same time as Simon and 'fetch' him home. The year was up and they were both meant to have been hit by the truck that day. Fred would return to his angelic form as Grim Reaper and do his job; the job in transport that was to *retrieve Simon and take him back upstairs!* But Fred had changed his mind! Somewhere along that year he had changed his mind! He didn't want Simon to die, and he *definitely* didn't want to be the one to do it!

Fred remembered his meeting with the Boss, back last year when he was still a Grim Reaper, just before Sarah and Simon were due to fly home from their honeymoon. In fact, he recalled, it was just before their wedding! He'd been told that he was being reassigned, but at that point he hadn't known where he was assigned. He remembered saying bye to Clarabelle and Nat as they sat on the cloud watching the honeymooning couple. He remembered going from there to drop off his last collected soul. Now suddenly he remembered where he went next. He went into a female dog's tummy and became a puppy! He'd laid there for all sixty-three days getting bigger and fatter until he was pushed out into the world. That was just before Sarah's birthday, although he hadn't known them then, Sarah and

Simon. And then Simon had come for him two months later, when Fred the dog was eight weeks old. That would be late October, he remembered now, and that's when he'd chosen him - Fred choosing Simon, of course, chose him so that he could kill him, well, cause his death anyway, but he hadn't! Instead he'd grown to love him, protect him, and look after him. *Wow! I never expected to love him, not at all! Love a human, get attached? Unheard of for a Grim Reaper!* Wow, he *had* gone soft! Putty soft! He'd grown attached to not just Simon, but Sarah too and he definitely didn't want Simon to go and leave Sarah on her own, or the babies. He just couldn't do it to them, just couldn't! So he'd come to see The Boss, the 'All That Is,' and he'd asked, no he'd begged for a change of plan. Gosh that was months ago! Ages ago!

"Yes, Fred, it was a long time ago, my dear. This has been arranged for many months. Many months! We had an inkling that it would happen, that you'd ask for a change of plan, so we prepared angels Clarabelle and Michael in advance, just in case they were needed. Of course, they didn't know. No need for them to! We didn't let it develop fully mind, their romance, not until you showed up and begged for us not to take Simon. A few weeks after you got there that was. Just a few weeks, you old softy! Once you did, we let the reins off them and let their romance grow, in readiness to save Simon."

"Blimey! Gosh! Really? Wow!" Fred shook his head in amazement. He knew that all sorts went on behind the scenes, but he never realised just how *complicated* it was! It was all planned, every bit of it, right from the moment AA Michael stroked Clarabelle's feathers in the award ceremony! Blimey! "So do I have to come home now?" he asked quietly, not wanting to hear the answer, not wanting to hear it at all! "Now my year's up? Do I have to come home?" He grimaced. He didn't want to go home, not now! He wanted to be back with Sarah and Simon, and Granny Smith and the screamers, Angelica and David. He liked being with people, human people; they were just *lovely*!

Metatron looked at him in amazement. *Lovely? Had he said lovely? Oh my days!*

"You want to stay?" he shrieked, shock written all over this face. "You want to stay, down there! On Earth! With them, with the humans, as a DOG? But, Fred, you can come home, Fred, you can come home now! You can go back to your job, back to your team and be with the other Grim Reapers where you belong!"

Metatron simply could not believe his ears! What were the heavens coming to! First angelic romances, miracles, humans cheating death and now this, a Grim Reaper preferring to be a mutt! This was worse than he thought!

"I wouldn't mind a bit longer down there, if that's alright, Sir? A lot more to learn I reckon, especially from the little people, the twins," Fred was saying. "Be nice to spend a bit longer down there if that's alright with you, Sir?"

There was a tone in Fred's voice that was different, desperate almost. Metatron's concern escalated. *What Angel of Death could possibly prefer living as a Dog!* He just couldn't get over it!

"If that is your wish, Fred, if that is your wish." The 'All That Is' was saying.

Metatron was in shock! *He was agreeing? The 'All That*

Is' was going to encourage this? Allow it? No! But too late, He was agreeing, He was already agreeing!

"You may stay in a dog's life for its duration if you so desire," He said. "That would be another twelve years, three months and eighteen hours, if that is agreeable?"

"Yes, Sir, that is most agreeable," Fred beamed.

"But, Sir!" Metatron exclaimed, jumping in. "Can't you see that he's attached? He's getting soft! I know we wanted to soften him up a bit, but really! There's soft and there's soft!" He shook his head in despair and went on, arguing his case as best he could. "Another stint down there and he won't be able to do his job at all when he comes home! Another twelve years and he'll be mush! Just look what one year's done to him! He'll be no good to me by the time he gets back, no good at all! He'll have to resign and I'm short staffed as it is!"

"That's quite enough, Metatron," The Voice boomed. "There may be other plans for our Frederick, other plans! Plans that you do not yet see."

Metatron sat down quickly. *It just was not on to be arguing with The Boss like this, not on at all.* What was he thinking! It was all these changes, all these, these 'unknown things' and he was the 'All Seeing All Knowing' Metatron, well he was meant to be! He used to be! *Oh, pah!* Metatron gave in with a huge sigh. He knew when he was beaten. "Yes, Sir. I'm sorry, Sir. You know best, Sir."

"I do believe," said the 'All That Is' gently to the beaten Metatron, "that by the time our Fred returns to The Realms he may well be ready for an upgrade, a promotion. Time to leave Transport and join the Guardian element, don't you think so, Metatron?"

Metatron nearly fainted! *Fred, a Guardian Angel? You have got to be kidding me!*

"Perhaps Trainee Third Level Angel, Class 5 would be appropriate?" Suggested the 'All That Is' with a smile.

"Yes, Sir," Metatron said, through *very* gritted teeth, "If that's what you think, Sir. Trainee Third Level Class 5 then. Lovely!" he said, trying hard to hide the sarcasm in his tone but not quite managing it.

"You may go now, Fred," The 'All That Is' said kindly. "Use these years wisely. Grow with compassion, with care, with love. Grow in your heart, your soul and your spirit, and one day, when you return, we will look at a promotion for you, if and only *if* you have earned it."

Fred beamed, positively beamed. "Yay, promotion at last!" he yelled, forgetting where he was for a moment. "Guardian Angel-ship here I come! Smashing!"

"For now, for services rendered, Fred, I award you this!" He said, and a golden halo was placed gently around Fred's neck. Fred stared at the halo in awe. Grim Reapers didn't get halos! Wow, this was awesome!

"Goodbye, Fred, we shall see you in twelve years or so, my dear. And, Fred, dear, you will remember nothing, nothing at all."

Suddenly Fred felt funny and things began to go hazy. He could still hear 'The Voice' but it was fading now, fading, fading...

"A doggie *halo* collar for now, Fred, just for now! It will be our little secret," the 'All That Is' said from the distance.

Suddenly the light went out and he was back in the tunnel zooming along.

"Smashing!" he barked. A real bark, a full blown proper bark! The dark cloak was gone, his tail was returned. He checked his fur, his teeth and his ears. Yep, they were floppy and furry! He was back. "Smashing! Just bloody smashing!" he barked ecstatically, suddenly noticing the new golden collar around his neck. "Whoopee!" he screamed, legging it down the tunnel. "I'm coming home, Dad, I'm coming home!" Fred the Dog is back. "No more 'Grim Reaper' for me! Yippeeeeeeeeee!"

Fred opened his eyes slowly, rolled over, stretched all four paws in the air, shook his floppy ears and felt something prodding in his ribs. Slippers! Manky, smelly ones at that! Fred slowly woke from his dream. "Mum, Dad, I had a lovely dream!" he woofed. "But I don't know what the bloody hell it was about! I can't remember a thing!"

Then 'Fred the Fabulous,' 'Fred the Magnificent,' 'Fred the Fantastic,' Golden-Retriever-Doggie-Mutt rolled over and went back to sleep. "Smashing," he woofed happily as he drifted off. "Just bloody smashing!"

The End

Angel on My Shoulder

(Sarah's Story)

By
Julie Poole

The first book in the 'Angel' series ...

Sarah is having a bad day! At 37½ life is going nowhere fast. She's been dumped by her latest boyfriend, again! She's lost her latest job, again! And her mother's driving her mad, again! To top it all, she can't even have a moan in peace without Clarabelle piping up every two minutes trying to cheer her up, again! Clarabelle is, of course, Sarah's 'Guardian Angel,' whose job it is to constantly keep Sarah's spirits up - an annoying distraction to say the least! Clarabelle certainly has her work cut out where Sarah is concerned!

Having reached rock bottom, Sarah reluctantly accepts Clarabelle's help, growing gradually from a chaotic, lost young woman into the person she always wanted to be. With the angel's help she is ready at last for her soulmate Simon to enter her life. Throughout her journey a team of angels have regular 'inter-angel-cy' meetings, mapping out and planning Sarah's life for her, often getting it very wrong with hilarious results!

Sarah's story brings hope, magic and inspiration from the beginning right through to its uplifting conclusion; drawing the reader into an emotional rollercoaster that will make you laugh, cry and ultimately leave you with a smile on your face and quite possibly with an empty box of tissues!

Angel in My Heart
(Clarabelle's Story)
By
Julie Poole

The second book in the 'Angel' series ...

Following on from 'Angel on My Shoulder (Sarah's Story),' Sarah is finally having a good day! At 38¾ life is now going fantastically! She's just married her soulmate Simon, her store is doing great and she's even getting on with her mother. (Miracles really do happen!) And to top it all, she's pregnant!

Her 'Guardian Angel' Clarabelle is, of course, 'smashingly' happy, but is she risking it all with her crush on Archangel Michael? How will Simon cope with finding out that his new wife has a Guardian Angel that she can see and talk to? Will Nathaniel ever sort out his Gonk hair, and what will Metatron do when he finds out about Clarabelle's crush; will she be banished from The Angelic Realms forever?

In this sequel, 'Angel in My Heart (Clarabelle's Story),' it is Sarah's turn to help her angelic best friend Clarabelle and prevent a disaster. Can she do it? Enter 'Fred the Fantastic' to save the day. Fred is, of course, Sarah and Simon's new dog; a Golden Retriever, who being a genius can speak three languages (dog, angel and human). Whether he can help 'Mum' and 'Aunty Clarabelle' sort the mess out that they've got themselves into, though, is quite another matter!

Angel in My Fingers

(Frieda's Story)

By
Julie Poole

The third book in the Angel series

Clarabelle is on a mission! With the children now at school, it's high time that 'her Sarah' focused! Enter 'Cassie' the cat (much to Fred's disgust), here to help Sarah become the 'Best Tarot and Angel Card Reader' this side of Mars ... Can Sarah do what Clarabelle needs her to do? And can she do it in time?

Frieda has a secret ... a dark, foreboding, sinister secret ... and it is only Sarah who can unlock it ... Can she help Frieda find the peace that she has never known, or is she jeopardising a friendship that has lasted for nearly forty years?

In this sequel - the third in the 'Angel' series - it is time for Sarah to move to the next level. Can she cope with the pressure ... or with what she discovers!

Pain and trauma ... secrets and lies - no one knows what she's been through, and Frieda's determined to keep it that way! With such resistance, can Sarah repair a broken spirit and bring a happy ending, even with Clarabelle and Cassie's help? Clarabelle thinks so, but only Frieda can be the one to determine that!

A Note from Julie Poole

Thank you so much for reading Angel in My Fingers (Frieda's Story). If you enjoyed it, please take a moment to leave a review at your favourite on line store, such as Amazon.co.uk or Amazon.com

I welcome contact from my readers. At my website you can contact me, leave a review, and find all the links to my social media: www.juliepooleauthor.com

18503335R00173

Printed in Poland
by Amazon Fulfillment
Poland Sp. z o.o., Wrocław